A moody, atmospheric book, *Listen to the Dead* is inspired by one of the largest unsolved cases of serial killings in the United States, the New Bedford Serial Killings of 1988.

Praise for Randall Peffer and the Cape Islands Mysteries

"… *Peffer offers an unusual and intriguing version of star-crossed lovers beset by evil enemies.*"   —Publishers Weekly

"*[A] seductive tale that, while obviously not for everybody, will appeal to those willing to cross over to the dark side.*"   —Library Journal

"*Provincetown Follies Bangkok Blues, is wonderful, and deserves a place in your bookcase alongside Chandler, Cain, Hammett and Woolrich.*"
                     —The Barnstable Patriot

"*An intriguing, offbeat mystery.*"   —Booklist

Also by Randall Peffer

Watermen

Logs of the Dead Pirate Society

Killing Neptune's Daughter

Provincetown Follies, Bangkok Blues

Old School Bones

Southern Seahawk

LISTEN TO THE

DEAD

LISTEN TO THE
DEAD

A CAPE ISLANDS MYSTERY

RANDALL PEFFER

TYRUS
BOOKS

Published by
TYRUS BOOKS
1213 N. Sherman Ave. #306
Madison, WI 53704
www.tyrusbooks.com

This is a work of fiction.
Any similarities to people or places,
living or dead, is purely coincidental.

12 11 10   1 2 3 4 5 6 7 8 9 10

978-1-935562-19-1 hardcover
978-1-935562-18-4 paperback

For Anne Marie, Kevin,

Eric, Julia, Zig, Jenny, Peter, Charlie B & Ben on Buzzards Bay

Maria, Troy, Mac, Terry, Milo & Johnny R in the Bahamas

—inspirations, friends

William Moore was the lighthouse keeper on Bird Island in Buzzards Bay from 1819 to 1834. He had a wife who came from a wealthy family in Boston. At some point in her tenure on the island, she vanished. Visitors of the era report seeing a fresh grave. Some suspected foul play.   *—Cape Cod legend*

" ... the hunt for an unknown murderer was in full cry. Nine women were dead and two others disappeared ... Meanwhile the killer proceeded on his deadly course ..."

    —Carlton Smith, The Killing Season, *1994*

"... the flying particles almost choked me, are these the ashes of the destroyed city, Gommorah?"

    —Herman Melville, Moby Dick, *1851*

Prologue

HE TELLS HIMSELF it's only a claw. Or what's left of one. The nails digging down into the earth. The white digits, which seem to be clasping a large quohog shell, are just visible, rising out of the damp, stony soil. Like something grasping for purchase. A creature struggling to get back to the air and sea. To live again.

During the winter, much of Buzzards Bay had been frozen solid until a Coast Guard icebreaker cut a path through for ships to transit the Cape Cod Canal. A mound of ice gathered on the southwest side of Bird Island. Storms drove the ice floe halfway across the flat acre-and-a-half island, piled ice in heaps halfway up the sides of the thirty-seven-foot lighthouse. Chunks as big as cars flattened everything, including the fences erected to stop erosion and protect the nests of seabirds.

Now the thaw has taken hold. Late March and the first spurt of warm weather is settling over Cape Cod, the south coast of Massachusetts and Buzzards Bay that divides them. The ice has melted at last, leaving the island rutted, bruised. Great swaths of spartina, beach plums, and poison ivy have been scraped away, the guts of the island tilled to the surface. Rough patches of rocks, mud, and sand steam in the morning sun.

Bird Island always has remains of dead seabirds scattered about. Corby Church never pays much attention to them when he comes out from Slocums Harbor to tend the light. The island is an important nesting area for roseate terns. They are small spitfires of birds, their skeletons fine as mouse bones.

But this claw is much bigger. At first, he thinks that maybe it came from a herring gull, a cormorant, a merganser. But there is no sign of webbed skin between the toes. So perhaps it belonged to an osprey, an owl. Even an eagle.

A raptor might have been raiding the terns' nests last summer. Kidnapping fat little hatchlings. Maybe a flock of terns attacked it before it could get airborne again. Raptors are slow and clumsy getting aloft, especially with a load. He pictures them as heavy bombers. Terns are daredevils, stunt pilots. Fearless. When he comes ashore on the island during nesting season, they strafe him from all directions. Still, he loves the terns. They are great fishers, and they protect their families against all comers. They could kill a raptor if enough of them attacked it. So maybe the owner of this claw got his just desserts.

The terns have not returned to nest yet. So Church is alone on the island carrying a buttoned-up golf umbrella in his hand, like a trusty walking stick. He uses it as a poker to push at the claw.

"Who are you? What dirty deed brought you to your death on my island?"

Standing over the claw in his canvas field coat, khaki pants, and clamming boots, Corby Church looks rugged. A character of the New England coast like the fishermen in *The Perfect Storm*. Age—early-to-mid 40s. With his old-school wayfarer sunglasses, wavy, sandy hair just going gray at the temples, he puts some of the townspeople in mind of the actor Jeff Bridges.

His lips purse as he uses the tip of his umbrella to prod at the place where the digits sink into the soil. He figures that with a little pushing he could dig up the rest of the carcass and put the little mystery of this island interloper to rest. Pass on his findings to the Woods Hole scientists who monitor the tern colony out here.

Then he can get back to work. There's a lot to do this morning, his first visit to the island after the long, hard winter. He's the Slocums Harbor harbormaster. The town is the custodian of the island and re-lit the old lighthouse thirteen years ago after nearly seventy years of dormancy. It's part of his job to make sure the solar panels, wires, storage batteries, witching, and light are dry, clean. In working order. He likes tinkering with the equipment, tending to the tower itself. But the island is more to him than a job. After years of caring for the lighthouse, he has come to think of himself as the keeper of the island and the light. He knows every scrap of its history and lore, has a file drawer in his office dedicated to Bird Island. Subscribes to the *Lighthouse Digest,* even writes articles for it.

The tip of the umbrella catches on something beneath the surface. He drops down on his haunches, twists, jimmies the dirt. Pries at what has to be an even bigger bird carcass than he thought.

The earth erupts with bones—but not the leg bones of a raptor. Finger bones. Stubby little wrist bones spill out onto the ground in a mess. Then he sees the grimy, gray shafts of a forearm.

Radius and ulna, he thinks, remembering anatomy class at college. At Massachusetts Maritime Academy.

His poker's tip catches inside a metal ring chained to something still under the ground. It looks like an antique handcuff.

"Holly shit. Christ."

He drops the umbrella, lets it fall beside the bones, jumps to his feet and takes a step back. His chest heaves a wheezy sigh. Then, he listens to the morning's southeast breeze beginning to whir around the lighthouse tower, the rush of waves against the stone seawall. A sad smile begins to ghost over his face. It's the look of a man starting to face off with fear. With memory.

• • • • •

Mid-April, 1988. He's keeping a lookout. Standing by the bones on the beach at Whale Cay. Watching. The boat will come for the rendezvous … when the moon goes down.

He paces, circles around the carcass of a beached dolphin. Stares at the skull, the teeth, the spine, the ribs. But mostly he looks at what is left of the pectoral fins. In the fading moonlight the fin bones seem like arms, with wrists and hands and fingers.

His bowels ache with emptiness. He loves the warm trade winds and the mild blue days here in the islands. Everything about the pink sand, the palms bending in the breeze, the jacks leaping in the waves. The smell of salt and wild hibiscus. The potcake dogs with their broods. But at night it's a different story. The wind burns him. He feels the rhythm of this world lit only by smoldering stars, hot blood, a promiscuous moon.

The skeletal hands of the dolphin spread out on the beach. Lines and crests and loops of salt, a jagged script, trail away from the white digits. As if they were writing a message in the sand just at the creature's hour of death. A love letter, a confession, a warning from another world. In a language he cannot read this hot April night. In the Abaco Islands chain. The eastern Bahamas. Beneath the fading light of a pale moon. When the sharks feed.

1

"LOOK, Colón, do me a favor, ok? Try not to get all spiritual and Rican about this body, will you, hon?" The police chief paces, eyes his only detective over a mug of black coffee. It's an hour before lunch.

Yemanjá Colón sits at her desk in the miniscule squad room glaring back at Chi Chi Bugatti, her huge black eyes already starting to glaze over with wishes she had called in sick today. Some things she does not have to think about; she just knows. And she knows after six months on the job that this one may not work out. That this job in Slocums Harbor is no match for the one she left last October under duress. The detective detail with her partner Lou Votolatto and the state police Crime Prevention and Control unit on the Cape, the CPAC folks. There are days when she tells herself she's going to quit this gig in Slocums Harbor. Trouble is she needs the money, loves investigation. *So here you are,* jeba. *Stuck in* pergatorio *with Little Caesar.*

"Hustle your butt down to Town Wharf."

Hustle your own butt, gordo, she thinks.

He's a stumpy bugger. Almost as wide as he is tall. And thick.

The blue uniform shirt seems tight as the skin of a balloon stretched over his massive chest, belly bulging over his gun belt. But his face, with the high cheek bones and shiny, leathery skin, is handsome. The broad nose, and lips, the tight, short, black hair. Almost Puerto Rican. Abuela says his mother was from *la Isla*, from around Guanajuato. But the man only plays the Latino card when he wants a sniff of his detective's perfume or a favor. Mostly, he comes on like some kind of Roman gladiator.

"Corby Church is waiting for you with his boat. And Hank Cabot from the archeological society. They think this is some kind of old grave that the ice floes have opened up."

He tells her to go on out there to Bird Island. Do her thing with Corby's bones. Get something that will help to figure out who's buried out there. But try to be back here mid-afternoon. Chi Chi needs her working on the B&E they had out on Neck Road yesterday. Property owners are bat shit.

"Just cover your bases. Leave the rest for the archeologist types."

"He said there were maybe handcuffs, manacles, he called them, on the body. What's with that? Probably not death by natural causes. You think I'm going to give a soft touch to a murder investigation?" She tilts her head back, uses a hand to flick her long, dark hair out of her eyes, continues to hold her boss in her sights. Never blinking. She's thirty-five, but looks ten years younger. A babe in a cheap charcoal pants suit. A whole heap of attitude.

"Jesus H. Christ, Yemanjá. Why is everything such a drama for you?"

"I don't know, Chief. Maybe because I'm psychic."

"Or psycho."

She feels a growl starting in her chest, grits her teeth. Then she jumps to her feet. "I'm out of here."

"Wait! I'm not finished, Detective."

She already has her back to him, is heading out the door to her car, when he barks her name. This time she spins on her heels, quashing a sudden instinct to draw her gun. She grew up with a father who thought he was the king of Puerto Rico, and now she hates being bullied.

"What?" She pulls on her navy blue North Face anorak. Even in the bulky coat, she looks slender. Maybe it's the dark hair running to her elbows, the way she holds her shoulders back, the long legs that make her look taller than her five foot seven.

"Don't go pulling an attitude with me, missy. Just do your job and we are going to get along fine. You keep up with this moody Latina shit, you're going to be in a world of hurt. It don't make no never mind to me that certain white folks in this town get all dewy-eyed 'cause we got an honest-to-Christ, flag-carrying *Borinqueña* on the force. You're just another cop to me. Am I getting through to you?"

She rolls her eyes. This *payaso*. Clown. "Loud and clear, Chief!"

"Good. Give a call into the station when you've seen what's what with the bones. It looks bad, I'll call in the staties. Suppose I'll have to call them anyway. Get some boys in here with real on-the-job forensic skills. Not just textbook stuff. Or any of that voodoo *santos* shit you're into."

She gives a tight-lipped smile and beats it for her Honda.

• • • • •

Henry "Hank" Cabot stretches his hand to help her into the harbormaster's twenty-six-foot Grady White tied at the town float. He's a good-looking man in his early sixties, wearing an expensive red yachting slicker. Tall and muscular, with thick, auburn hair. A dye-job. Professionally done. The wire-rim glasses have Harvard B-school written all over them.

"You ever hear the story of the lighthouse keeper's wife, Detective?"

She shakes her head no as she takes the offered hand. The harbormaster, Corby Church, is nowhere in sight. The wind is up now, and even though it is the middle of April, the air suddenly feels like January. A shiver rips down her back, right through both legs. When she's in the boat, she flips the hood of her anorak over her head. Tries to pull it tight with the drawstrings, but her hair gets caught in the mix. A girl would not have to put up with this kind of nonsense back on *la Isla*. She wonders if they have gotten her application at San Juan PD.

"*Madre mio*."

"Beg pardon?"

"Nothing. What's this story about the keeper's wife, Mr. Cabot? I didn't know Corby Church had a wife."

"He used to. Name of Karen Sue. His ex now. But you've got me heading down the wrong track. I'm talking about another lighthouse keeper. The first one."

"Oh? *He* had a wife."

"Who legend says disappeared."

"Really. When would that have been?"

"Sometime in the 1820s. The lighthouse was built in 1819, the first light on this part of the coast. A man named William S. Moore was hired as the keeper."

"And there begins the legend." Corby Church bounces aboard the boat carrying three big paper cups of coffee from Java Joe's. He passes them to his shipmates. "Hope you folks take it regular."

"That a boy," says Cabot.

Colón seizes the offered coffee, wishes it were the way they drink it back in the West Indies. As Abuela says, black as midnight, hot as hell, sweet as sin. She looks into the harbormaster's blue eyes. Likes the way the tiny creases at the corners make them seem as if they are always smiling. "So what's the deal with Moore? The legend?"

Church looks at Cabot. "You version or mine?" A note in his voice gives her the feeling that there's something between these men, maybe an old beef. They know each other. For sure.

She rolls her eyes. "Competing testimony?"

"Something like that. You first." The harbormaster nods to Cabot.

"But yours is so much saltier."

"Come on, boys. Make up your minds. The chief has me on a short leash. I've got to be back in the office by three."

Cabot shrugs, clears his throat. He says that historical records place William Moore on Bird Island from 1819 to 1834. The job, it seems, was a political plum for which he was paid well, $350 a year. He had a wife. Her name is lost, but legends seem to agree that she came from a wealthy family in Boston. At some point in her tenure on the island, she died and was buried there. Visitors of the era report seeing a fresh grave. Some of the locals suspected foul play.

Colón feels a flash of heat in her cheeks.

"That gossip persisted until 1889 when the original stone house on the island was torn down to make room for a modern frame dwelling," says Cabot.

During the demolition, workers found a secret compartment near the stairs leading into the basement. In the compartment they found a pouch of tobacco, a musket, and a letter from keeper Moore. He blamed his wife's friends for giving her tobacco, which caused her death. There are pieces of the letter at the archeological society but according to Cabot, it's almost impossible to read.

"You think this is her body we're going to see?"

Cabot nods.

"Could be," says Church. "It would solve an old mystery."

"What's your version?" She does not know what to call him. He's a local fixture who everyone at the town hall just refers to as Corby. But in six months on the job, she has never been introduced. She takes a sip of her coffee, looks out at the bright blue harbor and Buzzards Bay beyond. She cannot see Bird Island. Maybe she never has. But she's picturing the lighthouse, a thick, white shaft, wishing she were out there already.

"The stories I've heard say that Moore was a pirate, banished to lighthouse duty for ill-deeds," says Church.

According to legend, Moore was a rake and conned his Boston society sweetheart into marriage and a fling on the island. But she hated the isolation and soon discovered that he was a sadist. She tried to escape three times with Captain Jarvis Blankenship, who brought supplies out to the lighthouse. Moore pleaded with her, maybe threatened her, and each time she returned to Bird Island. Then one day when Blankenship came out to Bird Island with a boatload of supplies, she was gone. And Moore had nothing to say on the subject.

"You can take it from there."

"He greased her."

"Yeah, maybe. Definitely the pirate thing to do, right?"

She thinks he suddenly sounds a little goofy. There's an odd hitch in his voice. What is that, nerves?

Cabot licks the muddy-looking coffee from his lips. "Murder on Bird Island. Well … isn't that a spicy idea?"

She gulps the last of her drink. Crushes the cup and jams it in the pocket of her anorak. "Is anybody going to drive this rig?"

2

ALL THAT THE THREE OF THEM can do is look at the pale white
bones of an arm and hand reaching out of the muddy earth.

Colón takes a bunch of digital pictures and records the coordi-
nates of the grave with her handheld GPS. Locks in the waypoint.
Everyone agrees that the rusted bracelet around the wrist looks like
what is left of an iron manacle.

"I wouldn't believe it if I hadn't seen it with my own eyes," says
Cabot. "It looks just like the kind of thing you see in museum ex-
hibits about slave ships."

She hates to do it, but she calls the station on her cell, tells the
chief he better alert the ME, the staties and their forensic team, including archeologists, ASAP. The challenge of unraveling a 180-year-
old mystery tugs at her. More than tugs. She hears something like a
voice whispering to her from beneath the muddy, torn earth here on
Bird Island. A voice begging for justice, pleading for advocacy. She's
never been in charge of a murder investigation before, but right now
her whole body is buzzing with the possibility. She hopes the chief will

not take this case for himself … or hand it over to state detectives in the local CPAC unit. Maybe if she loses some of her sass and gives him a few smiles back at the station, Chi Chi Bugatti will cut her a break. Fat chance.

The sky has started to spit cold rain. They take a blue tarp Church has in his boat, lay it over the bones to keep the weather and the birds out, pile rocks on the edges to hold it down against the wind. Then they race the two miles back to Town Wharf, the Grady's twin 250s screaming all the way.

• • • • •

Corby Church tells himself that some things ashore will just have to wait. He has a raft of jobs to attend to on the water, what with ferrying a truck-load of equipment, troopers, and forensic people out to the island. Trip after cold trip with an east wind tearing at him. But he doesn't mind the cold or the extra work. Mostly his job is solitary, so this work is different. He's enjoying assisting the Latina detective. There's something different about her, a brash self-confidence, an effortless grace of movement. An abiding soulfulness. He wonders how she'll react when they dig up Mrs. Moore out here on the island. Wonders about his own reaction, too.

"Sorry. You've got to stand back." A trooper stops him with a keep-out sign of his hands. The staties have sunken wooden stakes like fence posts and secured a circle thirty yards in diameter with yellow crime-scene tape around the grave. Inside the circle a team of fourteen people comb the ground with what look like small paint brushes, take pictures, and huddle around the grave like surgeons and nurses.

"I'm the harbormaster." Church points to the embroidered badge on his jacket. "I'm the keeper of this island."

The trooper looks at him, crosses his arms over his chest. "I have my orders. Nobody but the forensic team comes in until further notice."

Church scowls. He can hear Chi Chi Bugatti pestering the forensic crew, saying things like "Goddamn, don't mess up my investigation, boys. You're dealing with honest-to-Christ history here." The man has a Caesar complex that will not quit.

Colón breaks from the throng around the grave, looks toward Church, reads the distress on his face and walks over to the guard.

"It's ok, Trooper. He's working with me." She gives him a little smile. "You could be right about the lighthouse keeper's wife. It's a woman, as you and Mr. Cabot suspected. We're already sure of that. We've got her mostly uncovered. You want to see her in the grave?"

"Am I morbid?"

"It's sort of human nature, isn't it?"

"What do you mean?"

"Curiosity about death. You know, like Hamlet staring at the skull."

"'Alas, poor Yorrick. I knew him, Horatio.'"

The wind whips a rope of dark hair across her face. She brushes it back. "I'm impressed. A harbormaster quoting Shakespeare."

"Don't tell anyone." He winks. "I like books."

She cocks her head, looks at him askance … as if a change of perspective might give her some new clues about what makes him tick. It's a friendly look, a little shy. And he smiles back.

"Come on, Slick. You ever looked into the jaws of death?"

Once.

• • • • •

Church remembers. That beach again. Whale Cay. Winter of '88.

"I got to leave you here for a while, man. Got to go down to the south end of the island and check on the Princess. She seems a little freaked. The boat should be here any time."

The silhouette, a tall, thin specter, lurches away down the moonlit strand, a giant wading bird. A crane maybe, with the queue of his ponytail sticking out like a crest on the back of his head. Nose like a beak.

"You sure this is the place?"

"Yeah, be cool, man. This is the place. Don't you worry." The birdman swings a shotgun onto his shoulder and marches away.

3

THE FIRST THING he thinks is *What a weird way to bury someone.*
He expected a shallow, rectangular grave, torn open by the scraping
or great chunks of ice and something like 190 years of erosion.

But what he sees is more or less a circular pit, about four feet
wide, lined with a triple-thick wall of granite beach rocks. The forensic folks have excavated one side of the pit, removing the dirt to a
depth of about three feet. He can see the skeleton in relief against the
remaining dirt.

Colón shines her powerful flashlight from the top to the bottom
of the excavation. The body appears to be curled into a ball, sort of a
fetal position. Head near the top of the pit almost exposed to the air,
feet at the bottom. No sign of shoes. The arms are raised over the
head, the one he found yesterday is stretching out above the surface
of the ground a little, the other pressed firmly on the dome of the
skull, as if she were trying to protect herself from something falling
out of the sky. Wrists definitely bound with crusty, iron manacles
linked by heavy chain. The neck is bent forward. Chin on chest,

twisted to the side so that now it faces the open air. Mouth gaping open. A full set of very regular, white teeth poised to bite. The earth in the nose and eye sockets has a weird greenish tint. A skein of dark red hair sprouts from the skull and winds its way down and around the neck. Twice.

"Shit."

"Exactly."

"What is this thing that she's in?"

"The archeologists think it's probably an old cistern or well."

He nods. That would make sense. "Or maybe some kind of root cellar. For long periods of time supply boats couldn't get out to islands like this. The lighthouse keepers were on their own."

"Who ever put her in here was more than self-reliant. He was a sick bastard."

"Moore."

She flashes him a sharp look, just for a second. A little reprimand. "We don't know that. But your legendary lighthouse keeper is on my suspect list."

He can see that this is already a murder investigation for her. Not just a disturbed grave.

They both go down on their knees and stare into the pit, almost eye-to-eye with the victim. He is surprised that his nose can still catch the faint scent of decay. It smells like week-old chicken skin in a trash can. And ammonia. Something is starting to churn in his stomach.

"Do you see what I see?" She raises her eyebrows.

"It looks like someone tried to choke her with her own hair."

"But she was still alive when she went in the ground. Still trying to defend herself, covering her head."

Suddenly he's short of breath, hot and cold at the same time. Feels his face going pale.

"You alright?" She puts her hand on his back.

He shakes it off. Stumbles to his feet, starts toward the stony beach. He does not even make it out of the circle of crime tape before he heaves a stew of coffee and an Italian sub sandwich. Heavy on the hot peppers.

"Tough guy," says one of the troopers.

• • • • •

Colón turns her eyes away from Church, who's still heaving. Peers again at the bony face in the wet earth, hears whispers again calling to her. A girl's voice. With a story that she's just beginning to channel. But whose story? Why is her voice dripping with emotion? What's with the sex?

"I want you again." The man's voice has an impatient tone.

The young woman feels his arms draw her toward him in the dark. Inhales a long draft of musty, salty air. His lips are on her neck. She can smell nothing but the distinct scent of Myers rum on his breath, see nothing but a little starshine coming from somewhere. Feel nothing but his lips gliding up under her hair.

His hands are pulling it back, giving him access to her flesh. She cringes. Not sure she likes the way he strokes her head. His hands feel too heavy. Shaky. Not confident, but strong. Obsessed maybe. They rake through her long hair, until her scalp hurts at the roots.

4

GODDAMN THE TELEPHONE. When it rings, Church is curled up
under a sleeping bag. Bruins game flashing on the tube. The volume
off. Jimmy Buffett's crooning softly from the stereo. And the harbormaster is in no mood to move from this spot or answer to the
world.

For something like twenty-two years, on and off, he has lived on
a wooden harbor tug, the *Brutus*. Working on the principle that a
man who values his privacy does not live in the town where he toils,
he keeps the tug tied to a wharf at the boatyard in Quissett on the
Upper Cape, miles from Slocums Harbor.

But the phone won't stop ringing because he has turned the answering machine off. So now he rolls out of his berth in the fo'castle
and climbs all the way up to the wheelhouse to find the portable receiver. A stiff north wind rattles the windows and sends drafts swirling
through the cabin. But he feels warm in his blue long johns, all except
for his bare feet. He has tried everything, but the floor of the boat is
always cold. *What can you do? Hot air rises.*

"Hey, how's it going Sherlock?" he says, after he hears Colón's voice apologizing for calling him when he's off duty. She's at the police station. Still working, going over her notes on what she has seen today.

"You seem like a man of the world. A man who has seen a lot of nature. You've seen a lot of dead animals."

He remembers puking earlier. "Not like that thing today."

She pauses. "It was sickening. Most of us lost our lunches out there. Even some of those hard-boiled forensic guys."

"She was murdered? The legends are true?"

"Yeah, maybe. But I've got a problem. Will you help me? Corby?" It's the first time she has addressed him by name.

"What?"

"This Mrs. Moore theory isn't totally working for me."

"Really?"

"It's the hair."

"How's that?"

"You ever hear of hair staying on a skeleton for a hundred eighty years?"

He thinks. "Sure, look at all those pictures you get of mummies in *National Geographic*."

"Those bodies were embalmed, frozen or preserved in dry desert air. I'm talking about bodies in this kind of damp, maritime climate. Ever see anything left besides the bones after a few years?"

"Whoa. Hold on. You thinks it's not Mrs. Moore we found out there?"

"I'm covering my bases. The forensics will tell us the story, but the lab work isn't going to be in for a few more days. And I need to get a leg up on this case. I want to test a hunch. Thought maybe a salty guy like you could help me out."

"She's getting to you. You can't sleep."

"Yeah. I put my kid to bed an hour early, left him with my grandmother and came back to the station. I'm tired as hell, but the sleep thing isn't happening. I've been wandering around here talking to the walls."

"I know what you mean."

"You got a kid too?"

"I wish." The way he says this is odd. There's a hitch in his voice. "No. No kid. I know what you mean about talking to the walls."

A laugh of recognition bursts from her throat. A workaholic, a fellow insomniac.

"Can I ask you another question?"

Something makes him hesitate.

"Corby, you there?"

"Yeah, sorry. I was just spacing out. Ask away, Detective."

There's a pause. "You can call me Yemanjá."

"Right … Yemanjá."

"How long have you been taking care of Bird Island?"

He pauses, has to think. It was something like two years after his marriage went bust, six years after the boat trip from hell. "Ninety-four. 1994 I started. Summer of my twenty-seventh birthday."

"You've been on the job sixteen years?"

He says that he and Hook Henry were trying to get a little boat shop going on the Cape, but not a lot of folks wanted a wooden boat back then. Corby needed money. He tried starting a tow boat business for a while out of Hyannis. But it wasn't really working out. There was an opening for an assistant harbormaster in Slocums Harbor. They wanted someone with a captain's license for some reason. He was driving the launch for the Harbor Yacht Club to make ends meet. People knew him around the waterfront. So they sort of nominated him for the job.

"And here we are."

"You must like it."

He's silent for several seconds. Then says there are times he wishes he was sitting in the shade of a coconut tree on a beach down in the islands somewhere. Building a boat every other year or so. The harbormaster gig, it's a job. But at least a guy can get out on the water every day if he wants. A lot of different aspects to it. Always some new challenge coming along to keep him interested. Like a hurricane … or all that ice this winter. Watching over the shellfish beds. Rescues. And there's hardly anyone looking over his shoulder. He's pretty much his own boss. Got to love that part.

"Kind of like being a cop."

"You're joking, right?" she asks. "You've heard about the chief?"

"No comment."

"Staying out of office politics."

"Always."

"But back to Bird Island …"

He climbs down the ladder to the galley in his tug. Lights a fire under the tea kettle. He likes the the husky note in her voice. "Yeah. What about the island?"

"Ever see anything strange out there?"

He clicks off the burner under the tea, takes a deep breath. He does not feel like explaining the obvious.

"You've been there. You've seen. It's always strange on the island. Wild. Especially with the terns. It's like that Hitchcock movie, *The Birds*. Nature rules. What are you getting at?"

"Ever see signs of violence? Ever find another body?"

Whoa, he feels a little chill ripple through his shoulders, wonders where she's headed with this question.

"I found a doe one time, gut-ripped by a coyote."

"They get out there? On the island?"

"Sure, on the ice. They come right across from the Cape. Animals will go anywhere for food. Do anything to survive."

"People too, Corby. But as our lady in chains showed us, we don't all make it, do we?"

He's still enjoying the sound of her voice. But this is just about enough questions for one night.

"Ever hear about somebody local disappearing?"

He bites his lower lip for a second. "What are you trying to suggest?"

5

"THINGS ARE ABOUT to get what you might call *real interesting*."
Chi Chi Bugatti sits at his desk patting his round belly with one hand
and waving a pack of papers with the other. "The forensics are back
from the state boys in Boston."

Colón and Church stand before the chief, looking at each other
out of the corners of their eyes. It has been several days since the state
crime scene crew carted the bones of Jane Doe off Bird Island. Several days in which Colón has had to turn her attention back to the
B&E on Neck Road, has had to try to tune out the girl's voice in her
head, the sex talk. Church has been gathering together all his gear for
reseeding the market oysterbeds with spat. But now Bugatti has called
them both here for this ten AM meeting without giving them a clue
as to why.

"You aren't going to believe this. The lab rats say your vic has
only been dead something like twenty to twenty-five years."

Colón's eyebrows arch a little. She can't help firing Church a smug
little smile. Something inside her wants to say *told you so*.

Church's face looks a little washed out to her, confused. Maybe worried. "She's not the Moore lady?"

"So much for the legends of Bird Island. Yours and Hank Cabot's both."

"But what about those old handcuffs? How do the forensic folks explain them?"

"They don't." Bugatti rocks back in his chair. "The shackles appear to be the genuine deal. Probably made sometime shortly after American Independence. But the vic's front teeth have caps done after 1980. They're called Dicor dental crowns. By-products of research for the tiles on the space shuttle."

"The plot thickens," she says under her breath.

"I don't get it." Church says.

"Neither will the newspapers," says the chief. They are going to have a field day with this. I've already talked to the town selectmen. We have to call a news conference."

"Jesus. Why?" Colón wants the buzz she gets from investigation, not the heat from being in the spotlight.

"Because the selectmen think being up-front is the way to go. You ready to be under the microscope, *chiquita*? Ready to show them some of your keen, Rican sleuthing skills?"

She tries not to glare. Wonders if maybe Church will back her up as a witness if she files a harassment charge against the stubby bugger. "Bring it on."

Church winces a little. Maybe he thinks that she's pushing her luck.

The chief gives a puny smile. "Fasten your seatbelt, *nena*."

Nena? She cringes at the chief's use of this Latino term of endearment. She's not his *nena*, not his cute, little, freaking girl.

Bugatti plows ahead with his own agenda. He says that the

county district attorney's office has arranged for the help of the state police lab in Boston.

"I don't know why I'm doing this. But I told them it's our case to run. Not theirs. Your case, Colón. And, goddamit, I want to know about every step of your investigation. You do nothing ... without checking with me first. Hear?"

"Of course," she says, trying to sound neutral. But inside she's shouting, feeling that buzzing in her body again, the thrill of finding justice for this poor dead woman. *Carajo. My case.*

"And another thing. Corby, can you make taking care of this investigation your top priority? Can you put your shellfish seeding on the back burner? We solve this case quick, we look like heroes. We screw it up or drag our butts and ... Fill in the blanks."

Your campaign for county sheriff goes down the drain, thinks Colón.

"Anything you two don't understand?"

The detective and the harbormaster shake their heads no.

"Then leave me in peace. I have a press conference to prepare for."

They are already out the door when Bugatti calls. "Colón!" She slumps to a halt. Church too.

"Come back here a minute, gal."

Church catches her eyes, seems to ask her silently if she needs a wingman. She nods for him to go on. When she gets back to the chief, he throws the forensic report across his desk. It lands with a slap.

"Read this stuff and get back to me with an investigation strategy by this afternoon."

She's in the middle of reaching for the report when he speaks again.

"Hold it. Close the door."

Here comes my harassment case, she thinks.

"One little thing. Let's just keep what's in that report between the two of us for the moment. Especially pages sixteen and seventeen."

"What?" She gives him a look. Is not getting the picture.

He smiles with the power of having a secret. "Just read it and keep it to yourself, ok? It could be our ace in the hole."

"Really?"

"Yeah, really, my little *guapa*. Trust your daddy."

Not on your freaking life.

• • • • •

Church is waiting when she walks out the front door of the small police station on Wharf Street. He sees the thick, white report that she carries in her right hand. The one that she clutches to her chest and folds her arms over, pretending she's trying to keep warm in the raw, damp air.

"What was that all about?"

"Pardon?"

"That thing in there."

"You heard him. She's not your Moore lady. We got a cold case, but not some ancient unsolved mystery."

"No, I mean just now. After." He tries to catch her eyes, but they are already fixed on her blue Accord across the parking lot.

"Nothing. Just the usual. My boss trying to micromanage my life." She's on the move, brushing wind-blown hair off her face and neck. He follows her to the Honda.

"I don't like it."

"What?"

"You know. The way he calls you *chiquita* and gal. That sort of thing."

She gets to the car, opens the door. He can see a booster seat in the back, a small plastic basket full of kids' books, Disney CDs spread

over the passenger seat, about five empty coffee cups from Dunkin'
Donuts.

"Forget about it, will you?"

"It's not right."

She drops into the driver's seat, throws the forensic report on top
of the clutter in the passenger seat.

He puts his hand on the top edge of the car door.

"I don't need anyone to fight my battles for me, ok?" she says.
Take your hand off my car, gringo.

"What *do* you need?"

"I need to know where someone gets his hands on a pair of slave-
era manacles. I need to put a name on your island girl. I need to think
why somebody buries someone like that. When she's still alive. You
understand that?"

"Where you going now?"

"Hey? Why so nosy, pal?"

He gives her a sad-eyed look. He's still trying to figure out why
she called him at night on the tug. Wonders whether she's working
some kind of angle he's not aware of. He still feels unsettled by her
call. Like she was interviewing him. Like she knows things she's not
talking about. Like he's more than a witness. Like that time in the
Bahamas. April, 1988.

● ● ● ● ●

Besides the birdman Paolo—the captain, the leader—there are four of
them on Whale Cay tonight. It's a mile-long, deserted lump of coral and
brush and sand set at the dividing line between the roiling, indigo wa-
ters of the Atlantic, and the calm, turquoise bay called the Sea of Abaco.
A network of swirling tides. A catcher of dead bodies. Like the dolphin's,

whose bones are keeping him company. Like the ghostly wreck of the sport-fishing yacht tossed up on the coral. Its tuna tower now the perfect look-out post. The perch he climbs to. To keep watch. Like the others.

Four men and a woman are stationed at key points around the island in the dark. Watching for a boat, coming from an unknown direction to meet them. To exchange a seabag full of money for five one-pound plastic bags of white powder. The deal that has taken Paolo all winter to set up.

6

"COÑO." A cloud of cigarette smoke bursts from Colón's lungs. She snatches the lab rats' report off the steering wheel where she has it braced while she's reading.

She has been parked in the lot at Cormorant Beach for more than an hour since leaving the station, trying to digest the staties' forensic report without any hassles from her boss or any phone calls about her other investigations like the B&E on Neck Road.

Her eyes ache. She's tired. Last night she and Abuela—her grandmother the old Cuban *santera*—stayed up late in the shrine room of their apartment scattering the shells, *las conchas*, asking the saints what they knew about this dead woman who has begun confessing a litany of dirty stories to Colón. But the *orisha* had almost nothing to say on the subject. Especially nothing like this.

She draws the report up to within six inches of her eyes. "What the hell?"

This close the black words on the shiny white paper begin to blur and dance as she stares at them. But what they say here on the bottom of page seventeen does not change:

"Some metal items were discovered in the grave. They were actually in the lower body cavity as if they may have been swallowed by the victim."

She rolls down the window of the Accord, tosses her stale Dentyne, then puts the window back up to keep out the snow that has begun to swirl around the car, cover the parking lot at Cormorant Beach. Maybe the last snow squall of the year. For a full minute she stares out into the bay. The car's engine mutters, the heater floor vent hisses as the speakers pulse softly to the rhythm of UB-40 singing about red, red wine.

Two miles offshore the light tower on Bird Island is nothing more than a faint, gray shadow. She thinks that it looks like a tombstone. *What would it be like to die out there with the cold earth pressing in around you? Your mouth gulping for air. Coming up with nothing but the after-taste of sex and Myers rum.*

She stares harder at page seventeen again.

"One item found in the body cavity is a steel key consistent with ones used to open a bank safe-deposit box. It is seriously corroded from all of those years in the wet earth. The other is a gold, antique costume ring. The gold on the ring band has been worn thin from use. But under spectrographic analysis, we have been able to see the faint outline of an engraving of three, possibly four upper-case letters in script. Perhaps 'HIS?' Perhaps 'KLS?' or KIS?' We cannot be sure. We are sending the ring out to the FBI crime lab for further analysis."

There in the middle of the page are two color pictures, taken by digital camera of the key and the ring. She squints at them, wonders what it would be like to swallow metal like that.

"What are you trying to tell me, *guapa*? How did you do such a thing? Why? Did you swallow these things at the same time? Did they belong to you? How long can such things stay in the stomach?"

She thinks of sharks she saw on the Discovery Channel that had old beer cans in their bellies when they were caught and cleaned. Alligators found with dog collars in their guts. But maybe some things, like that key and the ring, would eventually work their way out into the toilet. Especially if someone had swallowed them in condoms or balloons. It was the old drug mule trick, gulping condoms full of cocaine packets to get the drugs through customs.

"Damn. You were into some kinky *cosas*, hon!"

"Excuse me?" A muffled voice from outside the half-open car window.

Her head snaps back as if something has hit her. But it's only her reflexes taking over, startled by the face just outside the window, the humiliation of being caught talking out loud to herself.

"You want this?"

Corby Church stands outside her Accord, bent over at the waist in his denim coat, staring in the window at her. He has a sixteen-ounce cardboard cup of Java Joe's coffee in his gloved hand.

She inhales a deep drag from her cigarette, stubs it out in the ashtray … then slaps the report shut, drops it on the floor beneath her legs and wonders if she's blushing as she lowers the window the whole way. Cigarette smoke roils out.

"Anybody every tell you that you could get yourself shot sneaking up on people like that?"

"Sorry. I thought you could use a coffee fix, working right through lunch like this. I got blueberry scones too. And spinach croissants."

Snow has begun to clot over his hair and brows. His nose is bright pink, and for a second she wonders whether he's a drinker … or just has a cold.

"You better get in here before you turn into a snowman." She leans across the passenger seat, unlocks the door on the far side of the car, pops it open.

UB-40 is still rocking "Red, Red Wine" on the U-Mass Dartmouth college radio station when he drops into the shotgun seat. He just sits still for a minute. She can tell that he's listening to the song, having a little memory. He's grinning strangely, the way the local swamp Yankees do when the winter has gone on too long and life feels like a cruel joke. It's a cute grin. An honest grin. She can tell he's glad to see her.

"Gotta love this weather," he says finally.

She plays along, glad to deflect the conversation away from the report that lies on the floor. "Only in New England. Snow—accumulating snow—in the middle of April. I've gotta get a job someplace warmer."

"You're Puerto Rican, right?"

She gives him a look like *yeah, so?* "Half," she says. "My father's side. My mother's side of the family is a *loco* mix of Cubans and Jamaicans. I got my name from the Cubans."

"You ever think about going back?"

"Excuse me?" *Is he coming on with some racist stuff?*

He seems to realize his questions are putting her off, passes her the coffee, a scone. Starts again. "What I mean is sometimes I wish I had roots in the tropics, in the West Indies. I'd like the excuse of family to call me back to one of those islands. I had this Taj Mahal album called *Mo Roots*. Caribbean folk music. You know it?"

She nods. "My Jamaican cousins played it so much when we were kids, I think I know every song by heart. Used to drive me crazy. That stuff about the St. Kitts woman 'puttin' suga in ha beer call it ale' still pops up in my head sometimes when I'm trying to think about a whole lot of nothing."

She catches him smiling at the way her voice slips into the musical Creole of the song for a second. "Can I flat out ask you something?"

"Yeah, sure. Shoot."

"Did you really track me down here at the beach to load me up on carbs and caffeine and reminisce about some islands so far from here they might as well be on another planet? Or is something else on your mind?"

His eyes roll, trace a streak of dirt that looks like a comet on the ceiling of the car.

"You're thinking about her, our lady of chains. Am I right?"

He shrugs. Nods. "Maybe I thought that we could talk a little. You know, since you called me at home the other night and all. With questions of your own …"

She tries to soften what must be an impatient look on her face. "Talk to me."

"I keep picturing that skull, the green mud for eyes. That red hair like some kind of horse's tail."

"Somebody really did her wrong."

"No kidding. And they may have put her out there since … since I started looking after the island. It's a creepy feeling. I never had even the slightest idea that something …"

"Hey, you don't have to make excuses with me. I'm not the town selectmen."

"Yeah, but maybe I should have seen something years ago. That's somebody's daughter who got buried on my island."

"And someone's mother." The words just slip out before she can stop them. She's surprised. What he said about the victim being somebody's daughter put her off her guard for a second. Touched her heart a little.

Most guys she knows would not imagine a life for a corpse. They would just see bones or a puzzle. Church seems different. Now, suddenly, against all the warnings she ever had at detective school, all she learned from Lou Votolatto when she worked for the CPAC unit on the Cape, she has told someone things he has no need to know about a case. Stuff from the report, stuff she promised herself and Bugatti that she would keep to herself. She has spilled. Like some kind of amateur investigator. So much for playing her cards close to the vest. At least for this hand.

"She was a mother?"

"Look, I don't think this is going to come out at the press conference. And I told the chief I would keep it to myself so he can control the flow of information. You know how he is. But he gave me the report from the state lab." She thinks she sees his eyes flick to the stapled pack of paper a few inches below her knees on the car floor.

"She had kids?"

She cocks an eye at him like *I'm mud*, cabrón, *if a word of this gets out.* "I'll tell you, if you promise to get out of here and leave me in peace."

"It's your game. A mother …? Jesus."

"Well, at least, almost. The report says she was about six months pregnant."

"How the hell can they figure that out?"

She stares out the window toward Bird Island, pretending she doesn't hear his question. Doesn't want to think about what she read on page sixteen of the report. Doesn't want to picture a little, half-formed skull, small as a kitten's. *Blood flowing from the hole over the eye. Pulsing, red as a valentine.*

"Probably her first. She wasn't much more than a kid. In her early twenties, they figure."

"Damn." His face has fallen a little. His nose turned pale. She can feel his mind working. Maybe trying to picture a young woman, with long, red hair. A life in her belly.

"Hey, I got a lot of work to do, ok?"

"Right." His voice wobbles a little, the hitch again. He sounds distracted as he scrambles out of the Accord, starts to close the car door.

"Corby."

"Yeah?"

"Thanks for lunch." Her lips spreading into a smile. She holds his blues eyes in her gaze, sees the sparkle rising in his eyes again … Cute. Really cute.

Now he's smiling, too. "How about dinner?"

"Are you asking me on a date?"

"Would tonight work?"

She's wanting to say yes. She hasn't been out to dinner with a guy for at least six months. But she doesn't have time to think about a date now. Doesn't have time to wonder why he's still squinting as if something is confusing or troubling him … Her mind is already feeling the tug of her murder case, her hand already reaching for the report she has to finish reading this afternoon.

"Can I get back to you?"

I've got to come up with an investigation strategy for the chief. And there's a dead girl whispering a sexy story in my head again, dragging me into her forbidden world

• • • • •

She tastes the rum on his breath again. The Myers. His hands move as if he's coiling her hair into rope at her back, and she thinks for a second of Rapunsel. A prince climbing her, hanging from her hair. Now his tongue is reaching into her mouth. Teasing. Probing her throat. Maybe she wants this. This desire. This love. If that is what it is.

His body presses her hips back against something hard. A table, a counter, something metal, nobby. Maybe a stove. She doesn't know. His prick uncoiling against her thigh. Somewhere a gull screeches.

She tries to pull away, get her bearings. Bites his lips softly. "Stop it!" His hand is in her thong. In her. My god. "You love this don't you?"

She is clawing at his back, trying to scream ... when something smacks her from behind. Her left ear's ringing. On fire. She opens her mouth to gulp the air just as a hand rises over her head. Then dives down, making a swift spiral around her neck, sweeping her hair beneath her chin ... Just before she feels her throat seize with a sharp jerk from the noose of her tresses.

7

SWEAT'S DRIPPING DOWN Chi Chi Bugatti's bull neck again as he faces the glare of the lights from TV mini-cams and lies.

"That's it, ladies and gentleman, I have nothing more for you at this time. You now have everything I know about the circumstances under which we found the body and what we know about her. Let me summarize: She's a white female, red hair, early twenties. No identification. Probably dead for twenty to twenty-five years."

"One more question, Chief!" a voice calls from the gathering of media people in the garage of the Slocums Harbor firehouse, which has been hastily turned into an auditorium for this press conference. The speaker is a grandmotherly woman, shaggy silver hair and a cane, whom everyone knows as the host of a Cape Cod radio talk show, a local curmudgeon.

He shifts his weight on his legs, heaves a sigh. "Ok, Rita." Now, he puts his hands on his hips and steps out from behind the podium. "Last question."

"Do you think this body is that of another prostitute? Another victim of the New Bedford Serial Killer active during the eighties, the one who has never been caught? Could this be the body of one of the supposed victims who was never found?"

For a second the chief squints his eyes. A pained look flicks across his face. It's clear to Colón, watching from her folding chair, that this is the dreaded question. The one that her boss has been dancing around for the last twenty minutes.

Just the thought that the body on Bird Island might be connected to the legendary unsolved serial murders of the late eighties could send Southeast Massachusetts and the Cape into a paranoid frenzy, turn Slocums Harbor into a tent show of TV trucks and mike-wielding reporters for weeks. The rampage of the New Bedford Serial Killer. New England's deadliest unsolved murder mystery. The cold case from hell. In its day, it toppled the political career of a high-profile district attorney. No telling what it could do this time.

"We're not ruling anything out. Beyond that I have no further comment. Now, will you please excuse me?"

"But Chief ...?"

He pretends he doesn't hear. Striding from the room, his eyes flash at his detective. She's getting up out of her chair along with the other officers on the force who have been sitting down front to make a show of solidarity.

"Don't fuck this up, Colón."

She bristles. "Excuse me?"

"The ante just went up by a factor of eleven."

No need to ask what he means. She grew up in New Bedford. Well ... after she had to leave *la Isla* and came to live with Abuela when she was nine. She knows that eleven is the number of women, known prostitutes and drug addicts, who disappeared from the streets of Nu Bej during the summer of 1988. The decomposing bodies of most turned up along rural stretches of roads leading out of the city, strangled. Two are still missing. After all of these years.

She was barely a teenager when the cops started finding the bodies. She remembers how Abuela would not let her go out in the streets of the South End after dark that summer, would not let her go on a date unless another couple came along. Unless they had a definite destination like the cinemas at the mall. It was just about the worst summer of her life. And now it could be starting all over. The girl's not just in Colón's head. She's getting under her skin. *Sí coño.*

The inside of her cheeks feel scorched. The air stinks of sulfur, stale smoke, fish. Somewhere not too far away, a seabird screeches.

• • • • •

"Look, didn't I say I don't want to talk about the case tonight? No more questions?" She raises the glass of *vinho verde* to her lips, takes a long drink. "I didn't come here so that we could talk shop over a bowl of *paella*."

He freezes with a fork-load of rice and squid halfway to his mouth. "Sorry. All this murder stuff is just getting to me. Especially the serial killer thing. I remember the summer when ..."

"*Basta.* Stop! Will you? Or I swear I'm going home. I have the luck of a babysitter tonight, Abuela watching Ricky. I thought it might be fun to go out to eat somewhere, when you asked. Share a few stories about the islands. Have some laughs. Find out why you love lighthouses so much. Or live on a boat. How come you seem to be doing life with a red, yellow, and green golf umbrella in your hand. That kind of thing. Keep it light, you know? When you have a six-year-old, you don't get out to play all that often. I want to have a good time. You know? For just a couple hours I don't want to think about the dead."

He nods, swallows his bite of rice and squid, calls himself twelve times the fool for messing up the evening. He had meant for things to go differently when he invited her. Not a date exactly. But something along those lines. Get to know this black-haired fireball a little, test the waters so to speak. Take her to his idea of the quintessential romantic restaurant.

They are at a window table in a hideaway called Vasco da Gama, South End of Nu Bej. The snow coming down in flocks of big flakes outside on the street. Inside it's warm. The smell of fish, steaming *linguiça* and garlic fills the air over a handful of candlelit tables. There's a glass cooler by the entrance, full of green wine from the old country. *Fado* music seeps softly from the kitchen.

"The umbrella stuff is easy." He smiles, refilling her glass with *vinho verde*. "I got in the habit of carrying it with me. When I go out to the island, it protects me from the terns. They dive bomb anyone who goes ashore during nesting season."

"You mean they drop little white specks of doo-doo all over your head?" She's got an odd look on her face. Eyes big and black, encouraging him. Flirting maybe. Begging him to tell her something to make her laugh.

"Not so little. Didn't you notice? The birds are back. When we went out to the island with the staties to dig up ..."

She pushes back her chair, stands up. Looks around for her coat. "You're impossible! You know that?"

"What? Come on, sit down. Don't be like that. Talk to me. I'm a nice guy. This is some of the best *paella* in the world."

"And some of the worst conversation. I thought I was obsessive. Jesus. Men. Are you just so consumed with your own agendas that you are too busy to listen and respond to someone else?"

Now the other couples in the restaurant have begun to stare.

"Yemanjá, please …"

"Please, yourself." She pulls her floor-length, black, leather coat over her shoulders, then fishes thirty dollars in small bills from her purse and throws them on the table. "That ought to cover my half."

A second later the door is swinging closed behind her. She disappears into the shadows cast by the streetlights and the snow. Walking the ten blocks to her apartment.

He sits there feeling dumb. And sad. He knows he has fouled up. Hates that the lady in chains keeps popping into his mind. She's screwing up everything. He keeps seeing her long red hair, the green mud in her eye sockets. It's enough to make him gag again. Not just the memory of seeing death and decay. But there's something more personal in those bones that he's fearing.

So he's a mess. But, damn it all, Colón's overreacting. It's not just because of him. *The woman's got stuff eating at her, too. She just won't talk about it.* He knows how it is. He remembers 1988, twenty-two years ago, He was just two years out of college at the Mass Maritime Academy.

• • • • •

The Princess is not the only one who's a little freaked—he feels like jumping out of his skin. For the last six months or so he has been telling himself that tonight would never happen. That Paolo's get-rich-quick scheme was just a fantasy to get a crew of Jimmy-Buffett types aboard a great, old schooner for an extended cruise in the tropics. A whole lot of don't-worry-be-happy, mon. Tropical breezes, sun, sailing, diving, palm trees, cheap rum, friendly natives, a little weed. And a crazy, beautiful girl to look at day-in, day-out.

He cannot tell whether things have been getting more intense grad-ually, or whether they have just changed suddenly. All he knows is that the last ten days have been a nightmare. Before they sailed away from New England in late October, Paolo had said the plan was to score a couple of bales of reefer and sail his sixty-foot schooner Fedallah *home. Some con-nections he has in New Bedford would be putting up half the front money.*

All they would have to do was sail back from the Bahamas and meet a fishing boat out on Georges Banks that would take the pot ashore. The Fedallah *would then sail on toward Cape Cod, finally meander home to Buzzards Bay. With a little nest egg for everybody. No problem. Enough for Paolo to pay off the loan on his schooner. Enough for Hook and Corby to set up a boat-building shop on the Cape. Enough for Spence to pay at least a year's tuition at his Boston med school. Enough for that crazy girl to finally get a place of her own and start skating seriously again.*

But suddenly the plan has changed. Paolo has set up a deal for coke, not pot. Right now Corby wishes he were back north on Buzzards Bay, working at his old job on the Hyannis-Vineyard ferry. He hates cocaine. Hates the way it makes you feel. Hates its lies of omnipotence. Hates what it does to people. Turns them into thieves and assholes and whores. Just look at what it's doing to the Princess. If he had the money, he would catch a flight home out of Marsh Harbour.

Well, maybe.

8

"WHAT THE HELL'S GOING ON?" Colón's talking to herself again.
And to a bunch of goats.

When she really needs to get away from things and try to clarify
her thinking, she comes here. The water treatment lagoons on the
dump road. It's the last place Chi Chi would ever look when he gets
in the mood to dish out more of his harassment.

Three large goats are nuzzling the palm of her right hand, pressing their snouts through the little square holes in the hurricane fence.
Their chin hairs and slick tongues tickle her fingers as they nibble the
pellets of dog food she offers them.

She thinks it's crazy that someone turned a small herd of goats
loose inside the fenced compound of lagoons. Goats in polished, little Slocums Harbor. They seem so out of place. Maybe that's what
she likes about them. Mangy little buggers, stinking of shit, like critters you might find dodging traffic in Mo Bay or Puerto Rico. Island
critters. Tropical souls. Displaced to a *Yanqui* swamp, just trying to
get by. And make babies. *You gotta love the little ones.*

"You want to get the hell out of Dodge? Join my tent show, munchkins? You want to team up with Gypsy Yemanjá and little Ricky, hit the road and follow the sunshine? Dress up in silk scarves? Shake some tambourine, read the shells for folks? Tell them all about the love and misfortune the *orishas* got waiting for them. Just like Abuela does, eh?"

Bright sunshine bursts from behind a cloud. She squints for a second, then shades her eyes with a hand as she drops down on one knee and puts her face next to the fence. A little goat about the size of a terrier rises on his hind legs, pushes his head through one of the holes in the fence and begins licking her cheeks, her ear.

"Ouch! *Coño*, Rocco. No biting!"

The goat backs off to his own side of the fence, steps away, gives her a hurt look.

"You trying to tell me something, *nene?* You think I was too hard on Corby? You think I should give him a second chance?" Her voice softens.

The little goat moves slowly toward the fence and the woman who is still just out of range, down on her knee.

"He's self-absorbed. A space shot, always drifting away from me into his own mind. A bit of a *payaso, sabe?*"

The goat starts licking her cheeks again.

A faraway look spreads over her face. She's picturing something. "*Aye, mi!* There's something about him, though …" *Like what kind of guy would live on a tug boat? Listen to Taj Mahal? And sometimes he seems* muy simpático. She remembers his bringing her coffee, a scone, spinach croissant. Sweet. And what he said about the dead girl. She was somebody's daughter. Not the kind of thing her ex Jorge would ever think of. So maybe she should give this lighthouse keeper another look. It's not like she has any kind of life outside of work, Ricky,

Abuela, and the *orishas. Besides, he's pretty easy on the eyes. In a gringo sort of...*

The little goat Rocco starts tearing at the rolled-up computer printout sticking out of her jacket pocket.

"Hey! Give that back. What are you doing? What am *I* doing?" *Thinking about some guy when I have a murder to solve, maybe a serial killer to bring to justice, somebody who might still be killing, who might freaking kill again? This is my case. My buzz ...with a dead girl getting into my veins, feeding me random pieces of the puzzle in my head. And part of me is running from her, from the case. Why? Get back in the game,* jeba.

The little goat keeps tugging on the printout with his teeth.

"*Dejalo*, Rocco! That could be just the clue to finding a murderer that you're trying to eat. Are you *loco? Am I?*"

She rips the tube of papers from the goat's mouth.

"*Chinga*!" A heavy breath escapes through her nose as she unrolls what is left of the printout. Dusts the flakes of torn paper from the crumpled mess. Looks at the list of eleven women from the New Bedford area considered to be victims of the serial killer during the summer of 1988. And if she doesn't find her redhead here, there are two more columns of names. Over a hundred women who just plain vanished off the face of the earth from Bristol and Plymouth counties between 1986 and 1991. And nearly as many from the Cape and islands. How many did the serial killer take? And is one of them Corby's island girl? The lady in chains, the mother?

If she could put a face on her, then maybe she could find the girl's history. Maybe catch the *cabrón* who killed her like that. Maybe stop the bastard before he half strangles and buries someone else alive. Stop these *hidioso* stories of sex and violence that keep scrolling through her head and will not let her sleep.

But where to start? Photos maybe. Redheads. Better yet, consult the *orishas,* the saints.

Deal with Corby Church later.

• • • • •

Colón's *abuela* is almost panting with haste as she pulls her flowing white robe over her house dress, the white turban over the gray hair tied in a bun on her head. "Only Elegguá, the saint of the crossroads, can help you now. Are the coconut and the water ready?"

"*Aquí.*" The sacred water is in a Bacardi bottle. A dinner plate holds a mound of shredded coconut and four triangles of coconut shell, the white meat still inside. Colón's wearing a white robe too, but no turban. She's a believer, but not yet a *santera*, has not yet made saint. She's still learning the mysteries and the rituals of the *orishas*, cannot practice magic alone.

Abuela lights a fat cigar, inhales deeply as she leads her grand-daughter into the shrine room and closes the door. In a low cabinet on the floor behind the door stands a life-size, black clay head on a plastic tray. It overlooks the statues of saints and soup tureens, the *soperas*, that collect offerings to the saints. The head is more or less cone-shaped, with cowrie shells for the eyes and mouth. There are three horns sticking out of the head. Elegguá, who Abuela sometimes calls *el Nene*, the child. One of the most powerful o*rishas*. A capricious spirit who, in his twenty-one different incarnations, holds the keys to everything from birthday surprises to life and death.

"Take a puff and blow some smoke in *el Nene*'s face." The old *santera* hands the cigar to her, bends down and blows a huge mouth-ful of smoke in the face of the clay head. Colón does the same, then leaves the burning cigar in the tray beside the head. She also places a ten-dollar bill and a box of Raisinets in the large tureen filled with booty behind Elegguá.

"Now the rest of the blessing."

The granddaughter sprinkles three dashes of water and three dashes of the grated coconut on the head as the *santera* starts to chant in Yoruba. "*Ibarakoo molumba Elegguá ...*"

The invocation goes on for several minutes as the two women take their places to either side of the hemp mat on which divination takes place. Meanwhile the air fills with smoke ... and Colón's mind drifts with the voice in her head, with the girl. Into the nightmare, again.

• • • • •

She feels something warm and wet is running over her forehead, nose, upper lip. Wishes she could wipe it away, tugs on her arms again as if she were trying to curl an immense barbell. But she's doubled over, almost in a ball. Her knees jut out, blocking her attempt to lift her arms. The hard things, the cuffs that bind her wrists, scrape against her shins, cutting them.

She does not care, tries to inhale as deeply as she can to gather her strength. The air she sucks stinks of sulfur and stale smoke and fish. As she forces her lungs to swell, she thinks she hears the clinking of a bottle against a glass somewhere not too far away. An angry voice. Possibly voices. Or maybe just the plaintive screeching of seabirds. She cannot tell. Her ears are ringing, aching with the sound of every new noise. Each one seems a command to find her will, focus. Pry her arms free. Stretch herself to ease the pressure on her baby.

Until now the baby was little more than a troublesome mystery to her. And a way to make a man keep his promise. But now she pictures her, pictures her girl child. She strains to break free before she and the child expire in this tight ball of bone and flesh. The smooth pink face of her daughter, the long legs. The gleaming white skates on her feet. Her little, blue chiffon skater's dress flashing as she steps onto the ice and the spotlights find her. Red curls rise in the air as she speeds toward center ice, the music filling in from a dozen speakers. A reggae beat. Guitars. And then Bob Marley's voice.

9

"YOU GOT A PROBLEM, buddy boy?" Hook Henry looks up from his work and stares at Corby Church.

The harbormaster shrugs, both hands jammed in his jeans pockets.

The boat carpenter stops turning a C-clamp to lock a fresh plank against the ribs of a Herreshoff daysailer that he's building. "You look like you've seen a ghost."

Church inhales the scent of planed cedar and stares around the little barn in North Falmouth where his friend turns piles of lumber into works of art that sail. The neat line of chisels, rasps, spoke shaves hanging on the wall over the workbench gleam in the morning sun filtering through the windows. What a place. Twenty-two years ago this was Church's dream. The only place he ever wanted to be, building boats with this man who is like his brother.

"Well, out with it. You need something?"

"Yeah, I guess."

The carpenter wipes sawdust from his hands on the front of his bib overalls and gives a cockeyed look, one eyebrow arched like a pirate. He has a sturdy, broad-shouldered build. Thick neck, balding dome wrapped in a red bandana. Bushy, broad, blond mustache. A solid six foot three tall. With soft hazel eyes that always seem to smile ... as if the absurdities of life constantly amuse him.

"Ten o'clock. A little too early for a beer. You know what I mean, jellybean?"

"I could be tempted."

"Oh, Jesus. Here we go. What kind of a mess are you going to get me into now? Don't tell me. Pusski trouble again."

"Fuck you."

"Not in your wildest dreams, pal."

"You know what I mean."

"Hey, you came to see me. You're the one messing up my morning."

"Come on, Hook."

"Hey, I have 'La Traviota' cooking on the stereo, a hot mug of Earl Gray and a bright, spring morning for hanging planks on this boat ... And you come stumbling in here, all out of breath, tracking a shit-load of mud. Messing up my Zen."

"Sorry."

"Right. So take what you can get or fuck on off. The maestro is at work. Not all of us can coast on the good will of the tax-payers ..."

"I've got to tell you something a little scary, ok?"

• • • • •

"No shit?" The carpenter pours them both a second mug of tea. He hands one to Church, who is perched on a huge coil of lobster-pot warp near the wood stove at the back of the shop, then he flops into his old rocker again. "You think the cops have any idea who she is?"

"Seems like they are chasing this serial killer thing. Like maybe she's one of the bodies they never found."

"But what about the red hair ... you know?"

"Yeah. "

"Damn."

"Exactly. This could get really ugly."

"Christ! I swear hardly a week goes by that I don't think about that crazy little slut. And that bloody trip."

"Man, you're taking this worse than I am. Calm down. It's old news. Really old news. I can go for months without ever thinking about—"

"You lying sack of shit. You mean you never think about the Abacos? About kicking back again under the fig tree on Guana Cay, staring out at the crystal blue water?"

Church shrugs. *Well ... maybe.*

"Don't you think she's going to turn up on some old missing person's list from the late eighties, and your new girlfriend's going to put two and two together?"

"She's not my girlfriend."

"That's what you always say. Next thing I know, she'll be inviting you to meet her parents, and you will be asking me how the hell you're going to break it off. Just like always. Tell me you don't have the hots for her."

"She thinks I'm a total bozo."

"Well?"

"Well, what?"

"Aren't you?"

"Give me a break. I came here for a little friendly counsel."

"Yeah?"

"Yeah."

"Well, then I have just one more question for you."

"What?"

"You going to tell her what you know?"

"Yemanjá?"

"Is that her name?"

"You think I'm crazy?"

"Don't you suppose she's going to find out?"

"I don't know. That's why I'm here. Aren't you the guy with all the bright ideas? The maestro? What would you do?"

"I'd stay the hell out of the hen house."

"What's that supposed to mean?"

"It always gets you in trouble, doesn't it, buddy?"

"She's not like anyone I ever met before."

"That's what you said twenty-some years ago about your ex-wife … and the Princess." He scratches the emerging beard on his cleft chin. "Man, you sure can pick them. What the hell kind of name is Yemanjá?"

"It's a Cuban thing. Maybe. Or Puerto Rican. Jamaican. I can't exactly remember. She said it's the name of some kind of voodoo goddess of the sea."

"There you go."

"What?"

"Messing with the devil in a blue dress again."

Once was enough.

· · · · ·

Part of him says he cannot quit now. Better see this thing through. He read somewhere that once you begin a gesture it's fatal not to go through with it. Ok. And he has to stay for the sake of the others, too. Hook, especially … Like stand by your friends, man. And the Princess. Well, because she has those amazing green eyes. A bonfire of red hair. And she's lost in the world.

The whine of an outboard engine cuts through the silence of the night. It's coming from the northwest, maybe from Green Turtle Cay or a more remote island. Moving closer. The moon is down. So maybe this is it. The rendezvous.

He touches the .38 tucked under his sweatshirt in the waist of his jeans. Jesus Christ, what is he going to do with a gun? Shoot somebody? Why has he let Paolo give him this thing? He detests it. But Paolo has armed everyone tonight. Even the Princess. Just in case.

10

SATURDAY MORNING and Colón feels like shit. No buzz from the hunt for justice. Just the freaking hang-over, the filmy memory of a daughter who never was. Gleaming white skates on her feet. A little, blue chiffon skater's dress. A voice inside her head crying, *Help me.*

Living with Abuela, and having regular visits with the *orishas* in the shrine room since age nine, Colón has grown accustomed to listening to the voices of the dead. But until now, until the island girl, the dead have almost always spoken through Abuela or answered questions through the patterns Abuela and she can read when they scatter the cowrie shells or pieces of coconuts on the floor in the shrine room.

She thinks she may have heard whispers from spirits in her head before, but only in brief comforting phrases, an occasional sentence. After she prayed to them. And only in places heavy with spiritual energy, like a *cemetario* or that Indian mound in Chatham where the disaster-prone fisherman and attorney Michael Decastro—her last fatal attraction—took her. But the stuff that she's hearing in her head is nothing like those other voices. It's smoldering, shrill. It won't stop with the stories. They are really starting to freak her out.

She spent half of last night in Abuela's shrine room trying to consult with the saints again. About the island girl. About the serial killer. About the sick stories that keep playing in her head. But the shells she cast offered vague, indifferent answers from Changó and Obatalá.

"You have barely talked to your son ... or me ... since we got here," says Abuela.

Colón looks around her. The grass green, the birds chirping, robins plucking worms from the earth. Air heavy with the perfume of wet earth, sunshine, sea salt, beasts in heat. And for the first time since last fall, the elephants are outside playing in their yard.

She brings Ricky and Abuela here to the zoo at Buttonwood Park as often as possible. It has been a family ritual on her days off since the time when Ricky was still in a stroller. He has always loved *los elefantes*. And she does too. There is something about their dimpled skin and the way they nod their massive heads back and forth. Mesmerizing. But today she just wishes one of those big boys would crush her skull.

"*Lo siento*, sorry," she says to Abuela. Then she looks to Ricky.

The kindergartener in the hooded Bruins sweatshirt stares up at his mother and rolls his enormous black eyes. He has her ex's Argentine genes. Wavy, medium-brown hair, olive skin, thin face. Only the eyes and the gleaming teeth speak of the various strains of Africa, Spain, and the West Indies that he has inherited from his mother.

"Come on, *nene*. Eat up." She hands him a bag of popcorn that she has been hording. "And smile please. *Sonrisa, por favor.*"

"Abuela is right, Mami. You're acting so weird."

You would be acting loco, *too, if you had the feeling a volcano was about to blow right beneath your feet*, she thinks. Then she scoops her son into her arms. "Tickle attack!"

• • • • •

The boy is still squealing with delight, Abuela polishing off the last of the popcorn, when the phone in her pocket starts to chime.

"Detective Colón?"

"Speaking."

"This is Johnny Machico."

She frowns, turns away from her family, takes a few steps back from the fence surrounding the deer exhibit. "Excuse me, who?"

"The chief didn't tell you?"

"What?"

"I'm sorry. I think maybe somebody dropped the ball. I thought you knew about me?"

"What?"

"Excuse me, ma'am. Am I interrupting something? You want me to call back another time? Just say the word."

She pulls the silver phone away from her ear, as if to clap it shut. Then she thinks, *If this were a picture phone,* hombre, *I would show you exactly what you are interrupting. My family.*

"Ma'am? Are you there? Should I call back? Is there a better time to update you on our case?"

Coño. Our *case?* "Wait, who are you, again? You work for the DA?" She thinks his voice sounds like a high school kid's.

"Johnny Machico, I'm the new hire."

"For what?"

"Slocums Harbor Police Department."

"What?"

"I'm a detective."

"What?"

"I was just finishing up crime school when the chief hired me.

But then my Guard unit got called up. I'm fresh back from deployment in Baghdad. Military Police."

He sounds so young. Why the hell has the chief saddled her with a newbie? As if trying to solve this case has not put enough on her mind. Now this? Babysitting? Who? The no-show that she got hired to replace? She tries to picture him. Cannot. The only images coming up in her mind are snapshots of burned-out Hummers and prison guards at Abu Grave perched atop a pile of Iraqis. *Jesus and María. That bloody war.*

"You're on the job now? The murder case?"

"According to the chief. I just found out myself yesterday afternoon. He hands me a whole stack of papers about the Jane Doe and says 'Start reading, boy.' Gotta love government work. Especially on Saturday, eh?"

She hears a human being on the other end of the line, has the urge to ask him if he has a family. *Like can't you find something to do besides police shit on the weekend?* As if she's much better at setting this dead girl aside ... Her eyes shift from the white-tail deer munching grass in their compound to Abuela who has a sad, impatient look on her face. She's leading Ricky away toward the pony rides, getting him out of his mother's space.

"Hey, look, can I call you back? I'm at the zoo with my kid."

"Whenever you're ready. I think I've found something about our girl."

She closes her eyes, hears the dead girl's voice getting louder. Sees the dream that woke her breathless this morning. *Carajo.*

• • • • •

The girl thinks she could live with this throbbing pain in her head, the ringing in the ears, the scorching heat in her throat, the metal cuffs binding her wrists. Even being trussed up in a ball like this, lying on her side.

If she could just pee. She has had to pee for as long as she can remember. And now it is just about the only thing she can think about. The fire burning between her legs. That she can't put out. Because it hurts so much that her pelvis refuses to hear anything her brain is saying.

She wants to scream.

And finally she does. Releases a high-pitched piercing wave of pain. Feels her eyes bleeding tears. Moaning. Until she knows this scream, this pain, for what it is. The howl as she leapt off the mountain, so to speak, her first time with her beloved Jared, back in high school. And the last time she took the plunge ... tonight. The amazing free fall into blackness that she has taken with all the other men in between. How many?

· · · · ·

"Ok, Johnny Match. You've got my full attention now." The words burst from her mouth in a torrent. "You said you found something."

She did not want to call him, wanted to wait until at least after she, Abuela, and Ricky got home for lunch. But she does not do suspense very well, especially after these flashes of beating and bondage and slow death that she has been having in her head all morning.

So here she is, biting her lower lip to shreds, watching Ricky ride a zoo pony. Around and around. The phone in her hand, her head pounding with blood, her voice barely holding off the trembling.

"I ran down the dental records yesterday of all the redheads on the missing persons list."

"*Carajo*!" She kicks her foot against one of the fence posts at the pony corral. Damn, this guy is way ahead of her.

"Ma'am?"

"I was going to do that this afternoon."

She hears him take a deep breath. "Look, this is awkward. I didn't mean to step on your toes. I should have talked to you first. It's your case. I'm here to back you up. I'm just a little bit obsessive when it comes to research."

The muscles in her shoulders soften a little. "Me too ... *Mira!* I'm feeling a little overwhelmed. This case went from an archeological discovery to a serial killer investigation in about four days."

"Crazy, huh?"

"You have no freaking idea." She waves to her son passing by her on his pony in the corral. Sees Abuela leaning against the barn, arms crossed over her chest, staring daggers at her like she is the worst mother in the world for talking on the phone right now. Or just a fool.

"So ...?"

"Tell me what you know."

"I might have found our girl."

She hears Bob Marley suddenly singing in her head and just blurts without thinking. "Was she an ice skater?"

"What?"

"You got a solid lead?"

"The state forensic guys are checking the dental records right now. We ought to have an answer in an hour or two."

"No shit? That fast?"

"I know some people."

"You're pretty useful, Johnny Match." She thinks maybe this is just what she needs, a partner. A go-getter who can charge ahead with the basic police work on the case, while she tries to get herself around this freaking voice unraveling in her head. Around Coby Church, too. He's a charmer, but he's giving off some dark vibes. Maybe even guilty ones. Rule number one of murder investigation: never trust the guy who finds the body.

"My mother says I'm a hound dog, ma'am."

"Call me anytime … But two things?"

"What's that?"

"Will you stop with the 'ma'am'?"

"And …?"

"Can you give me our girl's name?"

So I can get a bead on who's telling me this crazy mierda? *And what, if anything, she has to do with the serial killings and Corby Church?*

• • • • •

How many? How many guys? How many mistakes has she made? How many snakes has she charmed? In search of what? This shuddering letting go of all that binds her to the earth and life and dignity. So that she can fly. Like a young girl again in her mind. Like a virgin. To a place where everything is the way it used to be with Jared when she was sixteen. When he thought she was the brightest light in the sky. Before things started turning to shit …

She can feel the cool heat of the blue spotlight following her, following them both, as they glide across the arena ice. Partners, high school lovers. The sound system churning. Marley again, singing his love song. "Turn the Lights Down Low." She feels the warmth of Jared's hands. The kick and glide of his hip against hers. In synch. The skates flashing against the ice. Her blue skater's dress rising with the wind and heat of their dance as he spins her, lifts her to the sky, holds her over his head. Nothing but his hands, the reggae. The quivering in her loins. She's a bird soaring through the black space. A rocket to the moon.

Suddenly soaking in her own urine.

11

"HEY, SLICK, we going to be friends again?"

Church hears her husky voice coming from the telephone receiver. Not his cell, but the phone in the tug. She says she wants to make peace. But maybe she's lying. His brain is shouting for him to hang up. She knows something. *Stay out of the hen house, buddy..*

Yet some deeper part of him pictures her black, silky hair. Her dark eyes. Wants to see her, smell the lime scent of her body. *Goddamn.*

"Corby?"

God, he needs to end this conversation. "What?"

"Can I come over?"

"Where?"

"Your place."

"My tug?"

"The boat. Is that ok?"

"When?"

"This morning works for me."

"The place is kind of a mess ..."

"I'll bring breakfast. Or lunch. What time is it anyway? I lose track on Sundays."

He thinks she's lying. She's swimming in her case. She's chasing down some lead. This isn't cool ... But, damn, everything seems fresher and brighter when she's around.

"What do you like to eat?"

"You ever cook on a boat? It's kind of limited as far as ..."

"You like *tostones*?"

"What?"

"Twice-fried plantains?"

"Those big bananas?"

"With honey."

• • • • •

She watches him from behind as he climbs the ladder from the galley to the wheelhouse of the *Brutus III*. No question, he looks good in those tight, freshly-washed jeans, the red waffle shirt hugging his shoulder muscles. She can see his hips flex as he climbs with the tray of coffee, her *tostones,* grilled ham. Even with the loose-waisted shirt, there's no mistaking the way his broad back tapers to a thin waist. She bets he was a runner, a sprinter. In high school she loved watching the track boys do their thing.

"Welcome to a million-dollar view of Cape Cod's best kept secret."

She sits down on a small berth at the back of the wheelhouse, looks out on Quissett Harbor, Buzzards Bay beyond. Three scallopers in a line, steaming east from New Bedford to Woods Hole Passage just two miles away.

She looks across the bay, sees the high-rises of Nu Bej, pictures her house over there, fifteen miles away. Ricky's window. She gave him the only room with the sea view when he got old enough to sleep in a bed.

It used to be her room, and she misses waking up at that window, seeing the water, the boats, the gulls.

"This is pretty *fino*."

"And so is this," he says. His mouth is half full, and he is waving a fork with a piece of *tostone* in front of his face.

His nose is red again, and she wonders whether he was hitting the sauce last night. She'll know soon enough … if he can't get through the meal without suggesting mimosas or bloody marys.

"So do you think I'm a lunatic?"

Carajo. She wonders if he's onto to her suspicions about him, cuts a piece of ham to stall. Takes a bite. "What?"

"You know. Do you think it's crazy, me living on the *Brutus*?"

She shrugs. "It's different. But I never really thought about it." She's lying to him. The first time she heard that he lived on a boat, she thought about reruns of detective shows on TV. Didn't Magnum live on a boat, or was it McGyver? She can't remember. She had a crush on both of them as a kid. If she lived on a boat, she wouldn't stay here. She would be heading south as fast as the boat would carry her, to San Juan, or Santiago de Cuba or Mo Bay. Some place like that.

He sits down beside her on the bench. "What are you thinking?"

She's watching a flock of terns chasing a herring gull. They wheel and swoop just above the bright little waves on the harbor. "What?"

"You seem so quiet, like your mind's a thousand miles away."

"You really want to know?"

"How else can I get to know you?"

"Can this boat go? I mean do you ever take it out? Or is it just some kind of—what's the word? *Reina del puerto*, harbor queen. It seems pretty big for one person to run."

He sighs. "Are you trying to bust me?"

Shit, does he know? "For what?"

"Being a poser?"

"Are you?"

He stands up, walks across the wheelhouse, throws a knife switch mounted on a wooden consul in front of the steering wheel. Something grinds deep in the bowls of the tug. Then an engine barks. The floor vibrates beneath her feet. A ragged exhaust note begins to rumble through the funnel, the smokestack, behind the wheelhouse. She smells diesel fumes.

"Want to go for a ride, little girl?"

She feel the skin on her belly tighten, He's messing with her … maybe not just flirting. Maybe signaling that he knows she's here to snoop on him and doesn't give a flying eff. "You're bad."

"No, really, you want to get out of here? See some islands?"

A little frown flickers over her mouth. She pictures a skull the size of a kitten's.

"Well …?"

Maybe this is the moment to zap him. He's off his guard. But she's liking the way that the morning sun makes his salt-and-pepper hair sparkle. He stands there looking a little like George Clooney in the wheelhouse of a sword fishing boat, one hand on the huge wooden steering wheel.

"What will you tempt me with?"

His eyes roll.

"Really. Why do I want to go on a boat ride with a guy I hardly know?"

"We could go out and watch the seals playing on Penikese Island."

"And?"

A smile bursts over his face. "I could make up a pitcher of mimosas."

"*Coño!*" Her face drops. Turns pale, frozen. Her throat clots with the taste of orange juice and stomach acid.

"What?"

Damn him. The vic's name is on the tip of her tongue. The island girl's long, lovely French name. She wants to sting him with it right now and see how he reacts.

"Hey? Did I say something wrong?"

She sees that hurt puppy look in his eyes. Before she can stop herself, she jumps to her feet and gives him a kiss on that red nose. Makes an excuse. "No. It's just ... Abuela is expecting me home." *I need to talk with the saints and get a better read on a dead girl ... and what I'm doing here with you.*

He looks utterly confused. "Maybe another time?"

"Yeah, maybe."

She can't believe she just said this. But things suddenly seem both clearer and more complicated in her head. Could be she's the one with the booze issue. Because of her ex Jorge's drinking. Because of her *papi.* Just possibly, this truly interesting man, this Corby, might rise to the occasion when she finally hits him with the dead girl's name. Remy's name.

It's the name that Johnny Match has uncovered on a twenty-two-year-old missing person report buried in the files of the Bristol County District Attorney. Because it had been filed twelve years before Kristen's Law established a comprehensive database of vanished persons at the National Center for Missing Adults, Remy La Moreaux's name has been all but lost to the investigative world. It never surfaced on computerized data banks. But Johnny Match has found it. Her original case file is missing from cold case storage in New Bedford, but dental records have confirmed that Corby's island girl was La Moreaux.

Now what, girl? Do I try to talk to the orishas *again about Corby Church and all this sex and violence I've been hearing in my head? Or do I talk to your next of kin?*

12

THE OLD MAN'S HANDS SHAKE as he lifts the picture of a young woman off the top of the TV set. His thin, gray face is a field of ruts, scars, days-old whiskers. Thrift-store paisley shirt buttoned to the neck. Pant cuffs dragging through the cigarette ashes on the wood floor.

"All she ever really wanted was to skate. From the time I took her to see the Ice Capades in Providence when she was just a little kid. After her mother passed. That was it for her. The ice. The music. The silver skates."

"So … this is your daughter, this is Remy?" She takes the photo, stares into the green eyes.

There's something in them she can't quite describe. Something wild, maybe a little scared. Or obscene. Colón has a thousand questions. They have been racing through her head since Johnny Match came up with the name, and this address on the Cape in Harwich for her father. But now she tells herself *dejalo*, let it be, someone has died here. *Patience*, chica. Cuidado! *Let him unpack his memories and grieve, if you can. Have a heart, ok? You just came here to tell this man after twenty-two years of mystery and worry that his daughter's body has been found.*

"She was my angel. When she left, it all went to hell. I thought she just had enough taking care of me. I drink a bit. Her mother gone with the cancer and all. It was hard for a girl like her. With big dreams. Putting up with me. But then that boy Jared, her skating partner. Her boyfriend. When he graduated high school, he took off with another fellow. A queer. After that things just started getting crazy with her. But she done her best to stand by me."

"I'm sure she did, Mr. La Moreaux." Her fingers trace the smooth white skin of the face in the photograph, run down the waves and ringlets of dark red hair tumbling over the shoulders. She can almost feel the faint freckles on the bridge of the nose and at the base of that long neck where the seashell dolphin pendant hangs from a thick, gold chain.

"I always hoped that she had got on with one of those professional skating groups. You know, like Disney. Went on the tour."

He says that he told himself that one day he would wake up and see her on TV. Skating to the music she liked by that Marley fellow. Yes, he had filed a missing person report on her. He had contacted the New Bedford police when her employer called the day after that Labor Day so long ago to say that Remy had failed to show up for work and nobody knew where she had gone. But this wasn't the first time she had just lit off without telling anyone. She had done it two other times in the last year. Once for the whole winter when she went on a sailboat to the Bahamas with a bunch of local guys. But she always came back.

The police were worried. That was the summer all those other girls disappeared from New Bedford and a couple of their bodies had turned up. Initially the police considered her a possible victim of the serial killer, especially after seven more of the girls' decomposed bodies were discovered during the fall of 1988 and spring 1989.

"But they never found her or her body," says her father. "So I told myself she wasn't part of that serial killer insanity, part of that mystery. And I guess the police did, too. After about a year, I stopped hearing from them. They had moved on to other things … and I kept believing she would come home just like all the other times she left. Now … you found her and I don't …"

The old man drops onto the couch. It, the detective's chair, the seventies cabinet TV, and a wobbly coffee table are the only furnishings in the living room of this tattered frame house by the lumberyard.

She can hear the green eyes in the photo shouting, begging. *Find the bastard. Make the motherfucker pay.*

"How old was she when this picture was taken, sir?"

He waves his hand in the air as if to drive off a house fly, doesn't answer the question. There's a glazed look in his eyes as he stares out the front window to the street. As if at any moment he is expecting to see his daughter come walking up on the porch.

"Now she's finally going to be on TV."

Colón feels something burning in her throat. "I'm so sorry."

He seems not to hear. "Tell me, how does she look?"

Forgive him! Forgive my father. Poor tortured soul!

She closes her eyes, raises her hands to her cheeks, wonders what she can say. "Her hair is three feet long."

"It was always her best feature. When she let it free and skated, it looked like she had red feathers trailing from her back. Wings, you know? The coaches out here on the Cape always told her to pin it up. But when they saw the way it made her look—when it was loose—

like a bird, their jaws used to drop. Everybody's did."

Glancing at the photo again. "Your daughter's beautiful."

"A lot of people thought she looked like Julia Roberts in *Pretty Woman*. If she had lived, she could have been somebody. Like Tonya Harding and Nancy Kerrigan. She got to skate with them once. She could have been famous."

"I'm sure." She thinks of the all the press the New Bedford Serial Killer spawned in the late eighties, feels the questions burning in her throat.

"Now everyone will know her name."

"I suppose so," she says automatically. The investigation and the questions are starting to get the best of her, filling her head. She's used to investigation, but this one feels very different. Personal. Constantly demanding. Because of the voice that keeps echoing in her head. Because of her attraction to Corby Church. Because of his suspicious behavior, too. "Do you have any video tapes or films of her skating?"

He shakes his head no. "She took them all."

"She ran off then?"

"Not exactly. Just ... after high school. After Jared left her. She moved out."

"That must have been hard for you. Where did she go?"

"I was all alone then. Working part time with some contractors in Chatham. Building walls. I'm a mason."

"And Remy?"

"She got a job off-Cape waiting tables."

"Really?"

"She made better money than she could off-season here on the Cape. Enough to pay for a room, skating lessons and such."

"Where was that?"

"Mattapoisett. On the South Coast, you know? She worked at

this restaurant on the harbor called the Mattapoisett Inn. I been there once to see her. Had this pretty porch where you could sit and have a drink, look out at the sailboats. That sort of thing. You know the place?"

"It's changed its name."

He reaches out, takes the photo of his daughter from her, admires the image. "Nothing lasts. That's the truth, young lady."

She looks around the room, stares at the tarnished brass crucifix hanging on the wall.

"So she lived in Mattapoisett?"

"Sometimes. She rented different rooms around. On the Cape, Sandwich, Cataumet. And in New Bedford, too. Last place she lived was North End of New Bedford. What they call Weld Square."

"You know of any roommates I might talk to?"

He shrugs. "I didn't ask a lot of questions. She gave me money to help out with the house and things. So I didn't think I had the right to bother her none. Didn't want to know the details neither, I guess. But there were men, I can tell you that."

Her throat feels on fire again. "Why?"

"One time she came by to see me. Left her purse here."

"I don't understand."

"I knocked it off the coffee table by accident. A lot of stuff fell out."

"And?"

"And about four boxes of rubbers fell out."

"You mean condoms?"

"All different colors."

• • • • •

She really needs to talk to Johnny Match, get his read on this case.

Face-to-face, not over a cell phone that someone in the media might listen to.

Coming back from Remy's dad's house in Harwich, she calls Match and asks him to meet her at a Dunkin' Donuts in Bourne. Now, staring across the formica table at him, she's thinking her new partner does not look like she expected. He's small, almost slight. But he's fit. His arms long and limber in the gray V-neck sweater. The cords in his neck are taut. A narrow face, very Italian. With a thin little mustache, long razor-cut side burns. Short black hair, gelled up in little spikes over the forehead. He's self-consciously handsome.

"All we've got is his story about a waitress job and a lot of condoms?" His voice seems soft as the boys' in her theater class from high school.

"You think she was a hooker?" She pushes the remaining half of her glazed chocolate donut toward the middle of the table, has suddenly decided that it's poison.

"Most of the others were."

"So you really think the serial killer got her? Even though the media, back in the day, never counted her among the eleven girls always tied to the case?"

He shrugs. "It's a possibility. The timing's right. Most of the other victims had some connection to Weld Square. She was strangled— well, sort of, like some of the others. And, according to the father, she was seeing a lot of different men like many of the other dead girls."

"Right, but none of the other vics were cuffed in antique *esposas* or buried in a ball like her."

Match says he knows. They were all found alongside highways. Not on an island. Her killer had to have a boat, some knowledge of the bay. Some place nearby to keep the boat. If Remy's death was the work of the serial killer, then he was branching out.

"It doesn't make sense to me. The killer was on a roll. His ritual or routine or whatever you want to call it was working. Why would he change? Expose new details about himself by doing things different?"

"Maybe he got bored. Maybe he wanted to leave a legacy. A monument to his reign of terror? I've read the books, the cases. The really sick ones are like that. Ted Bundy. And the Green River guy, for instance. Killing was their art form. They went through different periods. Liked to embellish on their crimes. Maybe this guy made that mistake. Maybe this is how we catch him … if he's still around."

She's staring at the crescent remains of the chocolate donut, frowning. "You read the internet?"

"What?"

"About the serial killer."

"Sure. There's a lot of garbage and speculation out there."

"Did you see the stuff about how Interpol has begun to wonder whether this guy moved on to Portugal, Belgium, the Czech Republic, some other places in Europe?"

"Are you saying our boy's long gone?"

"What do you think?"

She pauses. "We have to focus on Remy's murder. We don't have the time, man-power, or money to go digging into eleven other cold cases."

Colón says that maybe the serial killer got Remy, maybe not. But many cops spent lots of time already working the cases of those other eleven girls. And in the end they couldn't find the perp. With Remy's body there's a chance to start a fresh investigation. Maybe what she and Match find here will lead to the serial killer. But not now. The best they can do is to focus on finding whoever buried Remy La Moreaux alive. The rest of those poor girls will have to wait.

"So where to next, partner?"

She pictures Corby Church. "I think we need to talk to some locals. I think we need to visit a seaside bar I know."

"Where's that?"

"It used to be called the Mattapoisett Inn."

"You think someone there might help us?"

Unless the saints, the voice inside my head, or Corby Church come through for us first.

13

"DON'T BE STARING AT ME with that squinty-eyed look, *nena*! *No me mira!* It says right here in the *ordun* of the shells: 'A noble king does not tell lies.' *Claro!* The *orishas* have spoken. He's a *gringo*, but maybe he's a nice man. Give him a chance. You want to spend the rest of your life as an old maid?"

Abuela sits on the floor wearing her flowing white robe and white turban. Her *Creolla* features looking very African just now.

Between the two women, on the floor in Abuela's big bedroom closet, the shrine room, lies the straw mat of the *estera*, the Table of *Ifá*. Eighteen pearly cowrie shells are scattered over the mat, the pattern making the *ordun*. Seven shells teeth-side-up. A foot-tall statue of Santa Barbara with red robes, double-edged sword, and castle, watches over the shells. A burning joss stick fills the air with the heavy scent of cinnamon.

"The shells' answer is only as good as the question, Abuela." She rubs her eye with her right hand. Midnight and she's dead tired. It was her idea to wait so late into the night before consulting the *orishas* this time. She had a lot of online reading to do tonight related to people who are compulsive swallowers. Besides, she feels that the saints speak more clearly when there are no distractions. And she does not want Ricky waking up and seeing one of these rituals. Sometimes they kill a chicken as a sacrifice. But not tonight. Abuela has consulted Changó. What he wants is twenty dollars, a bottle of mineral water and a little pipe tobacco.

"Did he or did he not leave a rose with a sweet, little note pinned under the windshield wiper of your car today, *chica*?"

She remembers how the rose made her smile when she found it as she came out of the station after work tonight. A huge, fat rose, not one of those tight little buds sold at a convenience store. But a rose in full bloom, smelling like heaven. And the little card. In Spanish. "*Viva tostones!*"

"Ok, Abuela. Maybe you're right. But can we ask again? About the murder, about Remy La Moreaux?"

"Another question? You have had your four. You know the rules. Why are you so full of questions, *nena*? How can you ever learn the ways of the *santera* if you cannot find patience in your heart? You don't think the *orishas* have better things to do than answer all of your questions? We must beg Changó for a favor. For the impatient one."

The old lady scoops the shells off the mat with the sweep of her two hands, draws them close to her lips and begins the invocation. "*Changó mani cote, Changó mani cote, olle masa Changó ...*"

Colón holds her breath, tries to frame the question.

Abuela stops the chant and looks at her expectantly. "Speak, *nena!*"

"What am I afraid of?" These are not exactly the words she hoped to speak. She wants to ask about a more pointed fear. About Remy. But her mind is stumbling between Spanish and English, between Remy's murder and this attractive, but suspicious man whose blue eyes and broad shoulders have started taking up almost as much space in her head as the voice of a dead girl. And now that the question has been asked, she cannot take it back. The *orishas* would not abide such disrespect.

Abuela gives the shells in her hands three gentle shakes and casts them on the mat. There is a little clatter, almost like muttering, as they tumble to rest on the mat. Twelve shells with their tiny mouths face up.

The santera claps her dark wrinkled hands together in discovery. "*Mira, nena.* See! Once again you get *ellila.* The *orishas* have had enough of you for one night."

She wants to curse, but says nothing. She knows all too well what *ellila* says. "You are defeated through your own fault."

It's the *ordun* that has haunted her life. *Hijo de puta,* she can't just wait for Johnny Match to do all the basic police work of running down leads. She has to get her *culo* in gear. But when she was back working for the state police with Lou Votolatto she learned that sometimes you have to put some of the day-to-day detective work on hold and follow your instinct. Let your emotional intelligence and your spiritual connections run free for a while and see where they take you. Well right now the *orishas* are definitely not cooperating, but maybe her heart knows a way.

It's telling her that before she goes dashing off to what used to be the Mattapoisett Inn to see if anyone remembers Remy, she needs to go back out to Bird Island for a private look around. If she gets Corby to take her, maybe she can get a little bit closer to finding out why he's acting guilty, whether it has anything to do with Remy's death ... and why her cheeks get hot every time she's around him. She can tell he's feeling hot around her, too. If she lets him close enough to her, perhaps he'll say something to erase her suspicions or move her investigation forward. But it could be she's kidding herself. Could be this is yet another disastrous instance in her life of fatal attraction.

· · · · ·

"So did you like the rose?"

She smiles at the man in the blue fleece pull-over at the controls of the Grady White. It swings out into Slocums Harbor and heads for Bird Island. She's glad it's just the two of them out here. That Johnny Match is off trying to track down former bar and wait staff from the Mattapoisett Inn who remember Remy. "It was sweet … Thank you."

"He grins. You're most welcome." He almost calls her Sherlock, thinks better of it. It might seem disrespectful now that he knows her a little better. Too cavalier. As if he's trying to hide something behind the teasing. Like a whole raft of secrets. He can tell that she's watching him, can feel her eyes on him.

"I want to look over the burial sight again. The lab report came back. They found an expensive, antique ring among the remains. The kind that jewelry hounds wear. I'm wondering if there's more jewelry around the grave site. Something the forensic guys missed before. Something that can tell us more about the island girl."

"So we are going to be digging."

"That's the plan. Any objections?"

He feels something twist in his stomach. "Well, isn't it still a crime scene? Won't the authorities blow a gasket if we disturb anything?"

She takes a deep breath, as if trying to summon her confidence. "Right now, I'm the authorities, Corby."

This doesn't feel legit to him, but what can he say without seeming guilty? "So … where are the shovels?"

"Haven't you ever had sand between your fingers?"

Jesus.

· · · · ·

He feels the gritty dryness of the sand and salt from the beach that have collected under his nails. Wishes he were still back at Hope Town or on Guana Cay dancing to cassettes of Jimmy Cliff at the little bar on Sunset Beach. Not this.

Not here on Whale Cay. Not up in the tuna tower of a wrecked sportfisher in the dark. Not watching the silhouette of the boat that is gliding toward the beach. It is a white Cigarette, twin outboards, maybe forty feet long. Big red letters on the side: NOBODY GET HURT!

"Cover me," says Paolo, climbing down the ladder from the tuna tower. "Stay down flat."

He nods, drops to his belly on the diamond plate, aluminum deck of the tower, pistol in hand. He wishes Hook were here. But Hook is on the far side of the island. Paolo sent the Princess to get him. It's a bit of a hike, maybe a half mile following the coast. They probably will not be back here in time to help ... if the shooting starts.

• • • • •

"Hey, I think I found something!" She's down on her knees, head and shoulders bent into the stone-lined grave. Knees of her jeans soaked with dampness, hands caked in mud.

"What? Where?" He's right beside her. So close he can smell the mix of coffee and Certs on her breath. A hint of lime cologne on her skin.

She grabs his right hand with her left, drags it into the dark, loose dirt that she has been excavating. Her hand feels like a warm glove over his. "Spread your fingers. Feel? I can't get it. Something hard. Can you help?"

He's not sure why he's doing this. Suddenly he's afraid of what he might find. But what can he do? He cannot quit now. It would look too sketchy.

"More to the right." Her hand drags his by the wrist, deeper into the cold, sandy soil. "Got it?"

Something hard scrapes against a fingertip. Two hard things maybe. Bound in a web of tiny roots. He curls his fingers, a claw around the metal mystery. And pulls. Until he hears something rip.

"Shit!"

"What?"

"I think I left a fingernail in there." He stares into the cup of his sandy hand. Counts his fingernails. They are all there. But one is oozing blood. The middle finger, which has snagged the mystery. As he uncurls his fingers, he can see two small metal rings flecked with dirt and pieces of roots. Feels a little sigh rising in his throat, the aftermath of fear. He lets it go.

"What are those?"

He fingers them one at a time with his other hand. "Brass."

"Costume rings?"

He feels their thinness. Sees the ridges where a machine has stamped the two sides of each ring together. "Grommets. Brass grommets."

She looks at these nearly flat rings the size of quarters, has no clue what he's talking about.

"You know. You put a draw string through them. Like on sweat pants or a bathing suit."

"Not jewelry, then?"

He shakes his head no. *Absolutely not*, he thinks. *Not the little dolphin pendant made of seashell that he once bought for the Princess from that artist and fruit vendor on Guana Cay. Thank god.*

Suddenly, a smile spreads across Colón's face as if some change of polarity has just overtaken her body.

He feels the heat of her hand on his again.

"You ever go out dancing?" she asks.

Jesus, is she playing me? The devil in a blue dress?

"You ever get a little wild at night, Corby?"

You have no idea.

· · · · ·

"Put down that gun, mon!" The driver in the boat cuts his engines. The needle bow slides up onto the beach. "Throw it in the sand."

A young black man is standing behind the windscreen in the Cigarette … with an automatic rifle pointed at Paolo. He can see the huge banana clip. A white guy sits at the steering wheel. He's in his early twenties, sandy hair, square jaw. Black bandana on his head. Little submachine gun in his right hand, pointing around the windscreen. Must be an Uzi.

"Come on now. Throw it down or somebody gone get hurt."

Paolo drops his weapon.

"Ok, then. Nobody move. Hands over your head, mon."

Paolo raises his hands. "Hey, man, I'm cool."

The black guy jumps out of the boat and starts up the beach toward Paolo, twenty-five yards away. "Yeah, you cool, mon. But don't be moving now. Where the rest of you posse?"

"Hey, amigo. Let's do the deal. Everyone goes home happy."

The black guy shouts over his shoulder to the his partner in the boat, "What this mon talking about, Skinny? Deal? What deal?"

"I don't know. Maybe he thinks we somebody else." The words come in abrupt, clipped bursts. The note of the voice rising sharply at the end of each sentence. Almost an English accent, but not an English accent. It's the peculiar speech of the white residents of the Abaco Islands here in the Bahamas, the Conchy Joes.

14

PART OF HIM FEELS even more strongly than ever that this Latina siren is playing him hard. And it's working ... because right now he almost doesn't care.

They have been on the dance floor for hours. Flamenco guitars are surging. Trombones, trumpets, drums blaring from the speakers all around the room. She's pressing herself, chest and hips, against him. Her black, satin cocktail dress the thinnest layer of skin between them. With her coaching, he has gotten past the basics of the *cha cha* and *merengue*. Until he feels like Michael Douglas dancing the *tango* with Kathleen Turner in *Romancing the Stone*. The red and green and gold disco lights splashing them with color. The music pulsing in his hips. Every muscle in his body on edge as their bodies surge to the music belly-to-belly. He does not want much. Just to rake her body with his hands, devour her flesh, steal her heart.

And she wants something too. Her hand slides down the upper plane of his thigh.

"Let's go," she says. "Live dangerously."

• • • • •

Paolo is acting up. "Come on, man. We both know Carlos sent you. Cut the shit."

"Who says we know this guy Carlos? I asked you a question, white boy. Where the rest of your posse?" The speaker is now within ten yards of Paolo. Automatic rifle pointed right at the man.

Fuck this, he thinks. He's as good as dead, and Paolo's as good as dead, unless he takes out this guy with the first shot. He feels the sweat running from his hand, soaking the wooden grip of the .38 special as he pulls back the trigger slowly to cock it. But forget it. This is just a dominance game. They won't shoot. At least not yet. They came for the money. And Paolo has it stashed.

"I'm asking you, mon? Where the posse?"

Paolo suddenly drops his hands, shrugs, sits right down on the beach, just feet from his shot gun. Like fuck you. "Where do you think, asshole? They got a bunch of guns on you right now. So let's quit dicking around. Show me the product, or my boys will start shooting. You think we're fucking rookies? We got cannons you never even heard of. Let's see the product or the deal's off."

He can hardly believe it. Paolo coming on like this all of a sudden with brass balls. Riding his own private snow storm.

• • • • •

All night she has been counting his drinks, wondering if he needs alcohol to have a good time. So she's surprised. After two rum and tonics, he has been the mad dancer. Drinking Perrier. High on something other than alcohol. She thinks that he's doing a good job making her believe it's her that makes him high.

"Come here." She draws him to her. His skin smells faintly of salt and some kind of oil. They are in the wheelhouse of the *Brutus*. Her fingers unbuttoning his white linen shirt, grazing over the hard muscles below his ribs. Dios mio! *Such a man.*

He spreads his fingers like combs, runs them up along the sides of her head, pulling at the roots of her hair. A thousand little explosions going off in her hair, her skin. She's on the edge of crying out with pain, with pleasure, when he draws her lips to his for a kiss. Butterflies in her mouth.

Cuidado! *Be careful, girl!* her brain is shouting. It's a distant call, a fading warning from the already dead. Something has begun buckling, melting in her loins. Monkeys screeching. The jungle on fire. She wants him here, now. On this little berth in the wheelhouse. Nothing else matters.

She steals a swift breath. Their lips quivering in the glow of a violet moon. Before they drag each other down into the wet wreckage of their own hearts. Remy's, too.

• • • • •

The girl smells the mud of low tide, hears the murmur of boats bobbing at their moorings. The key under the geranium pot as usual. She takes it, lets herself into the dark, little converted boathouse by the water. Switches on the light just long enough to go straight across the studio to the bar. Makes herself a vodka with rocks. Strips, crawls into bed. She does not know how long she waits before feeling his arms wrap around her from behind. She just knows that she has been dreaming of Jared and skating again. And that her glass of vodka is now empty.

"I was hoping that you might come." She smells the Myers rum on his breath.

"I told you I'd try to get away, didn't I?"

"You're my doll."

"I want you." She does not know whether this is a lie or not. After everything that has happened tonight, she is beyond questioning her own

motives, or her desires. She just knows that she cannot be alone right now. That she needs him. That he's her last hope.

So she reaches between his legs as she lies there beneath the top sheet, feels for him. Pulls him against her.

Then she rises on her knees. He tosses off the sheet, enters her from behind. The way she always wishes it. So that she never has to see him. Look at him. Only feel him covering her. His body a fur thing. A bear rug maybe. With a hot knife at its core. Cutting into her again and again. Until he roars. And roars.

Until something shudders inside of her. And she drops to her belly, feeling in love with death. And half afraid for the future of the child in her loins.

15

SHE MELTS into his arms.

"Are you alright?"

Her sobs come. Little ripples, circles out of a deep pool. Wet on his chest. "No."

"What's the matter?"

"I've got to ask you something."

He pulls the old, black comforter up over them. Hugs her to his chest. Tries to ignore the molten feeling in his stomach. The memory's smothering him.

• • • • •

The black guy turns back to his boat. "You hear this shit, Skinny? White boy, threaten us with annihilation? Telling us show him the product or else. You think he got gunners in them bushes? Or you think he bluffing?"

"He a lying sack of shit. His boys are down on the south end of the cay. I saw two of them lighting up an hour ago."

"That true, white boy?"

"What the fuck do you think? You want to take your chances, find out for sure, just keep pissing around like you're doing. Pretty soon you are going to see you got no boat, no money and no ass."

"That some outrageous trash you talking. Where the money, motherfucker?" The black guy is standing right over Paolo.

"Right behind you, you bastard. By the rocks. By one of my gunners."

The black guy turns to look up the beach for just an instant. He's looking at the rocks. Then at the wreck of the sport-fish. Then at the tower. At Corby—

—when Paolo seizes the shotgun off the sand, swinging it like a ball bat, cutting the brother right along the side of his left knee. Pounces on him even as the automatic rifle drops from his hands. And he howls.

Paolo's left forearm comes up, choking him from behind, making a shield of his adversary. His right arm pointing at the guy in the boat.

"Don't shoot, motherfucker!"

• • • • •

"Tell me the truth, ok?"

He thinks about the night they have just passed together. The *tangos* danced. The sex. Never in his life has he felt so utterly spellbound. Whatever she wants, she can have. He will say anything. No matter the cost.

"I've got a name for you." Her voice sounds shaky.

"I don't understand." He says ... But then he does. He fears what's coming next. Curses himself, the worst of fools.

She murmurs something he cannot hear.

"What?"

"Remy La Moreaux."

The words flash out through the dark, hit the walls of the wheelhouse and ricochet back against his chest. Collapsing his lungs.

"Shit."

She draws back from him, searches his face with her moist eyes. "Don't tell me you didn't know her."

Church needs three heavy breaths before he can speak. "It was a long time ago."

He lies. He says he hardly remembers her or those days together. Doesn't tell her about the gunfight he's reliving in his mind.

• • • • •

He doesn't know who starts shooting first. The guy in the boat, himself from up in the tower of the wrecked sport-fish or someone up the beach. Maybe Hook, maybe Spence, maybe the Princess.

Yeah, maybe Remy. He just knows that he has not squeezed off more than two shots from the .38 into the engines of the Cigarette boat before the air around him begins to buzz with lead. He jumps for cover in the bushes below. Falls flat among the dead leaves, cobwebs, swarms of gnats, fire ants. He's no stranger to guns, took a firearms course during college. But he's never been shot at before. And now the only thing he can think to do is pray and wish he were safe back on Cape Cod with his fiancée, the law student, Karen Sue.

"Give 'em hell, Remy!" shouts Paolo. "Hijackers!"

For a second the word hangs in the air. The terrible truth. There is no product. This is no deal. They have been set up, or maybe just shadowed by a pair of sharks. Who smell the scent of fifty thousand American dollars.

He hears the chatter of an automatic rifle, the sound he has learned to associate with the Fedallah's *recently-acquired AK-47. The shooting coming from somewhere off to his left, making steady clunks as the rounds hit the Cigarette, chew up the fiberglass hull.*

And the hijackers are firing back, bullets hitting the coral over his head, pebbles raining down on him. The air starting to smell suddenly dusty, damp, cold. The surf a dull roar on the other side of the island.

Another burst from down the beach. This time it's closer. And now the boom of shotguns. One near, one far.

The cough of outboard engines. The whine of props.

He gets to his knees and looks toward the beach. Neither Paolo nor the black guy are where he last saw them. The beach is empty. Except for dark spots on the sand. The Cigarette is roaring away to the south, smoke pouring from its engine covers.

"Fuck, man. You ok?" Paolo comes out of the bushes behind him. "Those assholes laid a load on you."

He stands up. Starts brushing the leaves and sand and seaweed off his body with his hands. He does not feel scared. Just pissed off. He has stings all over his feet, ankles, wrist, hands, neck, face. "Fucking fire ants."

"Better than a bullet. You know what I mean?"

He tosses his pistol on the sand. Wades into the water. Submerges, hopes the Sea of Abaco will take the pain out of the ant bites. "Jesus Christ, what just happened?"

16

"HELL YEAH I remember Remy La Moreaux. The little wench left town owing me about four hundred bucks."

The woman behind the bar at the Toad House in Dennis, thirty miles further out the Cape from Slocums Harbor, has the look of a WWF wrestler or a Viking queen. Middle-age, fit. Tall, rangy, strong neck, crew cut, bleached-blond hair, big blue eyes, soft lips. One gold earring. Breasts bulging under her Irish Pride hoodie, sleeves pushed up to the elbows. "You find her?"

"About a half-dozen folks said we needed to talk to you." Colón gives Johnny Match a look out of the corner of her eye as they drop onto stools, the only potential customers in the bar.

"Hey, that pizza smells good." Johnny Match tries to create a distraction so she will not have to give it out that Remy's dead, complicate the interview.

"You like brick oven pies, Detective? You ever try seafood pizza? You can try one on the house ... If you tell me what this is all about. Get me back my money."

Colón sniffs the pizza cooking in the oven. Realizes that it's the middle of the afternoon. She and Johnny Match have been running down leads all day. It's safer, saner, especially after that madness with Church last night. Especially after she didn't really push him when he admitted to knowing Remy. What the hell was holding her back? His strong, smooth arms wrapped around her?

She thinks she has to change her game today. Turn her focus to just plain, straight-forward detective work. Forget trying to be some kind of spiritual medium or secret agent. She and Johnny Match must talk to everyone who might have known Remy when she disappeared. And they've got to get started trying to track down where that safe-desposit key leads. As well as the ring and the grommets. So there has been no time for lunch. Like how good would a pizza taste right now? But work comes first today … and she's having this vague sensation that she has met this woman before.

"You still sound sore. I'm guessing you knew her well?"

The bartender tosses her hands in the air. "Damn that girl! You know how she is?"

The detectives do not answer. Colón is trying to place the bartender in her mind.

"That's what I thought. You don't know. You're out here on a fishing expedition. Trying to build a case for somebody. Maybe some district attorney or sheriff who's running for office, am I right? What the hell has she done now? No, let me guess. Grand larceny. Jewels. Right? That girl loved shiny things." There's an odd giddiness in the bartender's voice.

"Really?"

"Like an addiction. More than almost anything. Even more than vodka and men."

Johnny Match screws up his little mustache, pulls a notebook out of the jacket of his hounds-tooth sport coat. Starts scribbling.

Colón tries to get her mind off visions of sizzling pepperoni and mushrooms, this strong woman's face. "You said *almost* anything."

"Yeah, the girl—well I guess she's no girl anymore. Three things ruled her life when I knew her: ice skating, jewelry … and cocaine."

"How so?"

"It's been what, twenty years, something like that, since she split? But it seems like yesterday. We were both working at the inn over in Mattapoisett. I can still hear her begging me for a ride to that rink in Bourne. She was part of some synchronized skating team. 'Come on, Chelsea, I need this. Help me out. It's my big chance. Please, please, pretty please. Just one more ride.' Or else she wanted me to take her up to the Boston jewelry exchange so she could haggle with the Armenians for gold and diamonds. Damn, that girl could whine."

"So you helped her out?"

"Sure, what else could I do?"

Johnny Match looks up from scribbling. "Just say no?"

The bartender rolls her eyes. "You really don't get it, do you?"

"Excuse me?"

"Remy was—excuse the French—a fucking train wreck in the lives of everybody she came in contact with. Including her own."

Colón has her elbows on the bar, squinting at the flames in the brick pizza oven. Thinking pizza, but wracking her brain. *Where the hell did I meet this woman?* "I don't understand."

"What I'm saying is, yeah, I gave her a ride. Anything for …" A pause. A look away. A hand fluttering to wipe something from an eye. A tear maybe. "Anything for my baby."

Johnny Match shoots his partner a look. Like *holy shit*.

She jumps in before the downbeat. "You were involved with her?"

The bartender sighs. "Aw fuck, why am I going to tell you this?"

"You could help her. Really. More than you may ever know."

The tall, pretty woman behind the bar tosses her bar rag into the sink. "It was just one night. She was high as a kite. She had another fight with that asshole she was living with at the time. I was working the bar at the Inn and suddenly after about her fifth vodka, she started coming on to me."

"Sexually?"

"She was unbelievable, you know. Goddamn pretty ... and wild. With those sparkling green eyes. I knew she wasn't gay, but I took it for what it was worth. A hell of a night, ok? Trouble was ... for me it was like a taste of—what's the stuff they say the gods eat? For her it was a one-night stand. "

Colón's already there.

• • • • •

The lyrics of Whitney Houston's "Saving All My Love For You" is soaring from the stereo.

Strong hands, restless hands are sliding behind her neck. Playing in her hair. Gliding over her shoulders. The candle's flickering on the ceiling. The silk sheets are tangling around her bare feet. Her head spinning from the Stoli.

"Hold me."

The arms. Warm vines curling around her back, inside her tank top. Laying her down. A leg looping over hers. Bare and long in those cut-off jeans.

Lips. Soft lips kissing away the tears. Kissing the eyes, kissing the ears. Kissing the cheeks. Kissing the neck. Kissing the lips.

Oh, god!

Whitney Houston's rich voice going low down. A little bit terrified. A little bit lonely. Dreaming of something wild. Falling apart. Just falling apart.

Kissing back. Kissing those tender lips. Those violets. Kissing that slick tongue. That tongue of oranges and cream and plums ripening in the sun.

"*I don't know what to do.*"

"*Give me your hand.*"

The softest skin, the wettest skin.

"*Here?*"

She gasps.

A child in her arms, her hands. A mother. Sister. Sisters.

"*Oh, sweetie.*"

This skin of rose petals. Absolute rose petals. Smooth and sweet white chocolate.

A purple light blooming in her belly, rising through her chest.

"*Hold me. Please, hold me.*"

• • • • •

"I'm sorry," she says, still smelling the rose petals. Wondering where they're leading.

"Yeah, no shit, me too. Let me tell you. After that she just used me. For rides, for money to buy more blow, more gold. She even brought guys into my apartment to party when I was at work. Dopers."

"You remember any of the guys?"

The bartender turns away. Grabs a pizza paddle and slides a pie out of the oven behind her. She puts the pie on a butcher-board counter and starts cutting it with a pizza knife, slashing someone's face into very small pieces.

Colón's mouth waters for pizza now. Her head's trying to stay on the job, still searching to place Chelsea. "Talk to us, ok? Help us out."

She looks up from her cutting as if she has just heard the voice of a ghost. "Aw Christ, I don't really want to get into this. Can't we just leave the past alone?"

The detectives exchange glances. They are about to lose their source. Time to come clean.

"Look, I know this has to hurt. I'm sorry." Colón invokes her most sympathetic voice. "We found a body. And we think it's Remy La Moreaux. Someone killed her. Quite a long time ago. Talk to us, please. Help us get the bastard off the streets, will you?"

Both the detectives are watching Chelsea's face to see how she takes the news. The bartender's cheeks turn a flat white. Her throat starts to work, swallowing saliva uncontrollably. Little beads of sweat breaking out in the tiny hairs above her upper lip.

"Aw fuck … That was her? The body I read about that turned up near Slocums Harbor?"

"On Bird Island."

"When did she die? How?"

"We can't release that information, yet. Come on, Chelsea, I need this. Help me out. Please." Colón locks the other woman in her stare. Looks deep into her eyes.

It's so quiet, she can hear the hickory cracking in the oven flames. The bartender caught in her gaze. Finally, Chelsea turns away, starts looking around at the walls of the pub and restaurant as if she's lost in a dream.

"Chelsea?"

"I knew it. I knew this was coming. Her mother dead. Old man a rummy. Running off the way she did. A girl on her own. Living over there in New Bedford. Weld Square. What chance did she have?"

"Somebody killed her. It wasn't her fault."

"She ran with a rough crowd. Slimeballs. All those fucking guys. I told her she would end up this way sooner or later."

"Was she a hooker?"

"I don't know ... You mean did she stand on street corners in Weld Square? No. But, yeah, she did favors for guys. They kept her in drugs and booze. Gold. Gave her places to crash. Sometimes expensive vacations. Those bastards. I told her, stay with me, baby. I'll keep you safe. No hustles. Just stay. Get the hell out of Weld Square. We'll get a place way out on the Cape. I'll take you to the rink. To the Armenians. But did she listen? No. It was always 'Maybe next month, Chelsea.' And then one day she was gone. And never came back."

"It must have been very sad."

"I told myself she got smart and moved on. But in my heart I knew. I knew this day was going to come. Those fucking guys!"

"Can you give us names?"

Something like a little growl rumbles in Chelsea's throat. "You can start with Paolo Costa. We used to call him Paolo the Pirate. Guy listened to way too much Margaritaville music for his own good. He had a thing for big, old, wooden sailboats. And dope. Claimed he ran a charterboat business. Maybe he still does?"

"Where?"

"I don't know. Last I heard he was somewheres here on the Cape. Barnstable, Chatham, Provincetown. Or in the islands."

"You mean Nantucket and the Vineyard?"

"Yeah maybe. Them too. But also down south. Someplace warm. Barbados, Bermuda, Bahamas. One of those B places. I didn't pay much attention. The farther away, the better, from that asshole."

The bartender suddenly catches her eyes. Smiles, some shift taking over inside her, pulling her back to this black-eyed Latina sitting across the bar licking her lips unconsciously. "You want some of this pizza, sweetie?"

Colón doesn't answer. Another voice has her attention.

• • • • •

The sea looks like a fairy land of winking stars. A warm wind is blowing. It feels silky on the girl's bare skin. On the raw shoulders of the man she's holding in her arms. In this place between Heaven and Earth and sea, this lost world.

Here on her back with a man between her legs. It's almost as good as skating. In the old days. But he's not Jared. Not her real Jared. Her Jared of the night. Jared of the fog. Her Jared of sad-eyed vulnerability, Jared full of grace. Jared of awkward kisses. Jared who feels her pain, brings her pleasure. Not like all the others. Not like blow. Not even like gold. Better and worse.

He breaks the rhythm. Pulls his face from the shaft of her neck, looks around. "Someone's coming."

17

"I KNOW THIS IS NONE OF MY BUSINESS, but you got a problem, *nena.*" The old lady with the cocoa skin and purple head scarf sits at the kitchen table sucking a chicken bone.

She's looking up at her granddaughter the detective who has just come in the door of the apartment after work

"I got a hundred problems, Abuela. So what's new in *esta vida*?"

"I was talking with the shells."

"Abuela!"

The old lady shrugs. "It's what I do. Just like you. I solve mysteries. I'm worried about you. You're acting crazy."

"Can you leave me out of your visits with the dead? Unless I ask, ok? You know sometimes the *orishas* scare the hell out of me. I don't need to hear any more *ellila*. 'You are defeated through your own fault.'"

"You did not get *ellila* this time, child."

"You asked about me. Specifically about me?"

"*Claro que sí*! Who else?"

"Oh Jesus!"

"Not Jesus, *mi guapa*. Obatalá. Saint of saints! He spoke through the shells."

Colón drops into a chair opposite Abuela at the kitchen table. Peels out of her blue anorak and shoulder holster, drops the holster and Glock on the table. Another day of fighting crime down the tubes. She can hear the TV muttering from the living room. Ricky's home from kindergarten, watching the *Shark Tales* DVD for about the twentieth time.

"Ok, Abuela. What was the *ordun*?"

"*Muy estraño*. Stranger than strange. Twice in a row you got *osa*. 'Your best friend is your worst enemy.'"

"Terrific. What else?"

The next time that I scattered *las conchas*, it was number eleven, *ojuani*. 'Be distrustful; carry water in a straw basket.'"

"And the last question. The fourth *ordun*?"

"Very mysterious. Number four, *ellorozun*. Right from the mouth of your namesake, Yemanjá Mother of the Waves. 'No one knows what lies at the bottom of the sea.'"

She thinks back on her day. The pizza party with Remy's lesbian admirer. The faint memory of a Whitney Houston song, skin like rose petals, sex in the fog, the name Jared. Going down buckling and torn in a hail of blood. "Like really, Abuela, the *orishas* truly nailed it this time. I think I'm going backwards with this case. Nothing makes sense."

"Well, let the *ordun* help."

"What do you mean?"

"Your best friend is your worst enemy."

"Wait. What question did you ask?" She lifts the holster and gun off the table, hangs them on the back of her chair so that there is nothing between her and her grandmother.

The old lady lowers her head.

"Abuela, answer me." She reaches across the table and takes her elder's hands in her own. "What?"

"About your friend. I asked about your friend. The one with the boat. The dancer."

"Corby?"

The old lady nods.

"Jesus Christ. First you send me off after him like a cat in heat. And now this? Now 'Your best friend is your worst enemy. Be distrustful; carry water in a straw basket.' No wonder I feel like I'm going crazy. I feel like ... like Papi is back."

The old lady casts a dark look. "Forget about him. He's never coming back, you hear? This is not about your personal life."

She feels the flames rising in her cheeks. "Then what the hell is it about, Abuela? *Dígame.* What?"

"About work. Your case. This dead girl."

The one having sex in my brain. Carajo. *Even as I sit here in my grandmother's kitchen.*

• • • • •

"*Don't stop. Please don't stop.*" The girl, Remy, is almost out of breath.

"*It's Paolo! He's coming.*"

"*To hell with him. Don't stop.*"

A figure lurches up the beach, a shadow in the starshine.

"*Remy. Hey, Remy. Come on, girl. You here? Come on, baby doll. Don't be like that.*" His breath is heavy, puffing.

The man, this not-Jared between her legs, tries to pull away, reaches down to his knees to haul up his shorts. But she locks her legs around his hips. Squeezes him into her. Welds herself to him as she claws at the curls on the back of his neck, draws his lips to hers. Bites.

"Hey ..."

Her tongue in his mouth. Legs feeling the death rising in her. The howling. Doesn't care if Paolo finds her. Finds them.

"Fucking Remy. Where in hell are you? You stupid bitch."

Her lover is stiff with terror.

"Don't stop!" Jesus god almighty, not now. Not now, Jared love. Don't leave me. Kill me.

"Remy, you fucking whore. Your ass is grass. Stop playing games." Paolo's talking to himself.

"Don't stop!"

Her lover's body begins to yield, cannot stop itself. She knows this body like her own. Their bodies shredding each other in uncalculated fury. Breathless. Trying to kill, trying to die. Trying to disappear into the starry sea. This Jared who is not Jared. This new Jared who can love her beyond death. Beyond her papi. *This slave. This man who smells of salt and something else. Like olive oil. This body that sweeps her right into the heart of the storm. Until they go down leaking and torn in the silent sinking of their pleasure. A hail of blood.*

18

"WHAT ARE YOU HOLDING BACK ON ME, Corby?" Colón's pupils are immense, as if she's just witnessed unthinkable carnage.

She's standing at the galley door to the tug. The wind whipping her hair, flashes of chestnut against the florescent glow of the dock lights tonight.

Church rubs his eyes, is not sure what time it is. The last thing he knew he was in his berth reading a Dewey Lambdin novel of the sea. Must have nodded off until her banging at the door.

"You want to come in?"

She grumbles in Spanish. Steps into the galley, staring around at the stainless counters, the diesel stove, the rust-stained white fridge. Like she's looking for something.

"Hey, what's the matter?" He looks at the ship's Chelsea clock on the wall, its tarnished brass bezel. Sixty years old at least. And still keeping perfect time. It's five minutes before eleven.

"You said you knew her. From your drinking days at the Mattapoisett Inn."

He does not have to ask who she's talking about. The name Remy hangs in the night air. It seems to follow him everywhere. Especially since last night after he told Colón that he had known Remy back in the day.

"I already told you. She was a waitress, tended bar, too, at a place I used to hang out. You didn't seem upset when we talked about it last night. What's changed?"

"Cut the shit, ok? You think I want to be chasing down your sorry ass in the middle of the night? You think just because we took a tumble, you get to lie to me about a murdered girl?"

He stands there in his dirty, white long underwear. Feet feeling cold on the steel deck. Maybe she has a right to be pissed. But goddamn. He did not lie to her. "You want some coffee?"

She looks at the coffee maker, the Pyrex pot still half full of a muddy mix. "Don't try to distract me, Corby! You have no idea what kind of hell your life will be if I go public with what I already know. How would you like to be picked up as a material witness … or charged?"

"I don't know what you're talking about."

Her black eyes glare. Her hand unconsciously grabs a steel spatula out of the frying pan and starts shaking it in his face. She can smell the garlic oil and cheese of the *quesadilla* he made himself for dinner. "You and Remy, Slick. Don't lie to me. You were into her!"

"What?"

"Screwing her. Right? She wasn't just some barmaid who brought you your pops. Was she?" She's shaking the spatula in his face again.

"Would you put that thing down? You think crashing in here and shouting at me is going to make me feel cooperative? Maybe bullying works where you come from, but it just plain pisses me off."

She throws the spatula on the counter. "You bastard!"

He can see tears welling in her eyes. Feels the urge to comfort her, tries to hug her, forget his own fears about what she already knows.

But she straight-arms him in the chest. "Don't touch me! I must have been crazy. I thought you were different from other guys. Something tender. Something decent ... I've got to get out of here."

As she spins toward the door, he lunges, catches her by the waist with one arm.

"Stop!" She flails at him, nails his ribs with an elbow.

But he holds on, both arms around her waist now.

"You're in big fucking trouble, Corby. You're dead." Her voice is breaking even as she shouts.

He hugs her from behind. Feels the hardness of her Glock in the shoulder holster. "Please. Please ... Just take it easy."

"You want to kill me too?"

"Is that what you think? You think I killed her? You think I'm the New Bedford Serial Killer?"

Her body's going weak in his arms. She's starting to sob. "Christ, I don't know. I don't know anything anymore."

He wants to tell her that she's the freshest thing, the best thing, to walk into his life in at least a dozen years. More. But he can't say that. Not here. Not now. All he can do is loosen his grip on her a little and say, "Listen to me. I will never hurt you ... Remy and me? It wasn't what you think."

She turns to him now, her body starting to gain back some strength in the hollow of his arms. But still shaking. "You can't hold back on me. There's a killer loose. A bastard *pendejo*. How do I know you're not that guy?"

"Jesus. I swear ..."

"You better start telling me the truth."

"She came to me sometimes," he says. "Crazy out of her mind with man trouble. Drugs and big dreams. I was already engaged to Karen Sue, my ex, that summer. But I wasn't ready to get married. I was a sucker for Remy's wild vulnerability, flattered to be someone's confidant."

"But you slept with her."

"Only once. It was an act of desperation."

She growls, not buying his excuse. "Like on a beach, under the stars?"

"How do you know?"

She slides out of his arms. Does not speak. Does not say that she sees things sometimes, that she has been hearing Remy La Moreaux's voice in her head. That she fears the life of a dead *gringa* is getting really tangled up in her own shadows. Her own ghosts. Her eyes fix unblinking on his as if she is trying to read his soul.

Finally she says, "Can you help me find a guy named Costa? Or do I have to get you arrested to make you give him up?"

"Paolo Costa?"

"Who else?"

"That son of a bitch … I'd try the Vineyard. Maybe Edgartown."

"I thought he was a friend of yours."

"Not after the shit storm he started."

• • • • •

"The guy in the boat just let loose. Goddamn bullets all around me. One caught me in the fucking foot. And that black bastard got free." Paolo's missing the sleeve of his shirt, has it tied around his left foot. "If you hadn't started shooting, I would have been Swiss cheese. Then these guys showed up, thank fucking god."

In the starshine, Remy looks like some kind of superhero. Her jeans rolled up to the knees. New England Patriots sweatshirt bulking up her shoulders. Paolo's AK-47 in her hands. "I could get to like this son-of-a-bitching gun. Did I do any damage?"

Hook Henry stands there staring at the patches of blood on the beach. There's something bear-like about his thick shoulders. The shotgun looks like a toy in his mammoth hands. "I'd say that's one sorry hijacker." There's no conviction in his voice, just fatigue.

"What the hell happened, Paolo?" Spence is white with fear. His eyes out on sticks, a ghost crab. "I didn't fucking sign up for this duty."

Paolo has no answer. He drops on the sand. Unravels the bandage he has tied around his foot, pulls out a pocket flashlight, flicks the beam on the wound. "What do you guys think?"

There is a small purple hole on the bottom of his left foot, right in the arch. On the top of the foot is a ragged exit wound about the size of a penny.

"It went clean through," says Remy, her long, red hair falling in her face as she bends to look.

"You are one lucky bugger," says Hook. "Gee, isn't this exciting. Bush-whacked and gunshot in the tropics."

"Fix me up, Doc." Paolo's voice sounds a little ragged.

Spence is already bent over the wound. "This might hurt," he says. He pulls a pint bottle of moonshine rum out of his vest pocket and pours liquor on the wound. Nobody knows how strong the rum is. But every-one calls it "One-sixty-nine." Like that's the proof.

Paolo screams.

Spence lights a joint and hands it to him.

"We've got to get you back to the boat," says Hook. "Where Spence can clean that thing up." This is the counsel of a man who at twenty-four has already done a stint in the Marines.

"Shit, man!" Paolo grits his teeth. "We can't blow this now. Corby and Remy, you gotta hold the fort. Stay here and wait for the product to show. Do the deal. Carlos will come."

"You think I'll get to use this little darling again tonight?" Remy's eyes flash with the lime fire of her high. Her lips make a silly grin as she eyes the shabby Soviet weapon in her hands.

Suddenly, he feels like he could just drag her in the water with him and smack her one. Snap out of it, will you, Princess?

19

JOHNNY MATCH is smiling nervously at Colón. He sits across the table at the Dunkin' Donuts in Bourne that has become their rendezvous, their place to debrief and share with each other their individual work on the investigation. Almost every morning at eleven.

"You think it's safe we keeping meeting this way?"

"What do you mean? You think somebody's going to think we are having an affair? We're on the job. It's a public place. And the walls don't have ears the way they do at the station in Slocums Harbor."

"I mean somebody could be tailing us."

She looks at him. Like what the hell for?

"The media boys. They've smelled a story since the chief's press conference, but now they've got us in the headlights. Have you seen this?" He pushes the morning's *Cape Cod Times* across the table to her. Page one, left side below the fold. No, she hadn't seen this. She's been too overwhelmed by Remy's voice, too anxious over what Church has not been telling her about his connection to Remy. About her primal attraction to him, too.

SERIAL KILLER VICTIM 12?
New Body Reopens Cold Case

"Coño!"

"That and a lot more." He runs a thumb and forefinger over his thin little mustache, then pushes his other hand through his short, black hair. Fingers the little spikes gelled up over his forehead.

"You seem jumpy as a cat."

His hand leaves his hair, toys with the gold stud in his ear. "You better read on."

So she does:

NEW BEDFORD, MAY 2. The body of a woman found last week on an island in Buzzards Bay may well be the work of the serial killer credited with the deaths or disappearances of eleven other women in the New Bedford area.

Sources close to the investigation say that detectives have identified the body of Remy Anne La Moreaux. Slocums Harbor harbormaster Corbin Church discovered the corpse buried in a shallow grave on Bird Island.

La Moreaux went missing from her home and job in late summer 1988, the same time that the so-called New Bedford Serial Killer was raping and strangling more than ten young women from the New Bedford area. All were known cocaine or heroin addicts. Many were prostitutes who worked the streets in an area of the city known as Weld Square, just off Interstate 95.

La Moreaux, 22, was living in Weld Square at the time of her disappearance. She has been linked to drug addiction and possibly prostitution by people who remember her. "She was a red-haired fireball. Live fast, die young was her motto," said a former employee of the Mattapoisett Inn where La Moreaux once worked.

Officers from Slocums Harbor are working around the clock, trying to interview everyone who came in contact with the victim near the time of her disappearance.

Reliable sources say that Slocums Harbor detective Yemanjá Colón and corporal John Machico have already interviewed La Moreaux's aging father at his home in Harwich. They have also spoken with Chelsea Cullen, a Dennis bartender alleged to have been involved with the victim.

Slocums Harbor chief of police Carlos "Chi Chi" Bugatti has been in contact with a number of investigators, both retired and active, in the New Bedford area who were part of the original search for the serial ...

"This sucks."

"We're the entertainment *du jour*. There goes my private life." He rubs his eyes as if last night was a late one.

She suddenly wonders if he's gay. If he's a regular with the bare-chested boys in the rave clubs in Providence and on the Cape. "Where do they get this crap?"

He raises his hands. "Hey, not me, I swear."

"I haven't talked to a soul about this stuff." She wonders if she should tell him about Church, decides this is not the moment. Corby would not be the leak. He's already way too scared that he's getting sucked down by this case.

She thinks about what Johnny Match has said about being tailed. Maybe some news hound has been following her. *Coño*! Maybe her visits to the tugboat in Quissett are no secret. Isn't anything personal? Can't she just deal with Corby Church, and what he knows about Remy, on her own terms?

Colón reaches over the table and takes his hand. "I think this is going to be a wild ride. Stick with me, will you?"

"I'm glue." His eyes twinkle, then smile.

She grins back, likes this guy. "So what have you got?"

He says that he's been trying to run down the ring and the key. Jewelers tell him there's no sure way to date the ring. Best guess is that it is over a hundred years old. The key is a standard safe-deposit box key. The lab boys made Johnny Match a copy. "But it doesn't fit a box in any bank in New Bedford, Mattapoisett, Marion, Slocums Harbor, Wareham, Bourne, Pocassett, Cataumet, Falmouth, Sandwich or Mashpee. That's pretty much the local area."

She takes her hand away from his, rubs her cheek as if this man has just surprised her with a giant chocolate cake.

"You are really pretty amazing, Johnny Match."

He shrugs. "But now what?"

"I've got a lead. We're going to the Vineyard. Do a little bar hopping. Our Remy was quite a party girl."

"That so?"

If you could only hear a little of the stuff going on in my head …

• • • • •

Remy's high when she spins, spilling her glass of Stoli on a guy standing at the corner of the bar. He has a look. Faded navy flannel shirt, khaki pants, clamming boots. Wavy, sandy hair, soft blue eyes, a smooth, boyish face, deeply tanned. Expensive wayfarer sunglasses hanging from a cord around his neck.

"Oops, sorry!" She laughs, smiling. Like what the hell? Dabs at the stain on his shirt with the tail of the print sash tied around her waist.

It's the middle of July. The Mattapoisett Inn is jammed with party animals. The duo in the front of the room belting out "The Sultans of Swing." Scent of cigar smoke and piña coladas *in the air.*

"Hey, do I know you?" Her eyes flash at him. Her head switches left to right as she talks. Dark red curls whipping over her shoulders. She can already see that he likes the faint freckles dusting the pale plane of skin above her green tank top.

"I don't think so."

"Sure, I've seen you in here before. You come in with those shark-fishing boys. Am I right?"

20

"YOU WANT TO SPLIT UP … or do this thing together?" Johnny Match is staring out the window of a rented Jeep. Colón's driving. It's almost noon. Edgartown's a maze of closed shops and shuttered galleries.

Except for the bank, two bars, the post office and a store selling newspapers and sundries, Edgartown is still in hibernation. It has not yet blossomed again for another summer as the Vineyard's poshest resort town. Even though the temperature is sixty degrees outside in the brilliant sunshine. Early May. There are just a few people in the street. Construction workers and a couple of middle-aged women walking their schnauzers.

"You know this place?"

His left eye twitches a little. "Yeah, a little."

"What's that mean?"

"You really want to know?"

"Am I asking? *Coño!*"

"I used to come out every summer for a week to see a friend. Rent a room at a guest house. He was older. My math teacher in high school."

"Oh ..."

"Yeah."

This is getting awkward. But she sees a way out. "You said 'used to'?"

"Yeah."

"You still gay?"

He looks at her like *what the fuck.* Then sees the smile on her lips. "Bad girl!" He smiles back.

"Hey, sometimes I like men too."

"Like that buff harbormaster?"

Ouch!

She swerves to the curb and slams on the brakes. "We're here."

"So I see."

"Ok, why don't you do your key thing at the banks? I'll start with the bars. Got any ideas, Mr. Local Knowledge?" Her voice is flat, still pissed a little about his harbormaster comment. Match can read her as well as she reads him.

She looks at him. *This handsome guy. Gay.*

"You want to kiss and make up?"

"Why?"

"How about for Remy's sake?"

"*De puta madre!*" The words just fly from her mouth. She can't believe what her head's tapping into right this second. Can't believe the dead siren's bringing Corby Church into the mix.

• • • • •

Remy thinks she knows the score. This new guy Church, the one she spilled her Stoli on. He's standing with some dudes who think harpoon fishing for shark is as close to heaven as they will ever get. Spence Alpin is making a career of it. Well, at least when he's not crowing about going to Harvard med school. He has his father's Brownell sport fisher tied up down at the wharf. The rest of the guys go along for the thrill of the hunt. Almost every weekend. They have other jobs. But she can feel it. The sea is what they love. Fucking romantics.

She has heard them talking. What really gets them jacked is the rush of fishing for mako and great white when the sun is in your face, the harpoon poised to strike in your hand, and the shark a purple torpedo right under the bowsprit of the boat. Tonight they are heading out on another trip. East of Nantucket maybe.

"Hey, Popeye?" She's still dabbing at the stain on Church's shirt with her sash. "Are you another fish hound?"

She wonders if he can see the chemical fire in her big green eyes. Maybe they are too much for him because his eyes dart away. They look at her chest, the name tag pinned on her tank top.

"You work here?"

"Mostly week nights. I just came in to help with the porch crowd at dinner. But I'm off the clock now." She raises the remains of her glass of vodka and rocks, toasts the night. Downs the contents. "Cheers."

· · · · ·

The detective has been pinching her butt on the oak bar stool and trying to chat up the bartender in a dark little cave called the Wharf for twenty minutes. Nibbling at the edge of a conversation about Paolo Costa. No one else in the place until her long-lost partner shows up.

"Having fun yet?" he says.

"I wish I were drinking."

The bartender gives Match a questioning look. Bald guy, big gray mustache. "You want something?"

He looks at her. "Corona ok?"

"On the job?"

Johnny Match gives a sly grin. "How about we punch out early. You know, for the sake of improving relations?

She looks into his dark eyes, sees his confidence. Sees a friend and another crime-crazed detective. Knows neither of them can stop talking about the case for even a minute. On the clock … or off.

He signals for the two beers.

"What ever happened to the guy who used to call me ma'am?"

"He's been exploring an island."

The bartender brings the bottles. Match raises his. A toast.

She clinks the neck of her bottle with his. "And what did he learn?"

He takes a long sip of his beer. "We still don't have a box to fit the sacred key, Merlin. And nobody's seen our friend Costa since last fall. But they sure do remember him."

"He's an arrogant, careless son of a bitch," says the bartender, who has been eavesdropping. "That's what I've been telling your lady."

"And, surprise, surprise. Probably a bit of a pirate," she adds.

"He has a big black schooner called *Fedallah*, " says the bartender to Johnny Match.

"We're interested in one of his possible girlfriends," says Colón.

The bartender shakes his head. "That guy runs through women like AIDS in a prison."

She feels a jolt in her chest. A terrible hollowness, a sense of being trash. It's as if her heart is Remy's heart.

Her eyes, my eyes. Carajo. *Her whoring soul, my soul. But how does this all tie to the murder?*

· · · · ·

She sees a tall, dark blur in blue jeans, a white T-shirt gliding through the crowd at the Inn, coming toward her, toward the corner of the bar. His black, curly hair pulled back in a pony tail. A gold chain around his neck. Purple dragon tattoo on the right forearm.

He pushes toward her. Her stomach twists in a tight coil. For a second she hesitates, then throws her arm around his neck. What the hell.

Yeah, there's this new guy Church, with the soft face, the stained shirt. But here's her connection. He hooks her up. She's got to be loyal. Up to a point.

"I thought I told you to lay off the blow."

She pushes her empty glass into his hand. "I don't know what you mean. Buy me a Stoli."

"I'm going fishing." He gives a smile to Church.

Suddenly she wants to go to sea. Wants to stalk a fish as big as Jaws. Wants to feel the rush. Wants to be one of the boys. Why the hell not?

"Take me with you." She shouts over the music.

The guy with the gold, the ponytail, slides his hand over the small of her back and the rim of her hip, under the waistband of her shorts. Fingers gliding under her thong. Going deeper, hot, teasing. "I'm working on something I really think you are going to like."

Across the smoky room, the band is jamming away. Covering the Four Tops, "I'll Be There."

• • • • •

She feels the finger under her thong, bristles with more questions. "Has Costa been around here, Edgartown, a long time?"

The bartender opens a Sam Adams for himself. "Too long if you ask me. Seven or eight summers anyway."

"And before that?"

"I don't know. I kind of remember something about Hyannis. He was working over there."

Johnny Match clears his throat. "What do you mean working?"

"His boat, you know. The schooner. A pretty thing. Shame for her to belong to someone like that." The bartender takes a sip of his beer. "He lives on it summers, charters it out on daysails. Night sails. Not walk-ons. Top-end private charters. Does big business in July and August. But I'd be surprised it's enough to pay for all his toys. I'd say he gets his real money somewhere else."

She cocks an eye.

"He rides a really tricked-out Beamer bike. Keeps some kind of fancy plane at the airport. A Beechcraft something-or-other. Two engines. Go-anywhere flying machine. He used to brag about it in here."

"So where *does* he go in that?"

"Off to do his Captain Jack Sparrow thing somewhere else."

She eyes the bartender. "You think you could be a little more specific?"

"He likes warm weather. He was always talking to folks in here about this-or-that island down in the Caribbean."

"Like where? What islands?"

The bartender shakes his head. "I didn't pay much attention. It all sounded like a crock of crap to me. Do you have any idea how much horse shit a guy like me has to listen to?"

Johnny Match takes a long swill of his beer. "We really need to talk to this guy."

"Wait 'til June. He'll be back. His schooner is hauled out for the winter at a boatyard in Vineyard Haven. Probably stores the motorcycle there, too."

"Sounds like it's all about the airplane for this guy, now?"

"Yeah. And fast women. They like his toys. Probably has a yacht or a place somewhere in the islands. He's the type."

"You say his boat is stored at some kind of marina?"

"Boatyard, near Five Corners."

She stands up. Knocks down the last of her beer, looks at her partner. "Maybe they know how to contact him."

"Maybe they know where he might have gotten his hands on a pair of two-hundred-year-old handcuffs."

"You smell blood."

21

THE MOORING barge pitches suddenly, spray erupting as a wave catches the bluff bow.

"Hey, buddy boy! City work getting you out of practice? Jesus, you trying to drown me?" Hook, down on his knees at the front of the barge, shoots Corby a hairy eye-ball. "Go easy there, will you?"

He adjusts the throttle more gently now. Steers the work skiff, and the barge that it is pushing slowly into the wind, approaching the mooring so that Hook can swap out the heavy twelve-foot three-by-three, the winter place holder, for the summer pennant that will tether a pleasure boat to its mooring. They have forty of these swaps today. A normal spring chore for a boat shop that also tends moorings in Pocasset on the Cape side of Buzzards Bay. A two-man job. The kind of thing he likes to help his friend with when he has a day off. It's always a good time to catch up, talk. He needs to talk.

"She asked me about Remy ... and Paolo."

"Well, you knew that was coming. So?"

"So ... what?"

"You tell her?"

"What?"

"Everything."

"Not yet."

Hook gets up off his knees. Folds his arms across the slime-stained, yellow foul-weather overalls. "Why am I starting to get a sick feeling in the pit of my stomach?"

"I don't know. Maybe because you were there?"

"Not for all of it, pal. Not by a long shot."

"Me neither. When we got back home I'd had enough of her for a lifetime."

"Yeah, right. Don't give me that shit. I know. You think your ex Karen Sue wasn't all over me with her stories about your secret assignations?"

"Whoa. Big word!"

"Screw you. I got a brain. I use it. You? Half the time you think with that thing between your legs."

"Like you never had a piece of the pie?"

"I was trashed on that cheap-ass rocket fuel we used to buy from those moonshiners up around Powell Cay. She got me at a vulnerable moment. That's my story, and I'm sticking to it."

"Saint Hook. Is that it? He who once was lost but now is found?"

"Fuck off! You know what I mean." The usually playful note in Hook's voice is gone. "It took a while, but I grew up."

"What are you saying?"

"Forget it, bubba. Drop it, huh? We got a pack of work to do here before the wind gets up. Just steer us over to the next mooring, ok?"

"Come on. Don't be like that. What are you trying to say? Tell me."

"Are you going to get mad at me?"

He looks out toward the lighthouse on Bird Island. "I'm way past that. I'm scared. I mean, it has taken me almost forty-five years to possibly find a girl who I could really love. But she could bring the sky down on my head. You know?"

"Aw shit, man ... You really like her? Didn't I tell you to stay out of the hen house?"

"It's too late."

Hook rubs his eyes, leaves dark green streaks of slime and grease on his cheeks, nose. "Are you telling me you would consider making babies with this voodoo goddess?"

"It's not like you and Amy don't have a whole minivan full."

"But my wife and kids are not interested, either personally or professionally, in how I misspent my youth. You go out and pick yourself a detective. Christ."

Hook snags another winter mooring stick with the gaff.

Church drops the engine control into reverse. "This isn't going to get any better, is it?"

His friend stands there, holding the mooring stick with one hand and waving the gaff with the other. He's so frustrated he's ready to toss the thing off into the sea. "Look, I gotta ask you something ... Did you put her out there?"

Church feels a spring snap open in his heart. "Jesus. What kind of question is that? I *found* her, remember?"

"Hey, I'm just asking. People do weird stuff. You ever see little kids dig up their dead pets? We block all kinds of nasty stuff we've done out of our minds, you know?"

"What are you saying? You actually think I could have ...?"

"Hell, I don't know. No. Forget about it."

"Then why did you ask?"

"Karen Sue came to me once. It was a month or so before you married her that crazy summer after we got back from the Bahamas. She was kind of drunk. She talked a lot of trash about you and Remy. It was right after she disappeared."

"What was I thinking? Why did I ever marry Karen Sue?"

"You got me, pal. But if your current girlfriend ever talks to your ex ... You may as well take that tugboat, head for the Bahamas and start looking for a place to hide. Because the storm is coming."

Like the last time down there?

22

CHURCH'S EYES *are pools of sweat, his shirt soaked with his own wretched oils and the after-glow of homebrew rum when Spence shakes him awake.*

The wind's still howling out of the northeast as it has been for three days, Fedallah *tugging at her anchors here in the settlement harbor at Great Guana Cay. A wild horse trying to break free. March, '88, and the crew of the* Fedallah *has been sailing locally here in the Abaco Islands of the Bahamas for about five months.*

"Hey, get up. I can't find Remy!"

He rubs his eyes, stares at the figure standing over his berth, wearing a T-shirt and gym shorts. The man is built low to the ground, with broad shoulders. Slender waist, handsome, chiseled face. Long arms of a wrestling champion. Delicate hands of a surgeon in training. The jolting, urgent voice of a man who never sleeps. A man who imagines demons. A man wired. A man bitten by love.

"Come on, Corby. Get up! She's gone."

"What time is it?" He drops out of his upper berth in the fo'castle, looks aft through the galley into the main saloon of the big, wooden schooner. Moonbeams filter through the skylight, bathing the dining table in a whitish glow. The table littered with empty glasses, champagne bottles, bread crumbs. A nearly empty bowl of conch salad. Rolling papers. A dime bag of ganja. Mirror. Razor blade. Short straw.

"It's three-thirty. She took the rum, the one-sixty-nine."

"Yeah? Like we need more of that stuff?" He finds the head, pisses for more than a minute. "I got to stop this partying."

"Yeah, sure."

"No. I'm serious. My freaking throat is on fire. We got any orange juice left?" He opens the lid to the icebox, starts fishing around in the dark hole with his arm, comes up empty except for a can of St. Pauli Girl. "Christ. How did I get in this mess?"

"With your eyes wide open, fella. Can the remorse, will you? We got a problem. She's not on board."

"So? She probably just headed over to the oceanside beach with Hook to knock one off in the surf. What do you care?"

This is a truly mean remark. Church knows the answer to his question. Knows Spence Alpin is tearing up inside with his crush on Paolo's crazy-ass girlfriend. And tearing up with jealousy because lately she seems to have taken a fancy to Hook. He should hold his tongue. But it feels so good to bring Spence down from his almighty cocaine high. Bring the doctor down to his own level.

"Hey, you think this is a joke? Hook's passed out in his berth. Maybe she's in trouble? You see the way that guy off the yacht was looking at her tonight?"

Middle of the effing night. He has been crashed for four hours, and now he's not much in the mood to get his brain around yet another of the Princess's sketchy moves. This is one of those times when he wishes he was

*back in Massachusetts shacked up with his fiancée Karen Sue in her
Boston apartment, working a real job while she finishes law school.*

*They've been in the Bahamas all winter, and Paolo has still not scored
any pot for the trip home. The cruise has been this constant* fiesta, *every
night a fog of rum and drugs. So tonight it's even a struggle to think back
to before he crawled off to his berth for sleep. There was a party on the
schooner. This tall, slender middle-aged guy, lots of wooly hair, and his
wife. They came over from a fancy Alden sailing yacht tied off the end of
the Guana Beach Resort dock. They were from back home. From Slocums
Harbor. On an extended cruise of the islands. The idle rich on a junket
in Margaritaville.*

*They came out to the schooner loaded with four bottles of a chilled
Spanish sparkling wine, conch salad, fresh Johnny cakes. They ate. They
told sea stories. Compared notes on their favorite islands, anchorages, bars.
Hope Town, Man-o'-War Cay, New Plymouth Town on Green Turtle.
Pete's Pub in Little Harbor, The Blue Bee. Captain Jack's. The best.*

*They loved it here. Guana Cay. So undeveloped. So out-island. The
fresh fruit and home-made shell jewelry that Milo Pinder peddles from his
little stand by the fig tree. The intimate Guana Beach Resort. Its bar on
Sunset Beach where cruisers mingle with the local lobstermen. The Conchy
Joes' daughters.*

*They killed off the champagne. They did some lines. They started
mixing the moonshine, the one-sixty-nine, with coconut water. They got
trashed.*

"That was some party!"

"The dude off the yacht was all over Remy."

"Who isn't? She's pretty amazing to look at, you know?"

*"Yeah, but with Paolo gone back to the States right now, there's noth-
ing to hold her back."*

"What do you mean?"

"*After you crashed. Things got out of control.*"

He finds a dirty wine glass, pumps it full of water at the galley sink. Chugs. Tastes the rust from the boat's ancient tanks. "*I don't think I want to hear any more.*"

"*She started talking about playing strip poker.*"

He can picture it. Remy in her T-shirt and shorts, ready to test her luck. "*Oh Jesus. That's it, man. I'm going back to bed.*"

"*We've got to go get her.*"

"*Wait. You actually know where she is?*"

Spence grabs a handhold on the ceiling of the saloon to steady himself as the boat lurches in a gust of wind, shaking under their feet, the chain anchor rode screeching. "*Yeah, I think so ...*"

He says he was feeling a little paranoid so he went up on deck and waited for the wind to clear out his head. When he came back down below, all of them were stripped to their underwear. The poker game. He told them they were disgusting. Remy said he could go fuck himself. The games were just beginning. The rich dude said to hell with this antique pirate ship. Take the party to his boat. He had a killer collection of videos. Remy seemed stoked. Hook said he heard his pillow calling him to bed.

"*I said screw that, too. I wasn't going. These guys could be narcs or something. They've got this Polaroid camera, and they are always taking pictures, you know. Fuck that. Maybe they are trying to get the goods on us. Next thing you know, there goes any chance of getting a medical license. Right down the tubes. Bye-bye Dr. Spence.*"

23

"DID YOU REALLY ask me to come here to show me this fort?"

She's standing amid the rubble and graffiti-covered walls of an old gun battery at Fort Taber. It looks out from the South End of New Bedford over Buzzards Bay. The Elizabeth Islands stretch in a chain to the southwest eight miles offshore.

"From here those islands look like the Loyalty Cays in the Abacos. As you approach them from the northwest. Naushon looks like Great Guana viewed from Don't Rock Pass between Whale Cay and Treasure Cay." His voice has a wistful note. And something else. Something torn. Ripped cloth.

"You want to talk about the Bahamas. Is that why you brought me here?"

"I want this to be off the record."

"I've got a lot of phone calls and interviews this afternoon. Can we move this along?"

"The schooner cruise ... It was pretty crazy."

She reads the pain, the shame in his eyes. "I can't promise you anything. You sure you want to get into this?"

"You want to know about Remy, don't you? And Paolo Costa? You want to find the murderer."

She nods.

"Well, damn it all. I've made some mistakes. But …"

"But what?"

"I swear to God I didn't kill anybody. And maybe I can help."

Something's churning beneath her heart and in her belly, a hail storm of Remy's sobs again, a tiny daughter in a skating dress who will never be.

"Listen to me, Corby. I've got a job to do. You tell me something toxic, I can't protect you. The DA makes the deals. Not me. I'm just a cop. I follow the trails of blood and shit. If it's on you, maybe I've got to take you down. Don't put me in this position. I'm involved. I must be crazy. But I'm involved with you. I care. You know?"

He tries to take her hand, maybe hoping to feel its warmth and tenderness.

She snaps it away.

"See?"

He nods. Eyes fixed on the hand she has pulled back against the chest of her woolen pullover. The hand that she's shielding with her other one. "I've got to do this. I've got to take the risk. Otherwise you and me, we're going nowhere. You know that."

She gives him a look like *don't bullshit me,* amigo.

"I want you to hear this story from me, ok? What you do with this is up to you. But maybe it will help your case. I'm finished with hiding secrets."

She knows he will leave things out. Maybe not consciously. But he will leave holes. Nobody tells more than he needs to. But she gets this strong feeling that he's really trying to come clean. So she reaches out, takes his hand. "Let's walk. It's cold up here."

They head down crumbling, concrete steps to a lawn that's blocked from the wind by the ramparts of the main fortress.

"It was the fall 1987, the winter and spring of '88 …"

He says that there were five of them on Paolo Costa's schooner *Fedallah*. Most of them had met each other crewing together on shark-fishing trips aboard a sport fishing boat owned by Spence Alpin's father that previous summer. And now they were all taking a year off from work after college or the service, sailing to the Bahamas on Paolo Costa's schooner with the idea that they could score a few bales of pot, bring them back to New England and sell them to the drug boys. Thought the whole trip would be an adventure in paradise … with some profit on the side. They left the Cape in late October. Remy was the ship's cook.

• • • • •

"So you finally got a boatload of dope in April, after waiting all winter for a connection? After the shootout with the hijackers? And the dope was now cocaine, not marijuana? You and Remy did the deal with this Carlos guy. Then you and she were alone on the beach. Under the stars. Doing the wild thing … until Paolo came back from getting his wound patched up, looking for his princess and his blow?"

"Can I plead the Fifth?" he asks.

They are sitting on the ground in a bright pool of sun, legs crossed under them like a pair of Indians deep in discussion.

"This is not a drug investigation."

He rolls his eyes. "That's what the DA said back when he was investigating the New Bedford Serial Killer in '89. Then he indicted a slough of people on drug charges. A lot of his witnesses."

For a while, when the cops and DA were looking into Remy's disappearance, Church and his sailing buddies were pretty worried the law would be coming after them next. The cops had already questioned Paolo about Remy's disappeance. It was just a matter of time before they wanted to talk to the rest of those who sailed with her and Paolo to the Bahamas.

Colón remembers. The on-going search for the serial killer was a big deal in the news at the time. The district attorney kept trying to pinch someone into a murder confession ... or at least producing a smoking gun. But he got nothing for all of his grandstanding, just defeated in his reelection. Then all the charges against the suspects were dropped.

"You felt like you had just escaped a total shit storm?"

"Relief is not a strong enough word to describe how I felt when I heard that the new DA and the cops were shifting their focus away from the serial killings and Remy's disappearance."

"You've been a lucky man."

"Maybe ... But I don't see how knowing whether or not we smuggled in some coke has any bearing on your case."

She slaps his thigh with her hand. "*Dios mio*! Are you just stupid, or do you just not get how cops think? It's no secret that your old friend Remy had a problem with blow. And that, at least sometimes, Paolo Costa was her connection. If she had witnessed Costa smuggling in, *and selling*, a large amount of coke, would she not be a huge liability to him? She could blackmail him for drugs or money or whatever. Right?"

His eyes are following a little girl and her brother running across the huge lawn of the fort, trying to launch a yellow diamond kite.

"You saying he could have killed her to keep her quiet? And you think Paolo could be the serial killer. He killed all those girls because they were liabilities to his business, his freedom ...? Or do you think he gets his rocks off on murder?"

"I don't know. It's a theory. A lot of people die because they know too much about drug trafficking, *sabe?*" She says that right now she's not chasing a theory. Can't let herself think about all those other dead girls. Not yet. At the moment, she wants to hear his whole story about the sailboat cruise and Remy. She doesn't like missing pieces. They always turn out to be the most important ones.

"Come on, stay with me on this, Corby. I'm not going to ask you where you got the money to buy your tugboat, ok?"

He gives her a washed-out, blank look.

"Let me put it this way: Do you have knowledge regarding Paolo Costa's use of his sailboat to smuggle cocaine into Southern New England?"

He nods his head. Yes.

"In 1988?"

Another nod.

"Do you think it was a one-time thing? Or do you have reason to suspect that he was a narco-trafficker?"

He feels her gaze on his face. Raises his eyes to hers, tries to see deep into them, looking for a little trust, a little understanding. Affection. "Christ, this is hard for me."

"I know." She could bully him here. A lot of other cops would. But, instead, she reaches out and takes his hand. Her touch is warm, strong. "Paolo was into the drug scene up to his eyeballs, wasn't he?"

"I don't know. We lost touch. When we got back to New England in May, I had had enough of the whole bunch of them. I've already told you. I tried to start a new life."

"But they wouldn't let you be."

"Who?"

"Paolo, Remy, Hook Henry, the doctor. What's his name? Spencer Al …?"

"Alpin."

"Yeah. That guy. And the others. They wouldn't give you space. Right? They messed with you."

"Not Hook. Hook was fine. We just needed to go separate ways for a while."

"Because you were ashamed?"

"Wouldn't you be? You heard the story. Would you want to be remembering you were part of something illegal like a major drug deal?" He gets up, starts to walk toward the empty beach.

"Hey. Wait!" She jumps to her feet, strides after him. "I'm sorry. Just a couple more questions. Then let me buy you lunch."

He stops. "Make it dinner … At Freestone's."

She smiles. "Deal." The raw bar, the onion soup.

"You don't mind being seen with a suspected felon?"

She thinks about her days with her ex, the con man. That *pendejo*, that *borrocho*. "Right now you're a material witness. You're cooperating. You're my big break in this case … And you have nice buns."

"So now you're trying to handle me?" His voice is only half serious. Flirting. A little relieved.

She takes a deep breath, tries to stop admiring the chords in his neck. "If Paolo Costa is not on the Vineyard these days, where would you look?"

"The Bahamas." There's not a nanosecond of hesitation in his voice.

"Why?"

"It's one sweet place to hide."

"And trade in a little of Colombia's biggest export? Get down with wine, women, and weed?"

"You said one more question."

24

"WHAT THE HELL'S this place, some kind of voodoo palace?"

Chi Chi Bugatti's tiny, brown eyes scan the apartment as he pushes his way past her into the living room. He sees two-foot statues of the saints draped in beaded necklaces. The life-size painting of the mermaid with the black hair. A big ebony carving of Elegguá, the god of the crossroads. Looking very African, several tiny swords stuck in his head.

"Chief ..." Seeing him here at her home, unannounced, forcing an entrance, has left her speechless. The stumpy bugger. Uniform squeezing his immense chest and gut. Gun belt all but hidden under a lobe of blubber.

"We got another problem, Officer!" He pushes a copy of today's *New Bedford Standard Times* in her face. She has been avoiding him since the article in the *Cape Cod Times* came out yesterday, but she sure got an earful of his anger over it on her voice mail. Now, *carajo*, there's something new in the press.

It's barely eight-thirty in the morning. Her first day off in a week,

and she's whipped after what seems like endless hours of trying to
track down folks that knew Remy and Costa. Whipped from trying
to get the truth out of Corby Church. Whipped from wrestling with
her unreasonable attraction to him, too. Ricky has already gone off
to his kindergarten. She's still in her pajamas. And so is Abuela, who
has just emerged from her bedroom, gray hair up in curlers.

"Who the hell are you?"

"Abuela, this is my boss. Mr. Bugatti. The chief of police in
Slocums Harbor."

"*Claro.* I know all about you and your *mami* from Guanajuato!"

He suddenly looks sheepish, takes a step back from the old lady.
Turns to his detective. "I'm already getting calls from the *Providence Journal* and the *Boston Herald.* Somebody's leaking our case to the media."

Abuela marches right up to his face. "What did you call my
house? A voodoo palace?" She has a hair-drying blow gun in her hand.
Points it at him. "You come in here without any invitation, you disrespect our home. Get out of here, *gordito!*"

"Abuela!" She's mortified. By both of these people.

The old lady glares, points to the door. "*Fuera.* Go! Before the
saints shit all over your head!"

"*Callate*, Abuela. Shut up! This man is my boss." She does not
know why she's defending him. But she pulls on her anorak and leads
him out into the hallway, closing the door on Abuela. "She's having
one of her bad days. I'm so sorry!"

"You ought to be, Colón. That old lady is a fucking menace.
What kind of house are you keeping anyway?"

That's it. Abuela's right. I'm going to slug him, screw this job, she
thinks. But then she remembers the case. Remy. The skating, the flying. The long-lost Jared. As much as she's dreading all of this noise in
her head, she feels a duty to herself, to Remy, too. No, not a duty. An

obligation to unravel this dead girl's memories, to see where they lead and how they match up with everything she and Johnny Match are uncovering in the their day-to-day investigation. She feels an obligation to those other dead girls, as well. All of those violets, those roses, cut down in 1988. Then there's Corby, hanging way out on a limb. She can't just quit them all. People loved them. Still do.

"What do you want me to say, Chief?"

"I don't know. But you better say something fast. Or you're going to be off this case. Johnny Match will go it alone or team up with some of the boys at the state CPAC unit. Jesus Christ. Did you read this?" He pushes the *New Bedford Standard Times* at her again. "How does this shit get out?"

Front page, above the fold:

Island Victim Shackled & Buried Alive
Antique Handcuffs, Key & Ring Found with Bones

"Well? Tell me! How does this get leaked? Do you know how we look when this kind of thing happens? Do you have any idea how pissed the DA is? Do you? He wants to take this case away from us, give it to the staties. Says we're the fucking Keystone Cops. Says we've blown it all to hell with these leaks. Is this your doing? Are you trying to sabotage us? You and that crazy, old voodoo freak in there?"

Her mind's screaming. Her hand tightening into a fist. "Hey. Will you just let me read? Give me a minute of peace?" She snatches the paper from him, her eyes already drawing her into the story.

He's not exaggerating. This is awful. The paper exposes all the investigation's aces in the hole, all the intimate details of Remy's death and burial. Right down to the bludgeoned side of her head, the engraved gold ring, the key. And:

Sources close to the investigation have told the *Standard Times* that the key fits a safe-deposit box at a Bank of Cape Cod branch in Hyannis. The box is registered to the victim's former boyfriend, Paolo Costa of Martha's Vineyard. According to his answering machine, Costa has left the country for an indefinite period of time, his destination undisclosed.

"Jesus! Chief, I swear to you on my mother's grave. I did not leak this. I told you about Costa the other day when I got back from Edgartown."

"Do you have any clue how this information getting out to the public compromises our case? Do—?"

"Shit. Just shit, Chief. I didn't know about this safe-deposit box. That was Johnny's job. He's running down the key thing. I've been doing interviews. We had so much stuff swirling around us yesterday, I guess he forgot to tell me he found out about this bank in Hyannis ..."

"Yeah, well the story he tells me is that he came up empty searching the Vineyard banks, but folks there said Costa had been running his boat thing out of Hyannis before he came to the Vineyard. So Johnny beat it over to Hyannis."

"And got way lucky ..."

"Come on, 'fess up. You knew. He told you. And then one of you leaked all of this shit. To someone else ... or the press. Why did you do it, Yemanjá? Do you hate me that much? You just can't wait to make a fool of me? You thinking about going back to your old job with the staties, is that it? Looking for a promotion? Maybe take over your old partner Lou Votolatto's job when he retires?" There's a desperate note in his voice that she has never heard before. His piggy eyes search hers as they face off here in the hallway.

She can see specks of fat glistening in his brown irises. Her old job with the state CPAC unit on the Cape is sounding very good right now ... even if it's for shorter money and longer hours. *But, be real, who's going to reinstate someone who resigned her job because of personal problems after the Tuki Aparecio-Michael Decastro murder case? And who would hire back a detective even faintly linked to a media leak?* Her career's mud.

"I haven't talked to Johnny Match since yesterday morning. He was still on the Vineyard. He was supposed to check in with me at the end of the day. That's the way we always do it, since I've got the lead on this case, but ..."

Suddenly a comet flares and crashes in her belly. *Last night. Coño!* Last night she was with Corby. For that dinner she owed him. Then on the tugboat. Late. Serious love medicine. Her phone was shut off. *Christ, it still is!* She reaches in the pocket of her anorak, pulls out her phone and clicks it on. It starts pulsing softly to itself, the screen telling her of five messages missed. Johnny's number.

"Your phone was off?" There's a look of utter disbelief in his eyes.

She replays the first message. "I'm in Hyannis, partner. At the Bank of Cape Cod. Thought you would want to know, we just hit pay dirt. Box 821. It's Paolo's. Do you think we can get a judge to give us a search warrant?"

"*Coño!*"

"You really didn't know ..." He sounds a bit befuddled by the discovery ... but recovering. "You fucked up. We're so screwed. You think Machico leaked this? Think he wants all the glory, bucking for promotion?"

She considers. She doesn't see Johnny Match as the kind of guy who would blow a case for personal gain. But what does she know? What kind of judge of character is she? Look at her ex Jorge. Look at who she was sleeping with last night. Not Mr. Clean.

"I kind of doubt it, Chief. This leak is going to be on his head too."

He coughs loudly. Nearly choking.

"You ought to take care of that cold!"

"I ought to fucking fire you, *jeba*. And talk to the DA. Get some help from the staties and send your pal Johnny out on road detail!"

She knows he has a right to be pissed, that it is S.O.P. when this kind of thing happens, a case is blown. The detectives get the shaft. But she has an idea.

"What if I can bail us out of this?"

"What do you mean?"

"What if I can find Paolo Costa?"

"And where would that be?"

"If I keep that to myself, then the leak won't be on your head if it comes out."

He steps back two paces and looks at her in the rumpled pajamas and dark blue anorak. Rubs his jaw. "What about Johnny Match?"

"Leave him out of it. Tell him I'm off the case, until further notice. Let him keep doing his thing, running down the evidence. The ring. The handcuffs. Those little brass grommets that I found. Tell him you put me on a leave-of-absence until you can clear up this leak business."

"And what are you going to do?"

She thinks about how her credit card balance is just about to sail through the roof. "I'll tell you after I nail this Costa guy, Chief."

"You like him for the serial killings?"

She thinks about the current madness playing in her head. "One case at a time, Chief."

• • • • •

"Just give me a little more of what you showed me in the Bahamas." The man's voice seems a distant echo. But his hand between Remy's legs is real. A hungry animal. With claws.

"Get the hell off me!" The vodka that had put her to sleep tastes like acid in her mouth. Her sinuses are aching, the blow way worn off.

"Come on, Remy ... Remember why you came here?"

She opens her eyes. He has her pinned on her back. They are out on a dock. Water lapping all around. Rough boards under her bare shoulders. She feels a cool wind, smells the sulfur of a New England salt marsh. This is not the Bahamas. Not at all. And his fingers are ... Oh, shit.

25

"SHOW ME SOME PIRATES," Colón says. "Find me Paolo Costa."

"After dark."

"Why wait?"

"Pirates are usually nocturnal."

"I don't have a lot of time or money to waste down here, Corby." Since this morning when she boarded the flight from Boston to the Bahamas, she's had this shaky feeling that she knows will only go away if she really gets moving forward on this investigation. She can't stand twiddling her thumbs when she could be working.

And right now that's what it feels like she's doing.

It's late in the afternoon. Church has bought her a banana rum drink that is already starting to knock her on her butt. She's staring out from the shady deck of the Harbour's Edge at the snug, sun-washed yacht anchorage. The candy-striped lighthouse beyond.

Remy probably loved it here.

"What do you think of this place?" he asks.

"What's it called again?"

"Hope Town. Elbow Cay."

"Maybe we ought to check in with the local police and see if they can help us find …"

He shakes his head. "You're not really going to find cops out here. Mostly they're back in Marsh Harbour."

"We're on our own?"

"It's kind of the ragged edge of the world, these cays."

"We have a *pueblocito* like this in PR. On the south coast, *La Parguera*." She takes a sip of rum punch. "I used to party with my cousins there on vacation. A bucket of beer for three dollars. But this is not a party, Corby. Got it? We have to get to work."

He adjusts his sunglasses. "Your gig, Detective. I'm just along for the ride."

She looks at him. That red nose again. But this time it must be from the ultra violets, not booze. They sat out in the sun, riding the little ferry. Just an hour ago it brought them to this cay from the "mainland," Marsh Harbour on Great Abaco, where their flight landed. He brought her to this bar the Harbour's Edge because he said it was one of Paolo's favorite watering holes when they were sailing down here twenty-two years ago.

"*Carajo*. I just got here … and I'm already feeling a little drunk."

"Trust me. You don't need the rum to help you feel this way. The sun, the heat, the hibiscus in bloom, the salt air. You know?"

She tilts her head back, tries to relax in her deck chair. "Like no shoes, no shirt, no problem."

"Sometimes."

"But we've got work to do …" In the back of her head she hears the dead girl's voice. *Make him pay.* She sits up in her seat, suddenly full of conviction. "Right, Quimesabe? Find a killer. Save my career."

"How about mine? How long do you think it's going to take the chief and the selectmen to figure out that you're not down here alone … or that you weren't alone when you found those grommets on Bird Island?"

"It won't matter to anybody if we find Costa." She looks around at the harbor, its little pastel buildings, hears her boss's question in her head. *You think Costa could have killed all those other women? You think he could be the serial guy?*

He tosses down the last of his beer. "I don't know. I just don't know."

"We need to collar this bastard and get back home with some good news for the chief. I'm already missing Ricky. He wasn't exactly thrilled to see me go this morning, and my grandmother gave me a look like I had lost my mind. I came for Costa's blood, not this." She raises her drink glass.

He nods, seems to get her urgency. "It will be dark soon."

Bring it on, she thinks … already slipping into Remy's skin again. Feeling the mad burn.

• • • • •

The trip could have been a battle against fall hurricanes. But this year the storms have stayed well south of the Bahamas and the US East Coast.

Warm westerly winds were the rule for most of the late October voyage in 1987. The big schooner reeled off the miles under her wings of white canvas. Ten days from Cape Cod to their landfall in the Abacos, arriving here the first week in November.

And whatever else Paolo may or may not be, a girl has to respect the way he runs his ship. He has demanded that the entire offshore voyage be drug and alcohol free. Remy has enjoyed being the cook, filling the guys' bellies with all manner of crepes, stews, fresh vegetables. Everybody is clean, sober, strong, and tan by the time they come to rest at last. Here in the lee of a six-mile sliver of coral, pink sand, bougainvillea blossoms, casuarina pines swaying in the trade winds, coconut groves. This island in the Central Abacos. Largely uninhabited. Virgin. Great Guana Cay.

"I think I could love this life," she says to Hook and Church, after they get the anchor down in the settlement harbor.

The three of them are lying on their bellies in swimming suits on the teak deck, eyes half closed, sipping from a shared bottle of Perrier. The last cold drink on the boat. A warm morning breeze tickling the hairs on their arms.

After who knows how long, Remy whispers. "Hey, look at that!"
"What?"

Remy's up on her forearms, her green bikini doing nothing to hide the chords of muscles in her shoulder blades, the two dimples at the top of her butt. Legs men dream about. Yards of oiled skin. Long red hair coiling like thick rope over her right shoulder.

"There, check it out, dudes. A fruit stand."
Church pulls on his shades, the wayfarers.

She's looking at a bright, yellow, wooden fruit stand right on the edge of this tiny cove of a harbor. Nearby there's an enormous fig tree. A half dozen men and women lounging in the shade.

"We are totally out of fruit. What do you say we launch a dinghy? Head ashore and see what we can come up with?"

"You go. I'm feeling the peace of the sea turtle," Hook mumbles.
"Come on, Corby!"

He drops back on his belly. "Talk to your boyfriend."

She gives a little growl. "The trip seems to be over. He and Spence just did up a bunch of reds and are crashing in their berths. Come on!"

"Maybe later ..."

"You could use a long walk on the ocean-side beach, right? Aren't you curious? Don't you want to see if the natives are friendly?" She runs the backs of her fingers along the small of his back.

"Are you stroking me?"

"Come on, be a good boy. Get off your belly. Paradise is calling. Just walk with me. Talk. Ok?"

26

DARK NOW. She's fully on the hunt for sharks, nursing a bottle of the local Kalik at the bar in Harbour's Edge. Sizing up the crowd, thinking about a dead girl's wink and wiggle. Putting her own body out here as bait.

There's a Red Sox game on the satellite TV, but she pays no attention. She sits on her stool like a barroom queen in a halter top and cutoffs, swaying a little to some reggae coming over the sound system. Hoping to attract a few pirates. It's Saturday night.

Corby has bought into a pool game. They figure that if they split up, one of them might get lucky. Stir up a conversation with one of the locals or expats that will lead them to Paolo Costa. "You never know. He could walk right in here," Corby told her. "Come in off one of the yachts tied at the dock. Unless he has been reading Cape Cod news online, he probably has no clue that the law might want to talk to him."

Ziggy Marley is jamming to "Tomorrow's People," when a shark takes her bait, pushes up to the bar next to her seat. He is sandy-haired, blue-eyed, square jaw, wearing a pink polo, Bermuda shorts, Topsiders, no socks. Medium build. Handsome ... if you like the distinctive genes of Scotland. He is quite tan, and she can see the faint outline of a wedding band that he has removed from his ring finger.

"You live around here?"

He smiles. "It's my pleasure." The accent is American, faintly Southern, maybe. "Can I help you?"

"I don't know. I'll tell you when I figure it out."

"You will, huh? What makes you think I've got all night?"

She picks up her Kalik, sips, looks over his shoulder toward the pool table. Corby has his eye on her. "You got a house or something? What's an American doing living out here?"

"You mean, am I wasting away?"

Her eyes twinkle, a coy smile. Enjoying the game. "You said it, not me."

He leans on the bar, bites his lower lip, gives her the eye back. "Do I look wasted away?"

She surveys him, head to toe, back up again. "More like dumb and happy. Do you have a name, jolly mon?"

His eyes warm. "My mother named me Malcolm. People here call me Skip."

"Ok, Malcolm. What do you do when you are not hanging out at the bar talking to stray women? You have a job or something?" As soon as she asks that last question she knows it is all wrong, too direct. Damn, she has been living in New England for too long, forgotten the social graces of the islands. It is the same on *la Isla*. In PR you don't ask people what they do for a living, because quite possibly you do not really want to know. And they do not want to tell you.

He takes her hand, squeezes it slightly, and gives her a very earnest look, lowers his voice. "Watch your step. That's not really a polite question around here. But if you want to know, I sell real estate, mostly on Guana Cay. It's hot. Everybody wants a piece of Guana. How about you?"

God, she hates realtors. But this is good. He must know everybody, he's got a cheating heart, the night is young. She sees a way to lighten things up again, keep stringing him along. Maybe find her boy Paolo. "My name is Yemanjá Colón. You want to dance with me?"

• • • • •

It's almost two in the morning when he hears her unlock the door and tip-toe back into their hotel room.

"You ok?"

"Are you going to start acting like you're my *papi* again? I thought we were over that. Like I'm a big girl, right? I can take care of myself. Got it?"

"Sorry. I was just worried."

"I was on the job, *me entiendes?*"

"You start messing with the pirates, sooner or later you are going to get burned."

"You mean like that story you told me about the shoot out?"

"Something like that, yeah. This isn't New Bej."

"It seems a lot safer to me. They've never had a serial killer down here."

"How do you know?"

"I asked."

"The blond dude?"

"Yeah, the blond dude."

"He looked like a dink!"

"Hey, are you jealous? *Carajo*! Don't go getting possessive or I'm getting my own room."

"Sorry." He means it. He stands up, wearing just his boxers. Reaches out for her hand, pulls her into his arms.

She yields, lays her cheek on his shoulder. "I know where he is."

"Who?"

"Your old friend. Paolo."

"Where?"

"Ever heard of a place called Great Guana Cay?"

He sees Guana again. The way it was when he first went ashore with Remy. November, 1987.

• • • • •

"Now don't you be messing with me, missy. You really aim to buy all these here mangos …?" A man with broad shoulders, shorts, faded Hawaiian shirt. He stands in the shade of his fruit stand, waving his hand at the produce. He has a broad, sunburned face, creased with smile wrinkles. Wild, curly blond hair. His English is the faintly Cornish dialect of the Abacos' native whites.

"I want them all," she says. "I swear I do. I'll make it right with you. Please save them for me. I just have to go back to the boat and get some money. But first we want to see the beach. We need to talk. You know what I mean?" She gives a look. Like this walk, this talk, is urgent.

The fruit vendor eyes the siren in the little white shift with the hemline just below her breasts, the blue sarong tied over her bikini bottom. He turns to her companion, to Corby Church.

"She telling me the truth, brother? She really want me to put a dozen pretty mangos aside for her? Or is this little dolly just trying to pass the time of day with me? Some of the boat people do that sort of thing, you

know? Chat up the local. Promise me the moon, then skip town."

He looks at Remy, wonders what she is in such a sweat to talk about. Knows this savvy islander can see danger in her wink and wiggle. "You really want the fruit?"

"Didn't I already say that? Please!"

He cannot tell whether this plea is meant for him or the vendor. But he feels her tugging at him with invisible tendrils.

"Count on us." He takes off his watch, offers it across the tray of tomatoes and pineapples. It is not a Rolex, but it is a serious time piece, a diver's watch.

The vendor steps back. Raises his hands. "I don't want your watch, friend. I just want to know who I'll be saving all these mangos for. Or maybe I could interest you in some of my handmade jewelry." He nods to the tiny dolphin pendants carved from shell. "Milo Pinder at your service. Welcome to Great Guana Cay. You got a name, missy, or does everyone just call you Princess?"

"That works. Princess works!" She throws the islander, this Milo, a big smile as if he has put his finger on her secret name for herself. But her voice has an odd, shrill note in it. As if she is almost out of breath. She grabs her shipmate's hand and squeezes. Her eyes are already set on the hillside graveyard and the crest of the bluff beyond, rising above the little settlement. Her mind imagining the ocean beach just over the ridge. "Please!"

27

THEY CAN HEAR Toby Keith's country drawl singing "I Love This Bar" almost as soon as they step off the ferry at Guana Cay, long before they reach the pig roast. The music is coming from the crest of the bluff above the cemetery.

He remembers the cemetery from twenty-two years ago. From his time here with the Princess. The time he bought her the little dolphin pendant from Milo Pinder to cheer her up.

• • • • •

The surf crisps on the gentle slope of the broad beach, tickling his ankles. The sarong is off her hips now, trailing like a pennant in the winds from her free hand. Her other hand still holds his, towing him along the strand, with long swift strides. As if she is trying to skate with him. Trying to stride away from something chasing her.

"Paolo treats me like shit," she says. "But he says that if I ever try to leave him, I'll be sorry."

"I don't think this is any of my business." He feels her eyes on him. Looks away at a promontory of high, blue rocks way down the beach.

"I'm scared, Corby. I could put up with anything from him when he was keeping me in blow. But now ... I feel different. It's like two weeks since I've been high, and now I can't deal with his threats. The way he tries to push me around. But I'm stuck, see?"

"You want to jump ship?"

"Yes ... No. I don't know."

"What?"

"I like you guys. I like the adventure of the boat. I think I'm going to like these islands ... And I need the money from the deal, you know? I need it so I can get the ice time and a serious coach when I get back. Skating. It's all I really have. It's where I get my self-respect."

He stops, looks at her. "So what do you want to do? What do you want me to say?"

"I don't know. I just thought that if maybe we talked ..."

He looks out to sea. Watches the way the indigo swells roll in white plumes over the outer reef to the east, how the water softens to pale shades of emerald near shore. The white foam rushing over the pink sand, sweeping back. A small clutch of sandpipers are racing just ahead of the surf. Back and forth. Back and forth. Their stick legs a blur of scurry.

There are steep sand bluffs, maybe sevety feet high, all along this coast where the ocean has gnawed at the island. Immense pines toppled from the cliffs. Others standing proud. Dark green. Right on the precipice. Waiting their turn to face a hurricane. Clouds like cotton balls drift across the pale blue sky. The only noises the sowing of the wind in the trees, the rhythmic thud of the surf. No other souls in sight. Just him. Just her.

"Corby. Help me!"

A glazed look is creeping into her eyes. Despair, desperation, mania. Then tears. A storm of tears. He wraps her in his arms. And lets her sob. This lost princess. And him with no clue what to do next.

"Jesus, this place is unbelievable," he says.

• • • • •

"Nippers," she says, reading a hand-painted sign on a piece of drift-wood pointing up a sandy road toward the top of the hill. "This is the place everybody is talking about, right? This is the place we're supposed to look for Paolo Costa?"

He shrugs, half lost in the chorus of the Toby Keith song. Half lost in his memory of 1987-88. And Paolo. *That prick. What do you say to a guy like that after all this time?*

"Just listen to that, would you?"

It sounds to him like hundreds of people are singing along. "Somebody's having a good time."

Golf carts, the island taxis, loaded with people in party mode pass them, heading up the hill toward a clutch of octagon pavilions, a huge deck painted in pastel pinks and blues. Beach umbrellas shading picnic tables. From a hundred yards away, he can smell the scent of roasting pork, corn on the cob, coconut rum.

The deck at Nippers swarms with hard bodies in swimwear. Rich bodies is print shirts, gold, straw hats. Suddenly he feels stupid, dressed in jeans, carrying all his clothes in his backpack. The music switches from country to calypso and reggae. People start dancing. A crowd presses around the bar calling for fresh bottles of Kalik or strawberry-colored frozen punch. Waitresses hustle platters of pork. This is a great beach bar. And down on the strand below the bluff, families and lovers sunbathe, swim, snorkel around the coral heads.

What a difference twenty-two years makes, he thinks. Great Guana Cay, this outpost on the edge of forever, has been discovered.

A waitress sallies forth to their outpost along the railing overlooking the Atlantic.

"Are all these people from Guana?" he asks her.

The waitress smiles. "Only on Sunday, honey. They come from all over the Abacos by boat to make this scene." There is the look of easy money in her eyes. "What can I bring you?"

He has barely ordered two beers, when Colón asks, "Is he here? Do you see him yet?"

"Son of a bitch."

28

"WELL, you going to introduce me to this lovely, Corby? Or am I buying her a drink and doing this little number on my own?"

Paolo Costa is sitting at the back corner of the open-air bar beneath the octagonal roof, stirring a plastic cup of frozen pink punch with a swizzle stick.

The awkward first encounter is behind them. The two old shipmates have greeted each other, done the fancy-meeting-you-here routine. But his heart is still pounding. And suddenly he cannot find his voice as he looks at this bastard who surely put the Princess in the ground. The hair is shorter, frizzy, the black laced with gray. No more ponytail. There are lines and sun freckles on the forehead. The cheeks are a bit more hollow. And he is sporting a ragged beard. But otherwise Paolo Costa has not changed much since 1988.

Still a collection of gold chains around the neck. Same style of mutt-ugly silk shirt with the fly-away collar. Same baggy cargo shorts. Same crusty flipflops. Same dragon tattoo on the forearm. Same purple gunshot scar on the top of the foot. Same little, round, John

Lennon sunglasses. Same wise-ass grin as he sizes up a woman's bones. He licks the corner of his lip as he gives the once-over to this Latina in the cut-offs and the powder-blue tank top.

"You Brazilian. *Uma Braziliera, também? Fala Portuguese?*"

She drops her backpack at her feet, thrusts out her hand and gives his a firm shake. "*Sim, falo Portugues.* But I'm not Brazilian. My name is Yemanjá Colón."

"Interesting name. You Cuban? I really like Cuban women."

"Partly. And some other things."

He cannot believe it, she's smiling at this asshole. Flirting.

"Like?"

"Like Puerto Rican. And Jamaican." She tosses off the last third of her beer, looks at Costa's drink. Winks. "I'll take what you're having."

He signals the bartender, orders a round. "Dynamite gene pool, Yemanjá. What brings your sunny face to my world?"

"Remy La Moreaux."

He takes it right between the eyes. His hand ripping the sunglasses off his nose like his face is suddenly on fire.

Her face looks on fire. As if she has been waiting for this moment for years. As if she has a long, sharp knife in her hand. As if she's Remy fighting for her life.

• • • • •

"*Stop it, you prick!*"

He covers her mouth with his free hand. Drives down on her chest with his forearm until her breath comes rushing out. "Listen to me. You came here begging for it. Or don't you remember, you were so wasted?"

"No." It is all she can get out.

"Forget 'no,' Princess. I'm tired of your games, your teasing. You came for it. Now you are going to get it!"

She remembers. She was desperate. She needs her share of the money. Needs all the money she can get. She pleaded. She went down on him. Please just give me the money. He said head was nothing. She was going to give him what she gave him on the dock at Sunset Beach. What she gave him in the Bahamas. Love in the moonshine. Like it was the end of the world. Like he was the last man on Earth.

He rips open her shorts. He tears her thong. He's on his knees, pants down.

• • • • •

"I'm a detective," Colón says, still feeling the torn shorts. Her voice a blow torch.

"So?" Two sips of a new drink and Costa has found his rhythm again.

"We found Remy's body a few weeks ago." These are the first words the harbormaster can muster. The rum starting to free him too.

"The coke finally took her down, huh?"

"Somebody murdered her." She doesn't mention the other eleven women who are dead or missing, maybe connected. Doesn't say that the ME thinks Remy died shortly after she disappeared during the summer of the serial killings. She wants Costa to connect the dots on his own. Wants him to feel the fear, and say or do something hasty. Something telling.

"Really? I can't imagine why." The voice is flat.

She sucks on her swizzle stick, gives him a hairy eye. "We think you can. We think you know all about how she died."

Costa sets down his drink. "Let me get this straight. Did you come all the way here to Guana Cay to accuse me of murder?"

"We just want to talk."

"You're wasting your time."

"We don't think so. We found a key with the body. A safe-deposit key. To box 821 at a Bank of Cape Cod branch in Hyannis."

He shrugs.

She thinks back on Johnny Match's research. "The box is registered to Whale Cay Ltd. The company is owned by Fedallah Enterprises. And according to state records, you are president of Fedallah Enterprises. So maybe you could help us understand what she was doing with a key to your safe-deposit box."

"I don't know. Maybe she stole it. She was a fucking clepto."

"Yeah, but from where we found the key, it looks like she swallowed it. And it was not a little key. It had to hurt going down. She had to be desperate. What do you think of that?"

Costa takes a long sip of his rum punch, glares out to sea. Bounces back. "Why don't you ask your boyfriend about her?"

She shoots a pained look at Corby Church. Like she has heard just about enough of his involvement with this princess, this murder. Then she gives Paolo Costa her don't-mess look.

A nasty smile rises on his lips. "Oh, yeah, *guapa,* I remember the last night I saw Remy. It was on my boat. She came aboard totally toasted. I told her to clean up her act … for about the hundredth time that summer. We fought. You couldn't get through to her when she was high. I left to see some people. An hour later I get back. No Princess. But I forgot all about her when your boyfriend Corby's fiancée shows up at my boat and wants to get it on. Goes down on her knees and gives me a hummer. Me sitting down below in the fo'castle under the open hatch, looking at the stars. Smooth as silk. Karen Sue ever tell you how much she liked it, Corby?"

"You suck!" Church looks like Costa's just hit him in the guts.

"No, man. Karen Sue sucks. But I suppose you know that by

now. I'm betting she dropped your ass for some richer meat once she got to be a fancy Providence lawyer."

"You know what? You're scum." Some old jealousy's boiling up.

"Bite me, Corby. Maybe you saved my life once, but that was a long time ago. I don't owe you anything. You've been paid in full. And if you will remember … I never had a key to that box. I just rented it … or the company did. Spence had the key. The second key I threw into Buzzard Bay the day I got it."

Costa sneers. He takes another sip of his rum punch and watches to see the detective's reaction, her face go blank. Then he stings. "Have you told this little lady about Spence, or did you leave that out, too?"

"I ought to rip your head off!"

"Stop it!" She drops off her barstool, throws herself between the two men. Feet squarely planted on the floor, a martial arts defender. Her hand reaching for the shoulder holster, the Glock that is not there. Her voice loud, deep. People beginning to stare. Especially the bartender, a bronzed-cheek local with razor-cut brown hair, a trim beard, piercing blue eyes.

"Fuck off!" Costa pulls a snub-nose .38 out of his pocket, points it at the detective. "You have no jurisdiction here. Stay the hell out of my face or—"

"Drop it!" The bartender has a cut-off oar cocked like a baseball bat aimed at Costa's head. "This is a nice place. We don't need your trash here. I've had enough of you, Paolo. Get out of here and don't come back!"

Costa twists up his mouth, considering his options. Then pockets the gun. Steps away from the bar, heads down the stairs for the beach. "Piss off, Johnny!"

She grabs Corby's hand. His fingers feel dry, hard, shaky. "You want to start talking about your ex-wife … or this guy Spence, first?"

"Spence was our banker ... so to speak." He nods toward the beach. Wants to walk, wants to tell her another story about the last time he was in the Abaco cays twenty-two years ago with the crew of the *Fedallah*.

29

CHURCH FEELS *the heat rising in his chest as the first sip of rum in his Gombay Smash hits his empty stomach.*

Noon is way too early for him to be drinking, but the Princess has been soaking up Miss Emily's secret recipe in the Blue Bee for more than an hour already.

So has Spence. And now he has a half-cocked grin on his face as his fingers toy with Remy's under the table.

"Where the hell is Paolo?"

He squints, still trying to read the scene that he has just walked in on. What is going on here? "I thought he was with the two of you. Wasn't that the plan, meet here at noon? Set things up?" He looks around the rustic little pub in the heart of the village of New Plymouth. It is April, and they have been anchored at this settlement on Green Turtle Cay for more than a month trying to set up a deal. The village has the historic salt-water feel of Nantucket. At first, he loved it here. The nineteenth century cottages and churches, the picket fences, the rose gardens, the pastel church.

But after five weeks, he knows every brassiere hanging in the rafters of the bar, every business card tacked to the walls. He wants to move on. There are so many islands here in the Abacos to explore. He would like to just go back to Guana Cay, find what he had with Remy on that first beach walk. The day he bought her the little dolphin pendant. The day before they started all this drinking, Before she found someone to sell her blow. Before she started fucking around with everybody behind Paolo's back. Like what the hell has she been doing with Spence now?

Ok. So the guy's a stud. He's got the Miami-Vice-Don-Johnson look nailed. A face saved from too pretty by the shadow of a heavy beard. He is always looking casually elegant in his button-down denim shirts, Bermuda shorts, gator skin belt and Tevas … when almost everyone else in the crew gets by in random shirts, cargo shorts or cut-offs, and flipflops.

He's just five foot seven, but his broad shoulders, ripped arms, make him seem bigger. The Rolex watch is not a trophy, just the time piece of choice of a young man born to expensive tastes, a young man soon to attend Harvard's med school. A young man who comes from five generations of physicians. A young man hard to compete with.

The Princess must be boinking him again. She's hedging her bets on Paolo, thinking maybe here is a new sugar daddy. You can smell the pheromones fuming between their bodies.

"We're missing a great day on the reef. We could be down there with the slings taking some fish by now, if Paolo—"

"Did I hear someone mention my name?" The crane-like figure lopes up to his crew. Hook following behind.

Remy drops Spence's hand under the table, smiles. Waiting here half the morning has been no problem at all for her. She is blown away.

Paolo sees it in her eyes, frowns a little as he pulls an empty chair up to the table and sits. For just an instant his lip curls as he looks at Spence. It is not a voluntary thing.

"You want to hear about it? Or just sit there thinking about your hard-on for Remy?"

"Fuck off." Spence is not in the mood to take any shit. He does not have to. Everyone in the crew knows that Spence bought his ticket on this tropical junket by putting up twenty-five k to stake half of Paolo's get-rich-quick scheme. "Are we on?"

Paolo tilts his head forward, stares at his skinny knees for a full twenty seconds, adjusting the elastic hair band on his ponytail. A chair screeches on the floor as Hook makes a place for himself at the table.

"Well, maestro?" This time Remy is speaking. "Are we going to live like royalty?"

Paolo looks up. Gives a thin-lipped, toothy grin. His front teeth a little twisted at their roots. "Day after tomorrow."

"Who's the connection? Can you trust him?"

"He calls himself Carlos. Says he's Venezuelan. I've heard he's got a place on Scotland Cay. But then again I've heard he rents one of those fancy homes out on the peninsula at Marsh Harbour. I don't know. I met him over at Treasure Cay."

Spencer is up on the edge of his seat. "You don't fucking know? We're just going to hand over like fifty thousand dollars in cash to some guy. And you don't even know where to find him?"

Paolo jumps to his feet. "Look, man, you think you can do a better job, you go for it. But we've been down here all winter. and I ain't seen you do shit except get trashed and follow the Princess around like a love-sick puppy!"

Spence stands up, hands out in front of him ready to attack or defend.

Miss Emily, a vintage Bahamian lady who has been polishing glasses behind the bar, puts down her work and glares at the Americans who are starting to put a kink in her day.

"Hey, hey. Everybody sit down. Let's just calm down. Everybody take *a deep breath, ok?" Hook the peacemaker. "We need everybody together on this or we could be in really deep shit."*

Corby takes another swig of his Gombay Smash. What in the name of all things right and true is he doing here?

"This is how it goes," says Paolo. His voice is now almost a whisper. After months of searching, he is convinced that there is no reefer to be had in quantity here in the Abacos. The import/export boys, who it has taken him all winter to find and befriend, are selling cocaine. Supply is good, prices are within the budget, profits could be crazy back in Massachusetts.

Corby Church frowns, gives Hook a look like screw this.

"Hey, guys, we gotta take what we can." Paolo's eyes sparkle, promoting. "I don't know about you, but I'm down to rock bottom, and I ain't going home empty. It's just not an option. I'd lose the boat. And maybe get my ass shot by the money guys I owe in Nu Bej. You got a choice. You can feel saintly, catch the next flight out of here for Boston, or seize the opportunity of a lifetime. We sail as soon as we load the product. We go home and get rich."

"I don't like it," says Church. "We came for pot. Coke is a different game. This stuff gets people killed."

"How do you know we aren't being set up?" Spence toys with his drink, skidding it back and forth on the table, a hockey puck between his hands.

"Trust me. This is legit. Hook knows. He met the guy."

"I'm as skittish as the rest of you, but yeah, I think this Carlos is the real deal. Very professional with us," says Hook.

"I don't know ..."

"Don't fucking bail on me now, Spence. We gotta have your stake. Carlos said this was a fifty grand deal, nothing less. What do you need to make you feel better about this?"

Spence says nothing. Toys with his drink again.

"Come on, show some balls, Spence!" The Princess sounds out of patience.

"Ok, I'm in … If I get to guard the profits when we get back home."

Paolo bites his thumb, knows he's in a tight corner. "I'll get a safe-deposit box. We set up a corporate shield. My company rents the box. I'm the signator. We get one key. You hold it. So it always takes two of us to access the stash. No chance of a double cross. What do you say?"

30

SHE'S RUNNING, bare feet hissing through the damp sand. The beach on Guana Cay is pale blue in the moonlight. The surf crashing on the reef, rolling back into the black sea.

She needs to be out here in the sultry tropic wind. Walking so that she can clear her head and think. Maybe she's crazy to be on a deserted beach alone in the dark. But *quien sabe*? Right now she doesn't want to be around that man. Any man.

She has left Church back on Fishers Bay in the little blue cottage that they rented from Troy at Dive Guana. Sleeping like a baby, a soft snore bubbling from his lips. The son of a bitch.

But she can't sleep. Not even after the heat, the booze, the crazy revelations of this day. Too many questions, worries, strange stories from Remy racing through her mind.

Now what does she do? She walks. Briskly.

The way she sees it, she has three problems:

Paolo Costa. Corby Church. And where does she go from here?

Primero. Paolo Costa. Ok, she found him for Chi Chi, for the chief. But now what? Yeah, Costa is a *pendejo,* a slime ball. But he did not exactly cave in when he heard about Remy's death. He was quick to deflect the blame. Create doubt in her mind, make her think Spencer Alpin or even Corby had as much motive and maybe more opportunity to kill the Princess.

And the guy has a weapon. A crummy little detective's special. But still a gun. If he carries that in a bar, he is sure to have others where he lives. She has heard Corby's stories about the M-16s, the AK-47, sawed-off shot guns. And where is it that he lives? On Guana? Or was he just visiting by boat for the day? She doesn't know.

But one thing she does know. She has seen no police around on Guana. If she wants to talk to the local cops, she will have to take Albury's Ferry about ten miles across the Sea of Abaco to the port of Marsh Harbour. And will they cooperate? It's not like she's here on official business. Doesn't have any paperwork. No search warrant. No arrest warrant. No request for extradition of Paolo Costa. She was in too much of a rush to get down here and look for Costa to pull all the official paperwork together. It could have taken a week or more.

She's here chasing a desperate hunch. A hunch that Costa will do something to show his guilt. Something crazy to get himself locked up. So then she can call her boss and Johnny Match, get the paperwork rolling to take Costa home.

Que loco! Fat chance! She's seen it. The only justice on this island is a fierce bartender swinging a boat oar. But, hey, the man knows Costa's name. So maybe if she goes back to Nippers she can find out a little more about Costa. Where he lives. His habits. Maybe he's still running drugs. Like the guy keeps some kind of fancy airplane down here, right? Where's that plane?

She pivots on her heels, turns back toward the beach bar. In the distance, she can see the glow of the colored lights at Nippers up on the sandy bluff. She's going to talk to this bartender. She remembers his name. Johnny. He clearly does not like Paolo Costa. Maybe if she shows him some ID and comes clean with him about her investigation, the man will be in a generous mood. Help her fill in at least some of the blanks about Costa's life here in the Bahamas.

But what about her second problem? Corby Church. *Coño*. What the hell was she thinking, bringing him along? Sleeping with him?

Like this evening. Why did she lay her doubts aside when she felt his big hands drawing her against him? His stories. They get to her. They seem so sincere, so honest. He takes her back through time to Remy. To fill in some of the gaping holes in the narrative spinning through her head. To the Blue Bee. To all of that cocaine in 1988.

And booze.

You gotta know the booze was at work earlier tonight, nena. *Have you forgotten about what it did to you and Jorge, what it did to Papi? And all the rest?*

After the pig roast, both of them were way too high on the rum punches. Her peeling off his shirt, pulling him into that big bed with the sea view. The sun setting over the little island and the sailboats anchored offshore to the west, the room on fire with rosey light. Do you want me, *mi amor? Me quieres?* Do you want to feast on me? Eat my flesh?

And him. A *caballo*. Burning her. Searing her ovaries with his lightning. His tongue of coconut rum in her mouth. Uncoiling in fierce bursts. Until she is clawing at his back. Screaming in her head. Pues hodete, *Papi!* Venga, pendejo. *Fuck you. Fuck me 'til I die. Or I'll kill you, kill you tonight, you dirty, drunken bastard, Jorge.* Borracho! *Papi!* Her eyes busting open. The sun down now, the room draining purple.

And in the doorway ... the shadow. She sees it. Eyes as big as *pesos*. As her body thunders, moaning on top of this man who is a poison to her, a danger. A sickness. A love.

She knows.

Everyday she finds new things that he has been hiding from her. Things about his relationship with the Princess. Things that make him seem more than ever like a suspect. Maybe this safe-deposit box and the key are just a distraction. Her mind is just spinning, looping back on itself constantly, losing altitude.

What if Paolo Costa is the material witness and Corby did the crime? What if he killed all of those girls? Maybe he's trying to get her to blow the case. Maybe he's trying to get close to her so he can mislead her investigation, distract her body and her heart so badly that she gets so tangled up in her thoughts and feelings that she loses her bearings. She has seen it before. In her own pathetic life.

Like can we forget what happened with Michael Decastro last October, nena?

But she can't let herself believe this. No way. Not yet. Every time she asks, Church tells her what she needs to feel better. He just does not give her everything that she wants. Is he afraid of baring his soul to her, afraid of her judging his mistakes, his failures? Or is something else holding him back? Does he really care about her? How much?

Aye, coño! *He could drive a girl crazy!*

But first things first. She has to finish her investigation of Costa tonight. That's how it must happen. Talk to this barman Johnny. And get the hell out of here. She thought that she yearned for the tropics. That she is a *nena de la Isla*. But it's too hot for her here. Too much like her village on *la Isla*. Like her *mami's casa* by the lagoon. Now she remembers that she does stupid things in this heat, crazy things. Since she was a child. Things that she cannot explain to herself. She has to get back to the States, the cool of Cape Cod. Has to talk to this doctor. Spencer Alpin.

And Corby's ex. Karen Sue Adams, the lawyer in Providence.

Maybe soon she will know how big a fool she has really been. Whether or not the *ordun* tells the truth? *Your best friend is your worst enemy.*

Then maybe she will recognize the shadow that she saw while she was making love tonight. The hazy figure haunting her, haunting Remy. She does not even know if they are the same shadow. The same man. Men. Or maybe not just men. But they come. These shadows in the night.

· · · · ·

She strikes him in the groin … with the flashlight he has left lying beside them.

He rises in agony. She runs, dressing as she goes. For the big house on the shore.

"You fucking …"

His voice fading as she enters the library. Searching the shelves, the volumes in the light of a desk lamp. Looking for a book. A special volume. The Collected Works of T.S. Eliot. *The hollow book. Where he keeps the money.*

And there it is on the third shelf. In her hand. Opening its treasures.

"Put that the hell down!" He is standing in the doorway. A carving knife in his hand.

31

"LET ME ASK YOU SOMETHING, Detective. Are you fucking my ex?"

Colón's just a day back from the Bahamas. She thought she had the strength to plow ahead with both feet deep into good, old-school detective work, but this *anglo* bitch in the black power suit really knows how to deliver the low blow, knock a girl off her stride. She sits behind her gleaming chrome desk smiling wickedly, a queen bee.

The detective grits her teeth. "I'm just trying to understand why I'm not taking out a warrant for your arrest. Maybe obstruction of justice. Maybe murder."

Karen Sue Adams kicks back in her chair behind the desk. Looks out the plate glass window at the rich and stately cupolas of Brown University across the river on College Hill. Suddenly she's laughing.

"You think this is funny? You think I'm funny."

The lawyer jerks upright, glares across the desk, blue eyes full of lightning. "No, I don't think you're funny. I think you're way out of your league, Detective. And I think we are finished here."

Colón doesn't move. She sits in her seat and glares back. Crosses her arms over her Marshalls-sale ruby top. Just holds the lawyer in her sights.

"What?"

"What are you hiding, Counselor?" She watches the attorney.

There—for just a second—something involuntary. A rolling in of the lower lip. A secret sinking of teeth into the flesh, biting. Nerves. Then a quick smile to cover.

"I've told you all I know. Remy La Moreaux was a drunk, a drug addict and a slut. She fucked up my marriage before it ever got off the ground. You want to know who killed her, I'd start by asking Corby Church what he was doing with her on his tugboat the last night that you say anyone ever saw that wench. I remember that night. I watched Remy and Corby leave the boat, the wharf, in his truck. I'll testify in court. But you can forget about Paolo Costa. He was with me."

She can feel her brain starting to sizzle. *Coño,* Corby!

"All night."

Fuck this bitch. "Getting head from the loyal bride-to-be?"

"Is that what he told you?"

"Yeah."

"Actually, as I remember it, it was the other way around."

"Excuse me?"

"What girl could forget such a night? I had just found the man I was engaged to marry cheating on me with that bimbo. I was crushed. I needed a whole lot of TLC. Paolo was there when I needed him. End of story. You ever get good head? For hours? Nobody can give it like your Latino boys, am I right?"

Listen. Remy's shouting in her head. *Like this is how it really happened that night. Pay some fucking attention.*

• • • • •

She shows up on the tugboat just after dark. Falls into Corby Church's arms. Tears in her eyes, half-drowning in pre-mixed cans of Black Russians. Her day off work and she is wrecked after an afternoon of partying with some of her new friends from Weld Square. Now she's in a tailspin from fighting with Paolo.

She stumbles up the gangway to the Brutus, *shouting his name. Meets him on the deck. Sobbing on his chest, telling him she just cannot stand it any more. Paolo rambling on about sailing to the Bahamas for another winter. Just the two of them. She's not down for this. She knows there will be other girls. There are always other girls. He will coax her, or threaten her, to go down on some Conchy Joe's daughter or a tourist chick. Just so he can watch. His hard-on for the girl-on-girl thing out of control.*

And she has had enough of his moods, his distance, his mean streak, his hitting. His big deals. She can't take it anymore. All summer he has cut her off from his personal supply of blow, the miser. Well, fuck him. She has other ways to get coke.

Besides, she has got to get straight. The way she was when she first walked the beach back at Guana Cay. Clean up her act. Just plain take care of her body. She has to get out on the ice more. Start skating seriously again.

"You know what I mean? You are the only one who understands, Corby."

• • • • •

"Just calm down, *nena.* Let us see what the saints have to say about all of this."

It's two in the afternoon. A rainy day, late May in the South End of Nu Bej. Ricky still in school. Mercifully. And the door to Abuela's shrine room is open for desperate business. Yemanjá Colón has killing on her mind.

When she and Abuela have finished their chant, the old lady's eyes are rimmed with red from the smoking joss sticks, candles. Her voice sounds ragged. "Now let us see if we can discover why you are dreaming of murder, *nena*. And why you wanted to drive your car off the Braga Bridge on your way back from Providence."

"I'm so frightened."

Abuela lays a dry, bony hand on hers. She can feel its tremor. "We must trust in the grace of Elegguá. You can pick up *los cocos* and ask your questions now."

Slowly she gathers the four triangles of coconut shell into her left hand, touches Elegguá three times with her right, starts to chant in Yoruba.

"*Acuelle.*"

She puts her hands together on her chest and makes the sign of the cross. "*Onlle obi a Elegguá* … Is it right that I should think about killing?"

"*Asoña,*" says Abuela as her granddaughter casts the four pieces of coconut shell on the mat.

All four shells lie dark-side up.

"Shit, Abuela. *Oyekun*. I got *oyekun*."

The old lady has her eyes closed. Knows that *oyekun* is the worst possible answer the *cocos* can give. It means no. No, along with death and destruction to the person asking the question.

"What do I do?"

"Quick. I will light a candle for the dead. They will help us. Wash the *cocos*. Hurry. And try a different question."

"Are the living tormenting me?"

She throws the shells. A qualified yes.

"You must keep asking as long as the candle stays lit, *nena.*"

"Are the dead tormenting me?"

The shells clatter onto the mat. A definite yes.

"Am I haunted by Remy La Moreaux?"

The answer is *alafia.* All white sides of the shell triangles showing. Yes. In the sense of forthcoming peace and happiness. Definitely not what she expected. If the *ordun* is right, the Princess is an antidote, not a cause, for bloody thoughts.

"Hurry, *nena,* the candle is flickering."

She feels her cheeks burning. "Then who is tormenting me, provoking this thirst for blood?"

"Child, the shells can only answer yes or no. Give them a name! *Pronto!*"

She racks her brain for the names of the victims of the serial killer. But is coming up with nothing as the candle begins to sputter and spark. She squeezes her eyes shut, tries to see into her heart. Sees Corby Church. Wants to ask about him.

But no, he's alive. Her immediate problem is with the dead. She reaches into the darkness, for the hazy figures. The shadows that come to her. Are they the dead? The one in the doorway of the bedroom on Guana Cay. The one in her worst dreams. *Do you want me,* mi amor? Me quieres? *Do you want to feast on me? His tongue coconut rum in her mouth. And her clawing at his back. Screaming.* Venga, pendejo. *Or I'll kill you, kill you tonight.*

"Papi? Jesus Christ is it you, Papi?"

She throws the shells. They come up, one dark, three white. *Itagua.* It means yes. But more than that. *Itagua* means she has made some error in her questioning. Really, it means nothing. Because the candle for the dead is nothing but a trail of smoke rising into the cloud from the smoldering cigar.

"Papi?"

"*Qué vergüenza*! What an abomination. That man!" coughs the *santera,* scrambling for the open window and fresh air. "To even speak his name is to disrespect all that I hold close to my heart. Take your pain out on somebody else, *loca*!"

32

"YOU FILTHY PRICK! *Pendejo!*" The words are not yet fully out of Colón's mouth when she strikes.

Church is standing on the wharf, bent over an outboard engine, changing the spark plugs on his Grady White. The boat is tied to the town float for routine maintenance, and he is so deep into the chore, socket wrench in hand, that he does not even know she is coming until he hears her curse and feels the crack of her knuckles against the back of his head.

The first blow nearly knocks him into the harbor on this windy afternoon. But he catches himself, spins away, rising to his full height to face her. "Jesus Chr—"

She is in full Thai-bo mode. Catching him in the chest with a wheeling kick. Following with another smack to the side of the head. "Take that, you bastard."

He ducks and steps away as she launches at him a third time. "Hey."

She misses. But now she has him backing away toward the end of the dock.

"You lying shit. *Sí coño.* I ought to kill you now and save the tax payers the trial."

He sees the storm in her eyes. Holds up both his hands. "Come on, calm down, will you? What the hell is going on here?" But he knows his questions are useless.

Fists clinched, arms cocked for a strike, she's stalking him as he backs further down the wharf.

"Jesus, are you crazy?"

Her eyes scorch him. "You think I'm some kind of toy? You think women are disposable?"

He thinks back to the sudden end she called on their trip to the Bahamas three days ago. He knew she was having second thoughts about romance. Knew that Paolo's comments that night at Nippers were eating at her. So he went with the flow. He has been trying to lay low, give her some space. Hoping she would feel his genuine caring … and get over her worries as she had before, but …

"Why didn't you tell me she came to you the night she disappeared? Why didn't you tell me she was on your boat, in your fucking love nest? Did you think I wouldn't find out? What are you trying to hide?"

He shrugs, cannot find the right words, keeps backing toward the outer edge of the wharf.

"Did you think your ex was going to cover for you? Do you think I'm going to go to the district attorney to ask for a warrant for your arrest? Do you know what kind of fool I've let myself be? I must have been crazy to believe you that day at Fort Taber when you pretended to unpack your heart, pretended to tell me all about Remy and you. *Hijo de puta!*"

She feints at him with a right jab, then nails him the chest with a swift kick. It hits him with the force of a fast ball.

He falls backwards off the dock.

When he sputters to the surface of the fifty-five-degree water, his eyes are pleading. His body already starting to shiver. "I can explain."

"You better start talking," she says. "And don't think you are coming out of there until you finish. *Mi amor!*"

Shit. The last time I saw Remy ...

· · · · ·

He closes his eyes, feels her body, trembling. A princess folding up in his arms. The scent of fresh fish and the moist heat of Quissett Harbor lingering around them even as the sun sets.

"Help me. Please?"

He opens his eyes. "I don't know. This is a bad time. I'm getting married ..."

She is crumbling. He catches her. One arm beneath her knees, one behind her back as she falls. Red hair sweeping almost to the ground.

He's not up for this scene. Nine months ago when the cruise to the Bahamas on the Fedallah *had begun he loved her free spirit. But her addictions are too much. Really out of control this summer. And Paolo would* ~~go bat shit if he knew about her coming here. Not to mention Karen Sue.~~ *He has to get the Princess off this boat. Take her back to Mattapoisett. But he feels guilty that he let her think he might be a knight in shining armor.*

Christ, he's just an angry young man. A man pissed because his daddy walked, left his family shattered during his second year in prep school at Tabor Academy. After that he wanted to be bad for a while. But the past winter in the Bahamas was enough. Now he's bent on reinventing himself. Being engaged to Karen Sue has helped him regain some self-respect.

She will be a lawyer. A proper wife. A proper mother. He wants to have kids. Be the father that he lost, maybe never had.

He slides her into the passenger seat. Straps the seatbelt across her lap. Her head starting to nod off again.

Just as he starts out of the parking lot at the shipyard, he sees Karen Sue's red MGB coming down the road. And she sees him. With the Princess crashing on his shoulder. Karen Sue's eyes the flames of a welding torch. He can smell his burning flesh as he drives Remy to the Mattapoisett Inn. Maybe her old friend Chelsea can look after the Princess for a while.

33

COLÓN'S GETTING BAD VIBES. From the moment she meets Dr. Spencer Alpin, she's feeling that this bastard has had his hands all over her in another life.

His toothy grin, his extreme politeness, makes her feel like gagging. She knows the son of a bitch has probably read the papers about Remy's body, knows damn well he's likely to end up on a suspect list. But he's trying to come off all sweetness and light, apologizing for keeping her and Johnny Match sitting in his reception room for an hour. Says his secretary overbooked him with patients. He's so sorry, but he's due in surgery in an hour.

"This shouldn't take long, Doc," says Johnny Match. His voice is flat, matter-of-fact.

Colón can tell he's trying to keep everything on a strictly professional level with Alpin, just as he has been for the last couple of days with her. She thinks he has gotten skittish since the newspaper leaks and her little vanishing act to the Bahamas. He's trying to protect his career. Or maybe he's hiding something from her.

"We just want to clear up some missing pieces in a cold case that has landed on us. We hope you can help."

The doctor, she thinks, looks a little too cool and laid back in his Tommy Bahamas silk sport shirt. Open collar. At forty-three, he's still the blond-haired, barefoot boy with cheeks of tan. This guy is Johnny's fish. She is just here to watch him set the hook and take notes.

He waves his arm to sweep them into his corner office. It looks out on Boston baseball's Fenway Park from the sixth floor of this office building. The flood light towers nearly at eye level. "What kind of case?"

"Maybe you read about it in the papers. We found some bones."

She likes Johnny's low, slow delivery. Is glad that the chief has put them both back on the case together. Even if things are a little shaky between the two of them at the moment.

"I'm sorry. What kind of case?"

Is he faking ignorance?

"A homicide, actually."

She sees the doc's eyes widen a little.

"Really? Are you looking for expert testimony? I do that sort of thing. But usually it is a lawyer or a DA asking."

"She was half-strangled, buried alive. Twenty-two years ago."

"I'm a plastic surgeon. I don't understand where I fit in here."

"You knew the victim."

She sees the color starting to rise in Dr. Spencer Alpin's neck. Likes the way Johnny Match is teasing his fish. Poisoning his mind with anxiety so that maybe after he takes the hook he will flood, say anything.

"Really?"

"A bartender named Chelsea recalls seeing you with the victim at the Mattapoisett Inn the night she disappeared. I guess you two were pretty cozy."

"What?" His ears are going red.

"Remember Remy La Moreaux? The Princess. That ring a bell?"

• • • • •

"She was stoned and drunk out of her mind, ok? I saw her sitting at the far the corner of the bar, down by the fireplace," says Alpin. "A glass of ice water in front of her. Head in her hands, crying her eyes out. So I thought maybe I could help. I figured maybe she had a fight with her boyfriend."

"You knew her boyfriend?"

"Sort of."

She sees Johnny Match cock an eyebrow. "Come on, Doc. Don't hold back on us. We know all about your little Bahamas escapade aboard the good ship *Fedallah*. We know you had a crush on the Princess. We know she was boinking you behind Paolo Costa's back. We just need a little help figuring out where Remy was between the hours of about midnight and the time someone whacked her in the head, tried to strangle her with her own hair, bound her hands. And stuffed her in a hole to die on an island in the middle of Buzzards Bay. An island that is only a mile or two from your family's summer house."

"I think I need to speak with an attorney." The color of his cheeks and nose has gone from crimson to a chalky white.

"You can do that, if you want, Doc. But then we will have to take out a warrant for you. You know, homicide, that sort of thing. Then we can talk. Very official-like."

Match adds that the trouble with the official approach is that while he and Colón have been trying to keep the investigation quiet, the press has been all over them. They've had a problem with leaks.

"Ask your old friend Paolo Costa. The news boys have been smearing his name all over New England. You know ... in connection with this thing about the Princess. The New Bedford serial killings, too. You get an attorney; we have to get a warrant. A lot of people are going to know. What do you think the chances of a leak will be? What do you think that will do for your practice?"

The doctor leaps up out of his swivel chair behind the desk. Goes to the plate glass window, looks out at Fenway Park. The Sox are battling the Yankees down there. The flood lights on, weird blue flares in the middle of the day. "You bastards! You know Hook Henry was poking her, too? And Corby Church. When I saw her at the Inn, she said she had just been with Church. She was crying. What the hell do you think he did to her, Detective?"

She feels something slice through her gut, the urge to fight, the urge to kill. Cannot just watch and listen anymore ... even though this is Johnny's fish.

"Look, you piece of preppy shit, we're talking about *you* and the girl here. We know Paolo Costa gave you the key to safe-deposit box 821 at a bank in Hyannis. We know that some or all of the money from your Bahamas drug deal was in that box. We know Remy was looking to get her money, wanted to leave town. And we know she somehow got that safe-deposit key. Because she swallowed it. We found it with her bones. *Comprende?* You want to tell us how she got that key? Or do we get a warrant? And tie you to the New Bedford serial killings, too."

The doctor spins away from the window and points to the door. "Get the hell out of here!"

She can already feel the chill on Remy's skin, a man's arms sweep around her from behind.

• • • • •

The air has the scent of mildew and low tide and sea salt.

"I need some money."

"How much."

"Ten thousand dollars."

"You must be kidding me."

"No."

"I don't have that kind of money lying around."

"Come on."

"Why?"

"It's time to go."

"And you want me to just quit everything and ...?"

She gives him a look like he's welching on a promise. Sighs. "It is up to you. But I need the money. I've got to go."

"Is this about cocaine?"

"Maybe."

"Jesus Christ!"

34

CHI CHI BUGATTI's massive chest is heaving in heavy bursts beneath his tight blue service shirt. His paunch rises and falls over his gun belt. His right arm waves an imaginary sword as he paces.

The two detectives sit on the rigid aluminum chairs in his office. Morning sun blazing through the east window, burning a silvery pool on the rug in the center of the room.

"Tell me, what the fuck is wrong with you two. Apart, you do your work, everything is fine. No leaks, no media. Solid progress on the investigation. But as soon as you get together here comes the shit storm."

"Chief—"

"Don't chief me, Colón. Just bite your tongue and read this. Both of you!" He throws *The Boston Globe* on her lap. Front page:

Doctor & Harbormaster
Suspected in Serial Killings

"*Aye, coño!*"

"You bet your sweet ass!"

Johnny Match is shaking his head in disbelief, raking the fingers of his left hand through his spiky, dark crew cut. "I don't understand. We haven't even asked for warrants yet."

"Which of you deadbeats is selling us out?"

She looks at Johnny Match. She thought he was clean, but he could actually be the one, he could be talking to the news guys. He could be making a mess of the publicity so that she gets pulled off the case again, so that he gets the glory now that they are homing in on a suspect.

His eyes stare back at her. Tired … and scared maybe. She sees something there; something is wrong. But not the leak. She does not think he's leaking.

"Only the three of us know about the recent interviews with Church and Alpin. One of us talked to the press since yesterday. And it wasn't me or her."

The chief stops pacing, wheels on Johnny Match. "What the hell are you trying to say, Trooper?"

"I can vouch for her and me. I don't know about you, Chief."

"What?"

"I spent last night with Trooper Lisowski of the state police, we had a stakeout on Colón's apartment in Nu Bej. You can check the logs at Bristol County CPAC."

The chief's face sags with disbelief.

She feels something buckling under her ribs. She knows that the Commonwealth of Massachusetts can bring in the state Crime Prevention and Control boys at any time on any local case of unattended death. She was on those details back when she worked with Lou Votolatto and the staties. "You did what?"

"I'm sorry." He casts a dark look at the chief. "This wasn't my idea, 'Manja. The DA came to me two days ago and said we had to know if you could be trusted, you being tangled up with Corby Church and all. He had CPAC put a bug on your phone and cell."

"He didn't say shit to me." Bugatti still sounds stunned.

"*Hijos de putas!*" Colón stands up, fishes in her purse for her wallet. Rips her shield out of it. Throws it down on the chief's desk. "Fuck you guys and the district attorney, too."

"Yeah, fuck us," says Match. "You're right. It stinks. It was a dirty trick. I'm sorry. But it proves you are clean as far as this leak goes."

"No shit." *So this is why Johnny has been acting so weird around me lately?*

"No shit. You didn't leave the house after you got home from work yesterday. No visitors. You didn't even make a call. Only one call from your house. An old lady, your grandmother. Talking in Spanish, asking some old man whether he had any goats to sell."

"You speak Spanish and you don't tell me?"

He shrugs.

"I'm out of here!" She starts peeling off her shoulder holster. "*Pendejos!* Spying on me like I'm some kind of freak or perp. Playing dumb about Spanish. Leaking this shit yourselves, probably. Some kind of jackass power play. Like stick it to the *chica*. That old game."

"Honest to god, not me. I was just following orders."

She looks at Match as if to say *you pathetic tool*. Starts for the door.

"Hold on there, will ya, gal!" The chief has picked up her shield off his desk. Toys with it, passing it back and forth between his hands. "We aren't finished here yet."

She pauses, rolls her eyes, mutters something under her breath in Yoruba, a chant for mercy from Elegguá, god of the crossroads. If ever a girl were at such a place, she is the one.

"You going to walk on us just when we're ready to cull the clams? Just when its time to put the screws on your suspects? You afraid you can't make the case? Afraid to play hardball?"

"My kid's out of kindergarten in ten days. I think maybe I'll take him to the zoo. A lot."

"'Manja." Her partner's voice sounds ready to break. "Don't quit me. I need you!"

She bites her lower lip, stares at the door. *What's with the loyalty all of a sudden? Is Johnny Match twigging to my pain? He knows I've got this freaking fatal attraction to Corby Church. But can he sense the shit I've been channeling in my body and soul, too?*

The chief clears his throat. "Maybe we ought to just put this behind us, forget about the leak?"

She looks at him. Like why this sudden change of heart? Because if the dirty fingers of the media are not pointing at her or Johnny, then maybe they are going to point at Chi Chi Bugatti?

"Come on, 'Manja."

"Stop calling me that! Don't you know any Italian? How would you like to be called Eat?"

His eyes ask for forgiveness. "I think we've got to talk to this boat builder Hook Henry."

The chief presses her shield back in her hand. "Do that, would you please, Officer Colón? And do everyone a favor. Stay the hell away from Corby Church until this thing is all over, ok? He's on everybody's black list now … because of this leak. The selectmen have suspended him from work. The DA is impounding that tugboat of his while the forensic boys comb it for evidence."

Something claws at her guts. She feels her back stiffen. "I don't think he's our man."

"Then prove it. Find the killer. That's all that I want. I just want our little police department to find some justice for Remy La Moreaux."

And at least eleven of her sisters, she thinks.

35

AS SOON As he mounts the front steps to the triple-decker in the South End, rings the buzzer for apartment number three, he knows that he has made a mistake.

"*Diga!* Speak, *por favor.*" An old lady's voice crackles over the intercom.

"This is Corby Church. I'd like to come up and talk with Yemanjá."

No response from the intercom. Then, finally, "*Ella no está aquí.* Not home. Go away."

"Please. I need to talk to her. I am in serious trouble here. My life is falling to pieces. And ..." His words trail off. His voice dead.

The intercom crackles. No one speaks for what seems like minutes.

"Yemanjá? Please. I know you're up there. Talk to me. Or I'm coming up. One way or another. I swear to god I am! I can't—"

The door to the apartment house bursts open.

"Are you crazy? Do you know what time it is? I'm trying to put a six-year-old to bed. And you are making a drama on my intercom, scaring Ricky and Abuela. Threatening."

She is standing in the doorway to the building wearing a faded orange T-shirt and jeans. Her black hair back in a ponytail. Bare feet. The Glock is in her right hand.

"Jesus! What are you doing with that?"

"Trying to get your attention, Slick. Understand this. You can't be here. You are a suspect. You are under investigation. The media is probably watching you right now. Go away, Corby."

"I have no place to go. No job, no boat. I can't even leave the area. Chi Chi says he is a heartbeat away from getting a warrant to bring me in …"

He sees something soften in her face, her mouth open as if to say something. Then she seems to think better of it. Rubs her free hand over her cheek and temple. As if trying to drive off a killer headache.

"What?"

"I'm sorry. I wish things were different. I really wish things could be different for you. For us. But with all this stuff leaked out into the papers and TV … We're screwed. Really screwed. *Aye coño*! I can't imagine how your name got out. Or Spencer Alpin's either. But it's a mess."

• • • • •

She wonders if this guy ever watches TV. Not only are the Providence and New Bedford stations talking about the case, but tonight the New Bedford Serial Killer made the Boston channels. They had reporters broadcasting from in front of the New Bedford police station speculating about whether after twenty-two years the law might be closing in on the killer at last. And there were man-on-the-street interviews with folks in Weld Square saying they feared that if the murderer is feeling backed into a corner, he might start killing again. Like young women beware.

"All I've got in this world are the clothes on my back, my pick-up truck and a kayak," Church says. "Next thing I know, you guys are coming after that stuff too. If you need me, I'll be the naked guy eating berries out on Bird Island."

She gives a little smile, pictures him as a castaway.

"Damn, Yemanjá. This isn't funny."

She looks into his eyes, sees his hurt. "I'm so sorry. I didn't want any of this. Believe me. The chief sprung the news on me this morning, about taking away your job and your boat. I wanted to call you, but I thought someone could be listening on your cell. Or mine. I'm hoping you are going to get your boat back in a couple of days. Those forensic boys, they aren't going to find anything ..."

He shoots her a confused look.

"*Oyé*. Listen I ..."

His chest heaves.

"I know. I know you didn't kill her!"

A silent sob bursts into the chilly air of the early June evening. "How? How do you know?"

She almost says that she feels, sees, things deep in her *alma*, her soul. In dreams. Sometimes she relives unbelievable pieces of a dead girl's life. But he wouldn't understand. Week after week of these voices in her head ... and she doesn't understand. So she offers an undeniable truth. Something they both know.

"I know because of the way you touch me ..." Her voice a hush now. "So sure. So gentle."

He gives her a look as if he cannot believe how good it feels to hear her say this. "Can you help clear me?"

She takes a step forward. Her arms opening as if to hug him. But she stops short, remembering that someone might be watching them. "I have ideas. I need to talk to some people. Interview them, you know? You've taken me into the heart of this case. Into the night the Princess died. Now if I can just figure out who is lying to me ..."

His eyes search her face again, no doubt trying to find her tenderness, her concern. Most of all her faith in him. "How can I help?"

"Get lost for a while, *mi amor*? Find a lawyer." She almost tells him to go find Michael Decastro from the Provincetown Follies murder cases. But she hasn't seen Decastro since her truly unpleasant private encounter with him last October at the Chatham Bars Inn. She's heard that he's off the law. Fishing with his father on the *Rosa Lee*, drinking too much.

"Do you have some place to crash, Corby?"

"There's an old catboat. In one of the sheds at the boat shop. Hook Henry's place in North Falmouth."

"*Carajo!*"

"What?"

"He's on the suspect list, too, you know?"

Yeah, he thinks. *We were all criminals once.*

• • • • •

Early May, 1988. Church has already dropped into the leeward berth, still wearing a full set of foulies when Hook shuffles into the fo'castle cabin in the bows of the schooner, whispering.

"Nomans has come up on the radar scope."

The men are just off the eight-to-twelve watch. His eyes are burning from staring into the inky night in search of phantom boats. Now he wants to pull his sleeping bag over his head and let the music of the boat lull him into a trance, calm his nerves.

The schooner is closing with the coast of New England. The night foggy. After eight days at sea the Fedallah is bounding home, reaching more than nine knots, all sails set. Five one-pound plastic bags of cocaine hidden beneath a false fiberglass bottom in a water tank.

A fresh sou'west wind drives the boat. Bow rising and falling through the swells with low, muffled thuds, a bass line to an endless blues riff. Nomans Island, their landfall near the cliffs of Gay Head on Martha's Vineyard, lies dead ahead at about ten miles according to the green smudge on the radar screen. Visibility on deck remains less than twenty yards.

"It's a smuggler's night, mate," says Hook.

36

"THERE'S OUR BOY." Johnny Match nods toward the front entrance to Brigham and Women's Hospital on Francis Sreet in Boston's
Back Bay.

It takes them only seconds to exit her Honda, in the short-term
parking queue, and catch the doctor in a vice between them.

His eyes flare. "What the hell is going on here?"

"We have a warrant for your arrest." She waves a rolled up flyer
from Jordan's furniture store in his face. This is her bluff. There is no
warrant, the DA said there is not enough evidence. But she is desperate. Knows he is hiding something.

"What?"

"You want us to serve you right here in the street?" She pulls a set
of handcuffs from her pocket and a two-way police radio. "You can
cooperate, Doc. Or I can call for back-up. Bring in about three cars
of blue boys because you are resisting. You understand?"

"This is outrageous!"

Johnny Match takes his elbow in hand, gently. "You talk to us straight, you give us ten minutes, sit in our car, answer a few questions, maybe we don't have to serve you." His voice is calm, a buddy.

The doctor tilts his head, impatient, listening.

"If we hear what we need, then maybe it's like we can't find you. See, Doc? Maybe we can't serve you. Maybe we will never have to. Because you give us someone else to like more than you for this murder. What do you say?"

She has not stopped glaring at him with her black eyes. The fake warrant and radio in one hand, ready to call for back-up. Cuffs dangling from the other hand. People on the sidewalk in front of the hospital starting to look.

Beads of sweat are popping out on the doctor's forehead, his eyes darting around him.

"*Coño.* Let's take him. Maybe he will talk once he's in a lock-up and the media has his face all over the papers and TV again."

She's betting that this ploy is going to work. *Sí*, Alpin has had to deal with quite a lot of negative press that might make an ordinary guy feel as if he has nothing much more to lose … so fuck these cops. But she thinks the doc's vanity and arrogance have been convincing him that he can beat the heat. Here comes the moment of truth. Maybe he's going to finally realize how vulnerable he is … and cave.

Johnny Match looks at Alpin, who is still waffling, then at his partner. "Yeah, fuck it. This is a waste of time. Take him down."

She reaches for his wrist with the hand cuffs.

"Wait!"

"What?"

"Where's your car? I want to talk."

• • • • •

"We've had some chats with Corby Church."

"Really?"

"He thinks you are a piece of shit and a liar."

He shrugs. "He's a wharf rat. A tall child, stuck in the eighties."

"He says you never gave him his share of the profits from the drug run to the Bahamas. That right, Doc? You still got the money in box 821?" Johnny Match rolls down the car window, lights a cigarette as he sits in the back seat of the Honda with Alpin.

She sits shotgun and stares back at the doctor, watching for his reaction. For his tells. The question is a set-up. She and Johnny know that Alpin really gave Corby his money, Hook Henry too. And they know how much. They just want to see if the doc can play straight with them. If they have scared him enough to tell the truth.

"Doc?"

"That lying bastard. I don't know how much money is left in that box. I walked away from that whole deal after Remy disappeared. Like fuck Paolo, his deals, and his crazy girlfriend, you know? I was going to med school. I made a mistake ever getting involved. I wanted to put that all behind me. But I'll tell you what. Corby got his money. So did his pal Hook. All of it. As soon as Paolo could unload the stash. They each got twenty thousand."

"Really?" Johnny Match starts blowing smoke rings. They emerge from his lips in slow puffs.

"Yeah, really. It was right after Fourth of July. Paolo and I went to the bank box and got the money. We all went out to dinner at this place on the harbor in Hyannis. I gave each of those guys an envelope. They got five percent of the gross for being crew. That was the deal."

She catches her partner's eye. His story matches Corby's. So far so good.

"And you. How much did you get?"

The doctor stares out the window. Watches a huge Chinese nurse waddling along the sidewalk.

"Doc. How much?"

"I don't know."

"Bullshit." She's on him, radio antenna pointing at him.

Sweat blooms over his cheeks, bright sunlight flooding the car. "You think we could turn on the AC in here?"

"Not 'til you tell us the truth."

"I am."

"*Carajo*! Like you don't know how much money you made?"

"I never counted it—I never got it. I swear. It was supposed to be fifty percent of the gross."

"Two hundred thousand for you? Because you put up half the initial investment?" Johnny Match asks this question in a slow, matter-of-fact way.

"Are you trying to pin a drug charge on me?"

She rolls her eyes at her partner. "Why is everyone always asking us this when we are talking about a dead girl here? Tell him about priorities."

"It's like this, Doc. No one is going to come after you for a drug deal that happened twenty-two years ago when we can make you for murder."

"You don't have squat!"

"Did you forget the key we found?"

"She stole it from me. For all I know she took all the money left in that box. I never got a cent of it."

Match inhales deeply. Blows more smoke rings. "Ok, Doc. Let's forget about the Princess. Let me ask you something else. What about Paolo Costa? Did he get his money?"

"All but the forty thousand that he was leaving in the box for safe keeping."

"Really?"

"Yeah. He was going to pay off his loan on the *Fedallah* and take flying lessons. You know that song 'Treetop Flyer'? He got a hard-on over that kind of stuff. Wanted his own plane."

"And Remy. What about her—you pay her off?"

The doctor shakes his head no. "We told her she couldn't have it until she got clean. We didn't want her pissing it away on blow, making a spectacle of herself. Everyone wondering where she got all that money suddenly. Everyone looking at us ... A lot of folks around the Mattapoisett Inn knew about our cruise to the Bahamas."

"What did she say about that? About not getting her money."

"What do you think she said? She was strung out on coke. She was ripshit."

She's in his face. "So she threatened to rat you out to the cops and you killed her to keep her quiet, right? You and Costa?"

"I left her at the Mattapoisett Inn shortly after midnight. We smoked a joint together out back in the parking lot. I went home. Alone."

"In your black Z-car?" She's testing the accuracy of his story again. She has already paid another visit to Chelsea the bartender in Dennis, knows Alpin's car.

"Yeah," he says ... as if he, too, sees that lethal night replaying in Colón's mind.

• • • • •

Remy stares into the empty hollow within the book by T.S. Eliot.

"It's goddamn empty! Where's my money, Spence? You owe me my money."

"So you can piss it away on booze and blow?"

"I earned that money!"

"Aw screw off. Drop the book." He is moving toward her, waving the carving knife with one hand, trying to hold up his pants with the other.

"You think I'd keep the money here? Give me that thing!"

She has to think. There's no money here. Why does he want the book? Like look at it, girl!

"Don't make me hurt you!"

· · · · ·

"How do we know the Princess did not just get into that car and go home with you?"

The doctor is suddenly indignant. Really indignant. "How about my mother? She was working on a crossword puzzle when I got home. Alone. And she woke me up about noon the next day because she knew I had a sailing gig with friends at the yacht club. Are we done here?"

Something's wrong with this story. His sudden copping an attitude way out of line. This is his tell, his usual defense when he feels threatened. But what can she do now except talk to the guy's mother. Who would never give up her baby even if she knew he was lying. In Colón's experience, the rich close ranks and go into fortress mode faster than street gangs.

This cabrón *is leaving something out.*

She feels like putting her Glock to his head. Feels like making someone pay for the Princess. And all the rest of those poor girls, Maybe they didn't die at the hands of some madman like Ted Bundy. Maybe they lost their lives because they became liabilities to a drug dealer, just like Remy. Colón wants to make someone pay for their freaking misery. Maybe her own, too.

"Hey!" Match reaches across the space between the bucket seats, grabs her hand as it is going for her gun. Squeezes. "Doc, you see that look on her face. What do you think she aims to do to you? Pretty soon getting served will be the last of your worries."

Alpin sees the thunderstorm in her eyes. "What do you want?"

"You got to give us something we can work with." Match's voice sounds suddenly inspired. "Like you know Paolo Costa killed her that night. He had a boat. Easy for him to take her out to Bird Island and bury her? Am I right?"

"Except for one thing. Paolo was with Karen Sue Adams. I stopped by the *Fedallah* before I went into the Inn. Maybe about ten-thirty that night."

"Yeah?"

"They were having sex. Way into it. Right on the saloon floor. They didn't even see me when I came aboard."

"So?"

"So it didn't look like it was going to be over anytime soon?"

"How do you know that?"

"They were both wired on coke. I saw the mirror on the table and the razor blade where they laid out the lines. You do enough of that shit you can fuck all night."

"Or kill?"

"Can I go now?"

"No place very far."

37

THE COPS HAVE COME to crash a very fancy party. Women in their
cocktail dresses, men in their yellow pants and linen jackets, circle
among the torches marking the four cash bars on the lawn of Rosecliff mansion.

Another summer of fundraisers has begun for the preservation
groups that make up the social fabric of Newport, Rhode Island. And
Karen Sue Adams, with her pearls and little black dress from Saks, is
very much in the mix.

"You think she looks *muy bella*?" Colón has her partner's arm as
they exit the ballroom of the mansion, the lawn party spread out before them. Her, very Jennifer Lopez in dark slacks, gaucho top. Him,
a GQ badboy, in a black shirt, no collar, tan Ralph Lauren blazer.

"She knows how to turn up the heat. But all I see is plain white
bread."

She smiles. Savors his attitude, his gay cynicism, as she watches
the suspect and her date. Adams is with a local celebrity, a forty-some-
thing Rhode Island congressman with a shock of dirty-blond hair.

She cannot picture Corby Church ever making this kind of scene with the wench. Feels like a fraud herself. But *eso es la vida*.

The truth is that anybody can come to one of these fundraisers if she puts up a donation. This one cost her and Johnny Match two hundred bucks each. Which the Town of Slocums Harbor is paying. "Why the fuck should I buy you two clowns tickets to a party?" the chief complained when they pitched the idea. But he already knew the answer: You have a much better chance of squeezing a suspect when you catch her with her guard down, in a public place. When she might say or do anything to sidestep embarrassment.

"You ready for this, bright eyes?" She gives a little tug on his arm. The orchestra is playing a song called "What Will I Do?" from the film *The Great Gatsby*. It was shot right here on this lawn, with Robert Redford playing the tormented gangster Gatsby. Mia Farrow his beloved, cowardly Daisy. She loves that movie, even though everyone is a *gringo*. And now she's in it. Sort of.

"How about a gin and tonic first?" His eyes are on one of the bars overlooking Rhode Island Sound. The ocean turning violet in the last rays of sunset.

"Be my guest ... But I'm going to play this straight." She pokes her index finger gently at his heart. "Good cop." Taps her own chest, "Vampire cop!"

• • • • •

"Detective Colón ... What a surprise meeting you here tonight. You really get around!"

"You have no idea." A coyness creeping into the voice.

The women and their dates are standing at a long table with a white linen tablecloth. It is covered with appetizers and canapés.

Adams bites at a piece of chicken *satay*, eyes Johnny Match.

"Where did you find this cutie?"

"He's my partner." She says with a hint of attitude. *Like eat your heart out, bitch.*

He gives a boyish smile, innocence personified. Introduces himself. "Johnny Machico. I've heard a lot about you, Counselor."

The lawyer smiles back, a confident grin. Shakes his hand and introduces the cops to her date, Congressman Tommy McGraw.

"It is always good to meet members of the law enforcement community." The congressman has a gleaming smile … and a question in his eyes. He's already flirting. "What brings you out tonight? Did you get a tip that someone is planning to hijack the shrimp bowl? Or is *Al Queda* taking a bead on Newport preservation?"

Colón is opening her mouth to speak when Adams says, "Actually, I think they are here because of me. Am I right, Detectives? Snooping?"

She ignores the question, shoots a little hey-baby grin at the congressman. "I'm fascinated by people. You meet the most interesting people at places like this, don't you agree, Representative?"

"Call me, Tommy." The gleaming smile again. "I guess that depends on what you mean."

"Well-known attorneys, celebrities such as yourself, philanthropists, blue bloods, *gente de la noche.*"

"Excuse me?"

"Figures of the night!" says Johnny Match, taking a quick sip of his G&T. He drinks as if the time may soon come when he will no longer have a chance to finish it.

The congressman surveys her, top to bottom, up again. Eyes lingering an instant on her full hips. "Sounds a little wicked."

She pauses, sucks the meat out of a chilled shrimp tail. "More than a little."

"Tell me."

"How about murder? How about serial killings?"

"Here?"

She gives the attorney a dark smile. "You want to explain to the good congressman? Or should I? Don't you think he ought to know the company he keeps?"

Match winces.

"I beg your pardon?" The congressman's mouth is open wide enough to catch a sparrow.

"Come on, Tommy. Let's go." Adams takes his hand. "She's just trying to pick a fight to meet her own sick needs. She has backed herself into a corner. Mishandled the investigation into that body they found on the island in Buzzards Bay. The one some people are trying to link to the New Bedford Serial Killer. You've seen it in the papers. She's trying to make a name for herself by dragging prominent people into the case. People who have nothing at all to do with it."

"She's after you?"

"Let's get out of here. I'm not giving her anything she can make news over." She fires a coy look at Colón and starts toward the mansion and an exit. "Later, Detective."

"Maybe not, Counselor. How do you explain this?" In her hand is a small sandwich bag. It holds an antique, gold ring.

"What's that?"

"A ring that we found at the crime scene, Congressman. A ring that the victim apparently swallowed."

"So?"

"So. It has the initials 'K.S.' engraved inside it." Colón's lying. Taking a risk here, trying to push some emotional buttons. Fishing for guilt. There are possibly three letters in the ring. One is a "K," maybe. Another "S," but perhaps not. The lab guys still cannot be sure. The third letter is totally unreadable. Almost imperceptible. "Is this not your ring, Counselor?"

Adams barely gives the gold band a glance. "Not a chance."

"It is a pretty ripe coincidence. Don't you think the media would love to hear about this?"

"Are you threatening me?"

The congressman steps in. "Hey, calm down, ladies."

"Bite me, Tommy!" Adams's eyes flash.

The Honorable Tommy McGraw looks shell-shocked.

Johnny Match sets his G&T down on the appetizer table. This is his moment. He has just heard his cue. The suspect is over the edge. "I'm sorry, Ms. Adams, Congressman. Yemanjá, let me handle this, ok?"

Colón scowls, turns away, starts across the lawn toward one of the bars. As she walks, she makes a show of pulling a cell phone out of her purse, punching in numbers.

"Who's she calling?"

"I don't know, Counselor. She said something about a reporter at the *Providence Journal*. I'm sorry. She's a good cop. I've never seen her like this. She has gotten emotionally involved in this case."

"She's screwing Corby Church, Detective. Can't you smell it?"

The congressman squints his eyes, trying to bring things into focus. "Who's Corby Church?"

"For Christ's sake, can you tell her to put down that phone? What do you want from me?"

"We just want you to tell us the whole story of that Labor Day evening in 1988, Counselor ... You had a fight with Remy La More-aux that night, didn't you?"

"Dream on."

38

"WHAT ARE YOU DOING HERE?" Corby Church looks up from inside an ancient wooden Herreshoff sloop. It sits on jack stands in the middle of the boat shop. He's bending a new oak rib into the hull. And his avenging angel has just stepped into the boat shop.

"I need to talk to the proprietor."

"What about me?"

"I think you better just keep doing what you're doing. Is Hook Henry here?"

"Did somebody call my name?" The big man lumbers through the side door of the shop. His face is pouring sweat. Heavy leather gloves cover hands carrying several smoking six-foot lengths of oak, each an inch square.

"Have you got a minute to talk?"

His eyebrows pop up. "I got a fist-full of oak just out of the steam box to bend into this boat before it cools, and she wants to know if I can talk? Can you see I'm a little busy? Are you trying to sell me something?"

Corby rolls his eyes.

"You know her, bubba?"

"Hook Henry, meet Detective Yemanjá Colón."

The boat builder's cocky grin drains from his face. He slides the steaming oak into the cockpit of the old sailboat. "I knew this was going to happen. I knew it as soon as you started bunking in that old catboat. First you, then the law."

It's only ten-thirty in the morning but already hot. An early June heat wave is settling over Buzzards Bay and the Cape. She's trying to stay cool in khaki Dockers and a thin, white blouse. Her long, dark hair rolled up on her head in a twist. Wisps of hair curling around the ears and cheeks. Full breasts filling out the blouse. Tiny beads of sweat twinkle on her upper lip. There is no hiding the sensuous woman, but the look on her face is all business.

"Pleased to meet you ... But am I in trouble here, Detective?"

"I hope not. Why don't we talk?"

He cocks his head toward the out-of-doors. "Down by the cove. There's a breeze. A picnic bench. We can talk in private, and leave bubba to work out his worries on a bunch of steamed oak."

They have no idea Church is reliving his crime.

• • • • •

Like the old-time rum runners during Prohibition, they have waited off-shore for this weather to move in, waited for a front to stall over the south coast of Massachusetts. Now they have thick fog. And they can start for home. Perhaps the drug enforcement satellite cameras cannot see them very well in this weather. But the search radar on ships and planes are looking for smugglers. Ronald Regan's War on Drugs scrambling to stem the tide of narcotics coming into the US with Navy P3 Orions flying out of Brunswick, Maine. Coast Guard cutters from New Bedford and

Boston. This is an election year, and the Republican government aims to make a good show of drug interdiction.

But there are a lot of radar targets out here. A lot of innocent boats. Way too many for the Navy and Coast Guard to check visually ... track of. Fishermen work these waters hard. And this is the route to and from the offshore cod and scallop grounds. With the schooner's radar set on twelve-mile range, Hook has seen no fewer than thirty vessels on the screen. Even if the DEA has been watching Fedallah *with satellites as a "possible" since she left the Bahamas, they will have a hard time now. Paolo has sailed her into the middle of the offshore scallop fleet, hoping to cover his trail. Hoping to make the schooner look like just another scalloper to the government's electronic eyes.*

Now, he has tucked Fedallah *in among a loose convoy of four scallopers heading for home. For New Bedford. The scallopers can see him on their radars. But they cannot be sure he is not just another fisherman. They can't see him in the dark and the fog. And they have learned not to talk on their radios about an unidentified target. Fishermen have their own secrets to keep. Out here you don't ask ... don't tell.*

Hook rustles around in his berth for a few minutes, then jumps to his feet. "To hell with this, I can't sleep, I'm going back on deck and keep those bastards company. I didn't spend the last five months dicking around with these characters, getting shot at, playing nurse maid to Cocaine Sally to have these shitheads fuck it all up with us so close to home. This junket could be all over before our next watch, you know?"

Paolo and Spence are on deck, back aft in the cockpit standing the mid-watch together, midnight to four AM. *At this point each of them is so paranoid that the other guy might pull some shit, they won't let each other out of sight. Now Hook is starting to freak too.*

"I'm here if you need me." He mumbles from deep beneath his sleeping bag. Then he fingers the trigger guard of Paolo's snub-nose .38, the one

he has been carrying since the shootout at Whale Cay. Slides the gun under his pillow. He is almost asleep, dreaming of a great pod of dolphins playing in a sea of diamonds, when he feels someone slide into his berth beside him. An arm curl around his shoulders. Warm breath tickling his right ear. It stinks of vodka. And girl.

 "Can I stay here for a while?"

39

"WHY DIDN'T YOU TELL ME you had an alibi?"

Church has just finished bending the last hot frame into place aboard the Herreshoff when she gets back from the cove. "Sorry? What?"

"An alibi. For the murder night, *payaso*." Her eyes looking at him, bright and wet.

"What do you mean?" He scrambles out of the sailboat. Pulls the cotton gardening gloves off his hands, uses one to wipe the perspiration off his forehead and cheeks. Smears streaks of sawdust and dirt on his skin.

"You're a mess."

"I'm rebuilding a boat. What do you expect?"

"Why the hell didn't you tell me?"

He shrugs his shoulders. Still not following her.

"Why didn't you tell me about the night the Princess disappeared? Why didn't you tell me you took your boat out after you dropped her at the Inn?"

He shrugs again. "I don't know. Maybe because you didn't ask ... No, maybe self-preservation. Maybe because I'm an inch or two away from getting thrown in the pokey. Why would I volunteer that on the night Remy vanished—and ended up dead in a hole on Bird Island, I took my boat out and didn't come back for two days? Wouldn't that just about ice the case against me?"

"Not when someone can vouch for you."

"I'm still not getting you."

"Hook. Your friend. He says he and the woman who is now his wife were anchored at Cuttyhunk Island in his sailboat. You met them there in the *Brutus*. You had some beers that night with them, talked about your coming marriage to Karen Sue. You were worried."

"Yeah, so?"

"So that was before they went to bed. Before midnight. You couldn't have killed the Princess. Don't you know that we have found witnesses who put her at the Inn until closing time, about twelve-thirty? But you were long gone. And you stayed at Cuttyhunk for two days. The opposite end of Buzzards Bay from Bird Island, about twenty-five miles away."

"I was hiding from Karen Sue. She had never been happy about my going on that sailing trip to the Bahamas, and she was jealous of Remy. I figured she was going to raise hell about seeing us together in the truck."

"Did she?"

He heaves a sigh. Drops his butt onto a nearby sawhorse. "She almost called the wedding off."

"But she didn't."

"She said her parents would go bananas. Everything was set. It was too late to turn back. She wasn't going to look like a fool. I was going to have keep my mouth shut and shape up."

"Too bad."

"What?"

"Too bad she didn't dump you."

"You've met her, then?"

She grunts. "*Esa puta!*"

"She did her war dance for you?"

She looks away, out the open barn doors of the boat shop to the little cove and the bay beyond. Brushes a tear out of her eye with her hand.

"Hey, what's the matter?"

"Nothing."

"Talk to me, Yemanjá."

"I can't."

"Why?"

"*No comprendo.*" But I really need to talk to the saints.

• • • • •

The cowrie shells clatter onto the straw mat for their fourth and final time. Three land teeth up.

"*Orgunda,*" says Abuela.

"Arguments and tragedies are caused by misunderstanding," Colón interprets.

"*Sí. Correcto, nena.*" The old lady stares at the shells.

"What?"

"Shsssss. I must apply the *ordun* to your problem. Let me think!"

She runs her hands up under her long hair, lifting it off her neck to cool herself. The white robe a shroud, a blanket of fire, as she sits cross-legged before the straw mat on the floor of the shrine room. The burning candles and joss sticks adding to the heat that has not relented, even with the sunset. *This night from hell.*

"Will you stop fussing?"

"I'm burning up in here."

"Of course you are. Daughter of Changó. Child of thunder and lightning."

"Abuela, *por favor!*"

"You cannot rush the saints, *chica. Tranquila!*" The old woman squeezes her eyes shut. Tilts her head back on her neck. Her mouth whispering words in Yoruba, sighing, moaning. For minutes.

Suddenly her eyes pop open. She jumps to her feet.

"*Digame!* What?"

The little woman towers over her granddaughter. "Obatalá has spoken."

"And …?"

"He says that you must rethink everything. The *gringo* Corby Church is no killer."

"Abuela, I already know that."

"But you do not know that much depends on what you do next. Your mind is still full of misunderstandings and anger. The anger of the orphan child. You must find peace. Start with this *gringo*. He is the key. If you want him as *tu novio*, your boyfriend, the *orishas* have no objections. Clear your mind, heart and spirit of negative energy. Then look again at what you think you know about the murder. Look again at these other people you suspect. Listen to the islands … Listen to the dead."

"But where do I start?"

"The girl from the island, she still talks to you, doesn't she?"

• • • • •

What's in the book? Remy's eyes cannot focus. The hollowed-out core of the volume is empty. What's she missing? Her hands flutter over the binding, find something flat and hard under the binding, along the spine. She scrapes with her fingers. Has it. A key.

"You want this?"

His face is white with rage.

"Eat your heart out." She jams the key in her mouth, swallows it so that he can never take it from her. It is like a stone blade going down. Tearing at her guts. No matter. It's hers for keeps, like a secret stash of gold. Her legs are already sprinting toward the screen slider. And the dark beyond.

40

"WILL YOU STOP DEFENDING Corby Church? I don't want to talk about that knucklehead right now. Just give me this lawyer Karen Sue Adams' story, Colón. Jesus Christ, get on with it."

Chi Chi Bugatti is sucking on a stogie. The air in his office a foul congregation of vapors this June morning.

She looks at Johnny seated beside her in the fetid office. Wishes he would speak up, help her out here with the bully.

"We think she's still holding back," he says.

"But she gave you something, right?"

"Filled in an hour, maybe an hour and a half, that we didn't know about on the night the Princess disappeared."

"Talk to me."

"She said she followed her when she left the Inn."

"Why the hell would she do that?"

"You remember, she saw her fiancé, Church, with the Princess earlier in the night. Followed them to the parking lot of the Mattapoisett Inn. Took out her rage by having a sex party with Paolo

Costa at his boat down at—"

"Yeah, ok. So what?"

"So after her romantic interlude, she went back up to the Inn. She claims she was looking for Corby Church. Wanted to spit in his face for a while. Remy's too."

"Yeah?"

"But she didn't find Church. Only Remy. She figured maybe if she followed the Princess, Remy would lead her to Church."

"So ..."

"So according to Karen Sue, Remy left the Inn sometime after last call. A little after twelve-thrity. With—get this—Spencer Alpin."

"The nip-and-tuck surgeon?"

"Not back then, but yeah."

"She followed these jamokes?"

"Yeah. Got in her little MGB, took up the trail."

"Where?"

"To Slocums Harbor. To the Alpin family summer house out near Fearings Point. She says she saw them both get out of the car and walk down to the dock. Alpin left the Princess there, went in the house for a few minutes. Came back out with a bottle and glasses."

"This lawyer, she must have been one pissed off bitch."

Colón smiles. "Hell hath no fury like a woman ..."

"Get on with it, Colón."

"She waited to see what would happen next. I think she half-expected to see Corby Church wheel up."

"Sounds like she was just waiting for a chance to pop the Princess, that's what it sounds like to me."

"You may be right," says Johnny Match. "I'd bet she's holding out something on us."

"You've already made that point, Detective."

"Well …"

"Don't act so surprised, will you? She's a fucking lawyer. What else would you expect? But meanwhile … the good doctor and the Princess were having a shag down at the dock, right?"

"Maybe. Adams says it didn't end so well. She claims that sometime about one-thirty Remy came running out of the house from a side door, carrying some kind of book. Alpin chasing her with a knife, calling her a slut, a fucking bitch, trying to do up his pants and his belt as he ran."

"You think he killed her?"

Johnny Match shakes his head. It's an ambiguous gesture. "I don't know. Adams says that just as Alpin caught up to Remy on the lawn—like this is a big house, you know chief, a lot of property— she turned and winged this book at him. Clipped him right in the face, and vanished into the shadows."

"Where does Adams say she was to see all this?"

"Parked in under some big pine trees on the Neck Road. She says she had a clear view of the house, front yard and the dock."

"You believe that?"

Colón rises up on the end of her seat. "We scoped it out earlier this morning. She definitely could have been where she said and not have been noticed in the dark."

"So you think this is not just a load of bullshit? Adams deflecting the blame?"

She thinks about the book, her dreams. "I tend to believe her. You know like *mas o menos*, Chief."

"She could have wasted the Princess. Could be sending you off on a wild goose chase after Alpin."

"Maybe. But she couldn't have killed and buried Remy by herself."

"Why?"

"She doesn't know shit about boats, never had one." says Johnny Match. "No way to get to Bird Island."

"You sure?"

"I gave her a little quiz at the *soirée* in Newport the other night. She failed."

The chief pushes back his chair, his face lighting up like the Fourth of July. "Wait a minute. Just hold on here. What did Alpin do after the Princess winged him with the book? What about Adams?"

"She says she couldn't see very well. She says she thinks Remy went dashing into the forest out there. Alpin went after her."

"You believe that?"

"I think we need to talk to the doctor again."

"And where did Adams go after her little espionage?"

"She claims she drove home to her parents' summer place in Pocasset."

"But she has no witnesses."

"Right."

"So maybe this is all a crock of shit. Maybe you've got nothing but a pack of lies."

She throws her hands in there air. *Like what the hell, Chief?*

"Maybe we need DNA samples from Adams, Alpin, Henry, Costa, and Church. Let's not rule anybody out."

"Yeah, why not get samples from everyone in Slocums Harbor, Bourne, Mattapoisett, Pocasset, Cataumet, and North Falmouth. Like they tried to do after that glamour girl Worthington's murder out in Truro. Great idea, Chief." Her voice is loaded with sarcasm.

"They solved the case, didn't they, Ms. Wise Ass?"

"What are you trying to say, Chief?"

"I'm going to tell the staties to let Corby Church have his tugboat back."

"You are?"

"It's clean."

"And …?"

"And we've got something better. The forensic boys found some strands of hair on the Princess's remains. The hair wasn't hers."

41

THE FOGHORN at Butler Flats Lighthouse bleats into the dark, clammy night. Two figures walk along the top of the hurricane dike at the entrance to New Bedford Harbor. Moving out away from the land on a tarmac path atop the levee built of granite blocks.

They are more sound than substance to the solitary fishers camped along the edge of the dike with their rods and bait buckets.

"I shouldn't be here," Colón says.

Church does not ask her what she means. He knows. In the eyes of the world, he's still a suspect. Because of the press, it seems as if just about everyone on the Cape and the South Coast of Massachusetts has connected his name with the name of the Princess. Worse, with the nearly forgotten names of the eleven known victims of the serial killings in 1988. He feels dead ... like so many others linked to that unsolved case. It's a black hole that has swallowed almost everyone who comes near it. Now, he can tell, Colón sees it too. Sees that she has been sucked in up to her eyeballs. May never be getting out. May drown in the filth.

"I'm sorry," he says.

"My grandmother told me to follow my heart. And it brings me here. Into all of this blackness."

He squeezes her hand. "You want to go back, go home? I understand."

"It's too late."

"Why?"

"Because. Because I've fallen for you. You ... and your whiteness."

He wants to say he thinks that he may be falling in love with her ... and has no clue why. But the words will not form themselves in his mouth. So he slides his free hand along her dark cheek, to the back of her neck, and draws her against him. Kisses her. It's a kiss from another world. More air than flesh. More light than heat.

"*Dios mio!*"

"I feel ... blessed."

She nuzzles his neck. "*Mi amor* ... I fear it is the other thing altogether."

"Are you saying I'm cursed?"

He feels her head nod against his chest. "I don't believe in curses. We make our own heavens and hells."

"No!" She pushes him away.

"No what?" He reaches for her arm.

"*No se.* I don't know."

"What?"

"Maybe you should go away." She turns her back, looks into the black fog.

"Hey ..." Suddenly he wants to tell her in his limited Spanish. He's surer than he was just moments ago. "*Te amo.*"

"Don't."

"What?"

"Don't say that."

"But ..."

"Just don't. Ok?"

"Why?" He reaches out for her hand. But she's already moving away. Her footsteps in the fog. Birds' feet on broken shells. She's running.

And he's after her.

• • • • •

It's like another time. Not Remy's time. But her time. Back when she was married. *Coño* ...

He stinks of whiskey and the unmistakable scent of cheap perfume, lipstick and sex. Jorge. His hot hand plunging between her legs. "Tengo hambre, guapa.*"*

"You're drunk," she says in Spanish. Borracho. *Dirty, white Argentine son of a bitch.*

She tries to roll away from him in the bed. In the wet sheets of the hot Boston night. The July inferno that is this apartment in Jamaica Plain.

But he has her. Snagging her from behind. Pinning her belly to the sheet.

"Te quiero. *I want you.*"

"Dejame. *Leave me alone,* cabrón. *Get your filthy hands—*"

"I want to eat your flesh."

She looks at the clock. Three-twelve in the morning. He finally comes home at three in the morning. For this. Always for this. For her. Ripe with whiskey. Pockets emptied by the gamblers and whores on Blue Hill Avenue. Balls like mangos, gorged with seed. Ripe with pain and frustration. His voice a DJ's hustle. A son of Obatalá shouting for his goddess. For Yemanjá.

"Stop. You are going to wake the baby!"

"Te amo. *I love you.*"

Fingers. Scraping. Stroking. Kneeding. Teasing. Separating her from her alma, *her soul. She can already feel the breaking of the bond. The hot and sticky flow of blood as he cuts the cord, tearing her from herself. Until she's someone else. Another woman. Another one of his* putas. *The one men punish. The witness and the victim. The mother. The slut. She wants to scream, except for the infant sleeping in the crib across the room.* Diablo.

"Puta mia." *His pants are down to his knees. His weight crushing her from behind.*

"Fuck you."

"Como?"

"Fuck you, Jorge. Get off me." *She rises on her elbows, tries to shake him free. She can hardly think. Exhausted from the midnight nursing of the child.*

He wraps a hand in her hair, yanks. Her head snaps back on her shoulders with a crack. "Te amo."

"You bastard. Cabrón."

"He slaps her on the right ear. Her head ringing. Now her ear is weeping too. Like her breasts, her ovaries. Stinging her like the sound of her* mami's *screams.*

Her heart wailing. Remembering. Remembering ...

She's just a child standing in the doorway. The witness at her mother's room. Wanting to shout, Fuck you. Fuck you. Leave her. Leave her alone, Papi. She wants to kill him. Kill her. Kill the whore. Stop. Please. Papi ...

But she says nothing. Tastes the shame. Tastes the lipstick and the cheap perfume of putas. *It's she that he should be hitting. Not her* mami. *She wants the slap. The punishment. The love. Kill* me, Papi. *I want to eat your black soul.*

"Te amo," *he shouts. And hits her mother again. Herself. The skater. The princess with the red hair.* "You fucking whore." *Hits her again. Hits.*

42

"DON'T TOUCH ME." She wheels on Church and swings, a wild round-house of a punch, catching him on the heel of the jaw.

"What's wrong with you?"

"Leave me alone." She looks around. Left, right. The fog so thick she has lost her way here at the root of the dike in Fairhaven. Here at the ruins of Fort Phoenix. Earthen ramparts and cannons and blackness. The sound of a fishing boat's engine growling in the distance.

He throws his arms around her, this mad woman. This phantom he loves. This cop. This little girl, saint of the sea. Twisting in her own fire.

"You bastard."

He holds her as he has before. Hugging her from behind. Not with arms of steel. But with arms and chest turned pillows. Their softness absorbing her struggles, giving nothing back but insulation, padding.

She starts to scream. But it sounds like a sob. Her hands cover her face. And she turns, folding into him.

"*Finito*," she says.

"What?"

"I can't run anymore ... I can't fight."

He feels her tears on his neck. "You don't have to."

"How do you know?"

He wraps her tighter in his arms. She feels his heart beating through his sweater.

"I just have this feeling," he says. "This is going to sound crazy. Something is drawing us together."

She sucks in a sob. The words ringing in her heart. *Your mind is full of misunderstandings and anger. The anger of the orphan child. You must find peace. Start with this gringo. He is the key.*

"You hardly know me."

"Give me a chance," he says.

"Why?"

"Because death is a lonely business."

"Take me away from here?"

• • • • •

In the green glow reflecting from the radar scope in the wheelhouse, his face looks frozen, Colón thinks. The fixed jaw, thin lips, high cheekbones, eyes set on something out in the dark that only he can see. Church stands feet spread, at the big wooden wheel of the tug, navigating it into the black fog of Buzzards Bay. The *Brutus* heaves and rolls in the southwest swells.

She holds his waist—for balance, for comfort—with her right arm, steadies a huge mug of tea with her free hand.

"We'll be there in about an hour."

"Where?"

"You'll see." He takes a drink of the tea they are sharing.

"Can you talk?"

He checks the radarscope for traffic. The GPS screen for his position. "Alright. So …?"

"So … tell me about Karen Sue."

"You think she killed Remy?"

She pretends that she doesn't hear his question, gives his waist a little pinch. "What about you and her? How did you meet her?"

He sighs, figures that if they're really going to get to know each other, he has to start somewhere. The summer of 1986. He was fresh out of Mass Maritime, mate on the Vineyard ferry. She was working the snack bar on the boat. Still a college kid. Rich family from Providence. Summer place on Wings Neck in Pocasset.

"You seduced her with that rugged man of the sea thing you got going."

"Not exactly."

"Yeah, right."

"She had a boyfriend. Some tennis hotshot from Brown."

She wraps her arm tighter around his waist.

"I guess they were having some problems. One night after work, she asked me if she could buy me a beer. Wanted to talk, you know? Get some perspective about guys, she said. Wanted to get off the Cape, you know. Go over to the other side of Buzzards Bay where nobody knew her."

"The Mattapoisett Inn?"

"It was the mid-'80s. The Inn was the place. The Stunners jamming like the Sultans of Swing."

"So?"

"So I had nothing better to do."

"She was hurt, vulnerable. You took advantage of her."

His hands drop from the wheel. He peels her arm off his waist, turns and looks at her in the green glow. "Hey, come on. You make me sound like the big, bad wolf."

"I've heard your rep. A girl in every port."

He feels his mouth start to water. Nerves. She's getting to him. "People tend to exaggerate."

"But you got around."

"Aw, geeze, Yemanjá. It's the middle of a foggy night. I'm up to my elbows trying to get this boat to sea. Trying to take us somewhere the past can't track us down and ruin this little bit of goodness I feel when I'm with you. And—"

"You were a player."

He sees it all again.

• • • • •

"Match me." Karen Sue wants to throw down some shooters of tequila.

After five she asks him if he wants to go outside to her car and smoke a little weed. In the car she tells him that her boyfriend left for the family compound on Nantucket. For a fucking month. She's horny as hell. Masturbated four times today. Next thing he knows she's asking him to feel her panties, wet with fine oil.

• • • • •

"I was single. I was a healthy, young, American male. End of story!"

"You don't have to get all *loco.*"

He takes a deep breath, listens to the rumble of the big Caterpillar in the engine room. Feels the little shimmy of the prop shaft in the cutlass bearing where it's out of true. How come sometimes she makes him just wish he were dead? And still he thinks he loves her. Why?

Her hand circles his waist again. "*Lo siento.* Sorry! I've known some real bastards." She pauses. "I want you to be different ... And I'm afraid."

She's talking about him, about commitment, about relationship. But he knows that whether she realizes it or not, these things are all tied up with murder. With serial killing. The stuff no one should ever have to think about. Bad shit. The things you wish you could forget.

43

"DID YOU LOVE HER?"

"I guess she just blew me away." Church's eyes are staring into the fog and darkness. His hands moving the tug's wheel in slow, unconscious feints. "She was smart. She was pretty. She had class and money. And she said the boldest things. She feared nothing. She was a hurricane."

Like the night she proposed.

• • • • •

"It's time to fish or cut bait." He feels her hot breath on his chest as she slithers over him, an anaconda in his bed. "I think we should get engaged. Or quit here."

End of the summer, 1987, after Karen Sue's first year in law school. They have been playing house for the last three months in a little rental cottage in Cotuit. Now it's September. She's going back to Boston to finish her law degree. He's about to go sailing to the Bahamas with Paolo

Costa and company. She's clearly not psyched about his going, probably fears she may be losing control of his heart.

"Corby?" Her tongue licking the bone in the center of his chest.

"Yeah?"

"I want a commitment. I want to get married. I need to know you are up for this. So what do …?"

He hears a shrill grinding in his head, feels his tonsils about to explode. He's not ready for an engagement, let alone marriage. He knows it. He's too young, wants to see the world. Wants to ship out with the merchant service as the deck officer he has trained to be. Wants to be a mariner like his father. The amazing, disappearing dad.

"We don't have to set a date," she says. "Not yet."

He feels her breath in his ear, her teeth nibbling not so gently on a lobe. Smells the coconut-butter soap on her skin. Maybe I can ride this out, he thinks.

• • • • •

"While I was in the Bahamas, she worried about me out there in the singles scene. Worried about me and Remy. The *Fedallah* hardly cleared customs back into New England in May when she said, 'My mother and I are counting on an October wedding, Columbus Day weekend, with the leaves in Providence all on fire.'"

Colón holds his waist a little tighter with her right arm. She feels little jolts running through his body.

"When I got back from the sailing trip of '88, she was in Boston for the summer clerking in district court and studying for the bar. But she came down to the Cape and Buzzards Bay every chance she could."

He says that she liked to surprise him. He had just bought this boat, the tug. He was living on it in Quissett. He was trying to ship out on a container ship or tanker, but there were no jobs. No ferry boat job either. But it was ok. He started driving the launch at the Harbor Yacht Club. Hook opened his boat shop in North Falmouth. After a couple of months went by, Church started working with him part-time, building wooden Herreshoff sloops for the gentry. It was a screwy summer. And it ended with Remy. Vanishing.

"What was her take on that? Karen Sue's. She seemed weird about it?"

"'Good riddance to bad garbage,' she said the day she heard that the Princess had disappeared. The next thing I knew her mother was throwing a champagne-soaked wedding for us that had the folks in Providence talking for a month. Just like that I was a married man, moving off the tug into a duplex Karen Sue rented for us in Sandwich village. She was commuting to her job with a personal injury and divorce firm in Providence."

"You felt trapped."

He swallows hard. "It was a bad time."

• • • • •

"Why don't you sell that big, old boat or do something useful with it," Karen Sue says one night when she comes home to find him watching reruns of Gilligan's Island on TV. She's working hundred-hour weeks. They never see each other except to get a little trashed and have sex on the weekends. He feels itchy, lonely. And things are getting slow at the boat shop. The yacht club is closed for the winter.

"I'm going to start a business."

"Go for it," she says.

So he does. He starts a general freight and towing business with the Brutus. *Running barges to the Vineyard, the Cape, up and down the coast. It's hard. There's a lot of competition. The tug is a maintenance hog.*

Now he's never home. She makes him get a cell phone on the boat. She says at least he can give her phone sex.

Then one April morning in 1993 he comes home to the duplex after a miserable trip towing a leaky, old windjammer from Nu Bej to Greenport, Long Island. The apartment is empty except for the kitchen table and chairs, their queen-size bed, his old stereo, CD collection, clothes, boat gear. He can hear the faucet dripping in the sink. Until he puts on the Gypsy Kings and lets them wail.

There's a letter on the table. Written on her law firm's stationery:

We both knew this was coming. I'm sorry. I thought a clean break was the best way. I figure we split the assets. You get to keep the tugboat, and your business. I get the rest. Don't fight me on this, Corby. We had some great times. But we've grown in different directions. And with you always off somewhere doing your boat business, it is kind of the case of the invisible husband, isn't it? The rent is paid until the end of the month. Love, KSA.

● ● ● ● ●

"Harsh," Colón says.

He gives the big wooden wheel a turn. Two spokes to starboard. It squeaks as it turns. The sound seems to annoy him. He frowns.

"I moved back on the *Brutus*. Within the year the towing business went belly up. But I kept the boat, got back my job driving the launch for the yacht club. Pretty soon I was working for the town of Slocums Harbor. You know the rest."

All through the story she has been feeling his pain. Now she hugs this mariner, this man at the wheel. She presses her whole body against him from behind, as he steers through the black night. "I'm sorry. It must have been awful."

He shrugs. "A thing like that makes you feel worthless. A failure.

You're divorced. You know as well as I. There I was driving a yacht club launch. Her all over TV talking about how her law firm 'wins the big ones for its clients.'"

"*Coño.*"

"But, you know what? After I got over the rejection, I realized I didn't love her. Maybe never really loved her. It was something else between us. I think I was flattered that someone with so much going for her could ever want an ordinary guy like me."

"You're not ordinary in my book."

He gives a little grunt, almost a laugh. "Yeah, with you I get suspected of being a serial killer."

"More like a pirate ..."

"With a skeleton in his closet, right?"

She opens her mouth to say something, seems to think better of it. Kisses his neck softly instead.

His mind tries to shake the image of a pale face wreathed with moldy skeins of red hair. Eyes green as marsh mud.

44

THE SUN WAKES HER. Streaming in the wheelhouse window. Catching her in the face as she lies bunched beneath the comforter in the double berth at the back of the cabin.

Colón feels the tugboat rolling gently in a swell, hears the low, occasional clunking of steel as the boat pulls against its anchor chain. The air outside sparkles. The fog's a thin veil over the *Brutus*. The only way she knows that they are near land is the sound of waves hissing off a sandy beach, the chorus of gulls.

"I brought you some OJ." He has a tray with two glasses of orange juice, two mugs of tea, wheat toast, a large plate of eggs.

She brushes the hair out of her deep, brown eyes. "You made *huevos rancheros*?"

"Tried."

"How did you know I love Mexican?" She likes his pink, *anglo* skin this morning. The way his six pack looks, his buns in the dark green boxers.

"Just guessed. I'm kind of limited as a cook. I hope you like it." He sits down on the berth beside her.

"What else do you hope, *pirata?*"

He smiles devilishly, hits the play button on the CD player. Greatest hits of Elvis Costello comes up. A love song, "Alison."

"You want to pick up where we left off last night?" Her hand slides up the inside leg of his boxers, feels him flinch as the first blast of adrenaline starts to rock him with desire.

He bends and kisses her, sets the tray on the floor. Slides onto the berth beside her warm, nude body. She feels him bury his face in her dark hair as she welcomes him with her arms, her legs. They wrap around him. His body a dolphin running bait. Her mind a magnesium flare bursting. A signal of distress, a call for rescue.

• • • • •

They are still entwined, bare arms and legs and bellies, the *huevos rancheros* and the tea long cold, when her phone chirps. She fishes on the floor of the cabin for the cell in her jeans' pocket. It's the instinctive reaction of a mother separated from her child.

"*Sí, diga.*"

"I'm not one of your *amigas*, Colón. Speak English. Where the hell are you?"

Her eyes roll toward her forehead. It's her boss.

"It's my day off." She's still lying in the berth. Corby spooning.

"Don't you ever read the freaking paper?"

She doesn't answer.

"Colón?"

Her chest heaves. She's pissed. "*Eso es una tontaria! Dejame solo!* Leave me alone."

"I'm going to pretend I didn't hear that. Get you butt out of bed and look at the paper."

"I can't."

"What, you don't have the paper? What are you, illiterate?"

Sighs. "Yeah, I get the paper, Chief. But I'm out of town, ok. I have a life ... sometimes."

"Where the hell are you?"

She looks around sees the fog beginning to lift outside the port-hole, feels Corby's whiskers rubbing against her bare back as he holds her. "I don't know."

"Are you with Church? I told you to stay the hell away from him until this case is over."

"*Coño.*" *Maybe he has a point. The press could have a heyday if they knew she was here, but really. Jesus. Corby's not a suspect anymore.*

"She's suing us, goddamn it."

"Who?"

"That fucking lawyer. Church's ex."

"Karen Sue Adams?"

"That would be the one."

"Suing *us*?"

"Didn't I just say that?"

"For what?"

"Harassment. Stalking. Defamation. A bunch of other things."

"Us?"

"Yeah. You, me, Johnny Match, the town of Slocums Harbor, the District Attorney and the Commonwealth of Massachusetts."

"*Carajo!*"

"Exactly. You have no idea how pissed some people are. The se-lectmen were waiting in my office when I got to work this morning.

They said that maybe I should start thinking about resigning. Christ, I even got a call from the governor. He said some congressman from Rhode Island was all over his case to clean up this investigation. What the hell did you and Machico do to that wench?"

"We had a nice little chat down by the water at Rosecliff mansion. That's all. I thought she liked publicity."

"Maybe not when it ties her to a murder and possible serial killings. Maybe not when her boyfriend's getting set to launch his campaign for a senate seat."

"Hey, we haven't given her up to the press."

"But you threatened to."

"She can't prove that."

"You scared her. She doesn't want to play defense, doesn't like it. Not her style. So she's turning the tables on us."

"You mean she's coming after us before we can expose her, trying to makes us look like thugs."

"She called the press in for a little poor-me session. Her boyfriend, the good congressman, standing behind her. Shit. Just shit, shit, shit. Could you fuck this up any worse, Colón? Huh?"

She feels herself starting to shiver, a cold sweat seeping from her skin in spite of this warm man at her back.

"Screw her, Chief! *Sabe?* Right now she's one of the last two people to have seen the Princess alive. She can sue the world for all I care. Don't you see, she's up to her nose in this murder? She knows we know that she's still not coming clean with us. And she's raising hell with us to scare us off until she can find a way to get her skinny little ass out of our sling."

"That's what you say."

"*Sí claro*, Chief. Just give me a little bit more time. The *jeba* is going down … and soon."

"Soon, Detective. That's what the governor said. That's what the DA said. That's what the selectman told me. Soon. You don't have an indictment within the week, we can all kiss our jobs good-bye. How you going to support your *abuela* the voodoo queen and little Ricky?"

She turns to Corby, who has been listening, his chin on her smooth shoulder blade. "I got to go."

· • • • •

Colón looks around, a bit wild-eyed. The fog's lifting. She sees a pale, blue sea crisping on a long, white beach. Sun-dappled cliffs and rolling meadows in the background. Seabirds soaring and gliding in broad arcs. There's almost no sign of human intrusion, except a lobster pot buoy swept up on the beach. Except for the lack of palm trees, the place looks almost tropical.

"Where are we? What's this place called?"

"Nomans Island."

Her face softens a bit. "Really? Like No man's."

"Yeah. Look, I better get the anchor up."

"It's so wild."

"It's a nature sanctuary."

"Promise you will bring me back."

"Sure." He throws a switch on the consul. The Caterpillar diesel rumbles alive.

"I want to explore."

"You can't do that."

"Why?"

"The military used it for aerial bombing practice for a while."

"You mean like Vieques in Puerto Rico. The earth is full of poisons?"

"And unexploded bombs."

"*Coño!*"

"You can look, but you can't touch."

She thinks of Bob Dylan's song. "Just like a woman."

45

COLÓN HAS A WICKED SMILE on her face as she and Johnny Match tear down Neck Road in her Honda. Windows open, salsa blaring. Into the gated community out on the point that some of the locals call God's Country.

"Is he crazy?" Match seems to be feeling the *salseros'* drums pulsing in his shoulders. "You would think he'd be staying as far from Slocums Harbor and us as is humanly possible."

"Maybe he can't help himself." She knew her luck had to change. This is the moment. The *orishas* said it would happen. Well, sort of. A cruiser has spotted Spencer Alpin's gray Porsche parked in the driveway of the family compound on the Neck.

"Does he think we're not going to be on him like glue?"

"You said give him a little time to think we forgot about him, and he would do something stupid. Looks like you had that right," says her partner.

"Maybe he needs to clean up the place, you know? Like *pronto*. Afraid what we might find if we show up with a warrant."

"I don't get it. The crime is twenty-two years old. What would anyone find after all of these years?"

"Evidence is evidence. And I'd say our boy could be a little paranoid."

"Making hasty decisions."

"*Claro que sí.* Exactly, *hombre.* Balls for brains."

Johnny Match screws his lips. "Ok, our guy's not exactly Johnny Depp. But, yeah, this dog's a stud."

"*Macho* man. Thinks he's untouchable by the common *gente* like us. The surgeon's curse. The tragic flaw."

"What?"

"I read about it somewhere. Like in a news magazine or something. It's a recognizable syndrome. Some of these docs, big-time surgeons whacking themselves in high-performance sports cars and airplanes, they have the money and the ego for killer toys. But no time to really learn the game in any depth."

"So?"

"So they think because they're smart, and rich and *Jesus* in the OR, they can do anything. And they are pretty good at faking it. Until the pavement gets slippery … or they go flying into some ugly weather. Then they learn too late that there's no substitute for experience. And they ain't got it. *Sabe?*"

He scratches his chin. "You think our dog's the type?"

"I think we're going to know real soon. I got a storm of torment to unleash." Her mind thunders. *The room on fire with rosy light. And him on her. A* caballo. *Burning her. Red hair pulled tight around her neck. Until she's clawing at his back. Screaming kill me.* Pues … hodete! Venga, pendejo. *Fucking drunken bastard.* Borracho! *Stop, Papi. I want to die.*

Things are all mixed up.

• • • • •

"We got a search warrant, Doc." Match is smiling.

"You think I believe that? Why don't you get out of here before I call your boss."

She takes her phone out of her blazer pocket, offers it. "Just press three. Ask him if he wants us to bring you in on suspicion of murder, serial murder."

He gives her a hard look. His jaw muscles flexing. Arm stretched across the doorway into the Victorian summer mansion. "Save your TV-cop tricks for some other poor slob."

Match unfolds the warrant in his hand, passes it to Alpin. "We are really hoping you are going to cooperate, Doc."

Alpin pulls reading glasses out of the thigh pocket of his cargo shorts, puts them on. Starts to read. "How did you get this? This is a crock of sh—"

"You like the tarts, Doc?" Her right hand is holding a manila folder, kind of pointing it at him.

"What?"

"You know, your car comes up on the John list?"

"What?"

"New Bedford PD keeps a list of probable Johns' cars. You like to cruise Weld Square late night, Doc? Pick up a dolly? Buy yourself a hummer?"

His face, already gone pale, suddenly blushes with indignation. "Get real." He nods to the Porsche. "This car has never been in New Bedford."

She smiles. "No, Doc. Not this car. The SUV. Your local car. The blue Explorer. The one in your garage." She pulls some photos from the envelope. Eight-by-ten, black-and-white glossies. Five different shots of a Ford Explorer. Head-on, side-view, rear. Driver shadowy, plates clearly visible in several of the shots. Each shot shows a hooker leaning in the window, talking to the driver. Bars and restaurants marking the spot as Weld Square. The red-light district of Nu Bej.

"Other people use the car. It's a family car. The caretaker has a set of keys too. I don't know anything about this stuff." The edge is off his voice a bit. There's another note. Panic maybe. And he seems to be changing his strategy. "You want to come in? Then come in. I have nothing to hide."

She follows him into a large foyer, then toward a library on the left. "You pay for your sex back in 1988 too, Doc? You like to walk on the wild side? You think we look hard enough we're going to find you knew some of those girls that ended up dead back then? Are you the missing link—the one the cops never found in the original investigation? You like your sex rough? You kill the Princess and the others, Doc?"

"Damn ... No."

She feels the thunder rolling again in her head as she moves toward him. The old anger. At Jorge. And her *papi*. Always there. Ready to take over when she feels like just quitting. Tossing in the towel.

Suddenly she's backing him up against a huge desk, pressing within inches of this stud. She feels his body heat, smells the white wine and the Altoids on his breath. Her voice going low and raw. "Come on, Doc, make it easy on yourself. Tell us why you never married. You hate bitches like me? You want to jump us, *caballo*? Burn us? Wrap our hair tight around our necks? Fuck us until we claw your back? And die in you arms?"

Alpin stumbles backwards, his butt knocking over a pen set as he settles on the desk. Stuff clattering to the ground.

Johnny Match tries to hold her back as she keeps moving toward the doctor.

"That's how it is right, *mi amor*? You want us to die for you? That's how it was that night with Remy. And the others, you *borracho* motherfucker. Right? Right Papi?"

She could just spit in this bastard's face.

Alpin's hands flutter to his face. "NO. Jesus Christ, no." His chest heaves with the words.

Match hugs her from behind. She feels a tide of sweat seeping through her clothes.

"Everybody take a deep breath," her partner says. "Now, Doc … tell us what really happened to the Princess."

Alpin wipes his brow with his shirt sleeve. He's still catching his breath when Match hits him with a little piece of information he just sleuthed up last night. "Tell us why you have been making a bank transfer of ten grand every year since 1989 to two Providence law firms. Karen Sue Adams' office and Barney & Seigfried, where she started to work in 1988. Is she your attorney? She's a divorce and personal injury lawyer. You got those kind of problems?"

• • • • •

Alpin says that as soon as he and Remy got to the house, they went straight across the yard and out on the dock. He left her there, star-gazing. Went up to the house to check in with his mother who was doing a crossword, about to head off to bed. He grabbed a bottle of brandy from the bar. By the time he got back out on the dock, Remy was curled up in a ball, asleep. She was trashed on vodka, the coke worn off.

The doctor and the detectives have moved out onto the lawn looking over the long dock, Buzzards Bay, Bird Island and its lighthouse. It's as if he's taking them back to the scene of the crime. Cannot help himself.

"Then what, Doc?"

"I don't know. I sort of had a thing for her. I just lay there beside her, sipping the brandy, hugging her, remembering a good time we had together on a dock down in the Bahamas. An amazing night. A million stars winking, the moon just coming up to the east. Eventually she woke up. We started kissing."

Colón's recalling a piece of the dead girl's story in her head. "You're on top of her, forcing her."

"I don't remember that."

"Yeah, right, *pendejo!*"

"Hey, I speak Spanish."

"Congratulations. So do five hundred million other people."

"Well have a little respect, ok?"

Match elbows his partner.

"Sorry. *Lo siento mucho* ... Finish your story."

He walks them to the threshold of the dock, his eyes looking out over the water, seeing things from another time. "She said she was desperate. She needed her share of the money. She pleaded. 'Please just give me the money. I can make you feel like the last man on Earth.' That sort of thing. I told her she needed to sober up, find a little self-dignity."

"What a guy." She feels something tugging on her brain, shaking her.

"She told me to go fuck myself, started running toward the house, going to wake up the whole family. Going to rip me off. And split."

Colón's eyes brighten. Everything's starting to connect. She remembers. She has seen this in her mind, felt the struggle. "Is this the part where you rip open her shorts, tear her thong? Or was that earlier?"

46

"LET ME THE HELL OUT OF HERE, will you? You're going to get me in trouble again. I've got to go home. I got a family, you know?"

Hook Henry rises off the dusty sofa, eyes the wall clock, 8:17 in the evening. The last two full bottles of Guiness Draught on the workbench, ten empties lined up on the table saw in his shop. He frowns.

"One more." Corby Church is looking out the open barn doors of the boat shop, watching an osprey wheeling over the cove in the fading light. He's searching for one last fish, screeching to his mate nested in the dead swamp maple, promising dinner.

"Shit. What the hell are we celebrating. You get laid?"

"She said she loves me."

"Oh, Christ. Here we go again."

"Come on, be a buddy."

The boat builder twists the caps off the last two beers, hands one to his chum. He walks outside into the muggy evening air, nods for Corby to follow. "You been reading the paper? She's going to get run out of town, she doesn't come up with the son of a bitch who planted the Princess, those other girls, too. You want my opinion? I say heat shields up, brother. The fire storm has not yet begun to rage."

"You think the same person killed Remy was the serial killer?" There's an odd note in his voice. An exaggerated attempt at sincerity. As if he has wanted to ask this question for a long time, has been rehearsing it in his mind,

"I don't know. I'm not a cop, but I think the police are asking the same question. Just can't focus on the big picture until they figure out what happened to Remy."

"But you have an opinion."

"I think the Princess was flirting with danger, is what I think." He sits down on the end of the little granite wharf, dangles his foot over the edge. Blue crabs are darting over the muddy bottom in the shallows.

"Yeah, so?" Church sits down beside Hook.

"She got herself way in over her head with blow. You know how that goes, especially back in the late '80s. We've both been shot at, had people threaten us, am I right? People kill over that shit, pal. All those girls who died that summer. Coke was the one thing they all had in common."

"They were hookers."

"Not all of them." Batting a mosquito away.

"They were all part of the Weld Square scene."

"Where the hell you think Remy got her blow after Paolo turned her off?"

"I don't know. In the city, I guess. Weld Square?"

"Man, she lived there! I remember being at the Inn, having a drink on the porch after work that summer. She came in to do her waitress thing, face all red and swollen. You could tell she had been crying. 'What the hell happened to her,' I asked Chelsea. She was tending bar. 'They found another body out on I-195. In Marion,' she says. 'Remy's been all messed up over it. Says she knew the girl.'"

"I remember it took the cops months to make ID on most of those girls. So what the hell was Remy talking about?"

"How the hell do I know. I'm just saying Remy knew her way around Weld Square. The tricks and the drugs, you know?"

Hook takes a long drink of his beer.

"You ever go there?"

"What do you mean? If you mean do I like a couple of those Portuguese restaurants there, yeah. If you mean, did I ever cruise the hookers in Weld Square? Fuck off. You think I want to get AIDS? I'm a happily married man."

"You were never curious?"

"You mean you were?"

He shrugs, takes a drink. "Yeah, a couple of times."

"What the hell is wrong with you?"

"A lot of guys used to go there, you know?"

"Oh yeah, buddy boy, I know. I've read the John list in the papers. Doctors, lawyers, politicians, that famous pizza-parlor guy from Mashpee. Rich old fucks from the country clubs. The yachting crowd. I remember a bunch of the sailor boys got busted over there one night before the Marion-Bermuda race. So I guess you weren't alone."

"It's a pretty sad scene. Loaded with junkies."

"Tell me about it."

"I was just seventeen ... the first time."

"You were such a loser, you had to go out and rent a piece of tail?"

"I had a girlfriend."

"You went alone?"

"Yeah."

"What the hell were you looking for?"

"It's kind of weird."

"Are you drunk?"

"I don't think so."

"Then stop clawing at the back of your neck like a damn mon-key … and talk to me."

"I had this crazy idea I might maybe run into my dad?"

Hook almost chokes on his last sip of beer. "Oh, man." His voice sounds torn to little pieces. "Didn't anyone ever tell you, you can't bring back the dead and gone?"

"What do you know?"

47

"SO WHAT, DETECTIVE? I have done some legal work for Spencer Alpin. Since when is that a crime?"

Karen Sue Adams is sitting on a park bench along the River Walk in Providence. A container of Chinese take-out on her lap, a bottle of Perrier in hand. She was having a peaceful dinner in the glow of the June sunset before Colón and Match showed up asking nosy questions.

"Don't waste our time with a lie, Counselor. Alpin admits paying you off."

The attorney looks at them like they are speaking Martian.

"Are you blackmailing him? We know he has been buying your silence, hoping you would never tell anyone what you saw at his house the night that Remy disappeared."

"I beg your pardon."

"Now that you fingered him, I guess the deal's off. Ship's sinking, so to speak. And it's everyone for himself. You tell us the truth this time; it's going to be easier on you in court. Know what I mean?"

"Keep it up, Detective." She stuffs her chopsticks and a half-fin-
ished container of *yu shang* eggplant back into a paper bag, stands to
leave. "Give me more ammunition for my lawsuit. You can't just push
yourself into people's private lives and bully them to death with false
accusations. Hasn't your boss told you that?"

*Colón knows that Adams has a point here, but the detectives are run-
ning out of time to solve this case and, well, sometimes a little intimida-
tion gets quick results ... especially when you can back it up with hot
evidence.*

"Leave me alone! Stop harassing me. There are laws against this
sort of thing. If you really had anything, you would be waving a warrant in my face."

Colon smiles, hands the attorney a folded sheet of thin white
paper. "I guess you mean this."

Adams sits back down. It's almost dark now, and she fishes glasses
out of her purse to read. "You want to check all my client billing for
the last twenty-two years? I can't just ... How am I going to ...?"

Johnny Match shrugs. "Your firm has an office in Massachusetts.
Our jurisdiction. So we got our job; you've got yours, Ms. Adams."

There's lightning in the attorney's eyes. "Spencer Alpin didn't tell
you anything. There's nothing to tell. And I know you're off this case
and out of a job in a matter of days unless you get a break. You're just
trying to shake the bushes. But guess what, guys—this bush shakes
back!"

Johnny Match takes a seat on the other side of Adams, pulls a
small tape recorder out of the pocket of his chinos, clicks it on.
"Maybe you better have a listen, Counselor."

A scratchy voice, Spencer Alpin's, rattles from the tiny speaker:
"Yes, ok, this is for the record."

"You want to tell us about the night of August 30, 1988? Tell us what happened after you took Remy La Moreaux back to your parents' compound, about twelve-thirty in the morning? After you had the fight with her down on your dock?"

· · · · ·

"She hit me in the balls ... with a flashlight. Said go fuck yourself and started running up the dock toward the house."

"You followed her, chased her, right?"

"She was going to raise hell, wake up the whole family."

"Did she?"

"She went in the back door and straight to the library."

"Why the library?"

"She was looking for a book."

"What book? Why the hell would she want a book?"

"*The Collected Works of T.S. Eliot.* It was hollowed out."

"Your stash? Drugs?"

"Money."

"How did she know?"

"I had it on the boat."

"Paolo Costa's boat."

"The *Fedallah.*"

"But she knew it was in the library now?"

"When we were in the Bahamas, we were close for awhile. I told her things. She knew about the book. Thought it was pretty cool, the leather binding. I said it came from my mother's library."

"So she was after your stash."

"I told you. She said she had a problem. Said she needed all her money."

"What for?"

"How the hell do I know? Drug debts maybe."

"You didn't really know … You didn't give a shit, but you weren't going to let her rip you off. You got a knife from the kitchen. You went after her."

A long silence. "I didn't hurt her."

"But she got your book. This T.S. Eliot."

"It was empty. She started screaming at me. 'Where's my money? You owe me my money.' That sort of thing. I told her I didn't have the money. It was in the bank."

"Then what?"

"I wanted that book. I told her."

"Why did you want the book?"

He sighs. "I hid a key in the spine."

"You hid a key in the spine?"

"The safe-deposit box key. That key."

"The one we found in the grave?"

"I suppose."

"What happens next? She finds the key?"

"Yes."

"And …?"

"'You want this?' she was yelling. 'Eat your heart out!' She stuffed the damn key in her mouth. And swallowed. Crazy. Then she ran out the door. Into the woods. It was the only key."

"How much you figure was in that safe-deposit box? Cash?"

"Over $150,000."

"You never got the money."

"No."

"How come you didn't get Paolo to go to the bank and ask them to drill out the lock? It only costs about $150. Because you were afraid that box might connect you to a murder?"

"We talked, Paolo and I. He wanted the money. I told him about Remy and the key, said let it go, man. Walk away from it. But Paolo wouldn't do that. He said if he stopped paying the rent, sooner or later—like three years or so—the bank was going to open that box. 'They see money, they are going to tell the cops. You aren't supposed to keep money in those things.' So he said his dummy company would keep paying the rent. If nothing about Remy surfaced for twenty-five years, we would go for the loot. But as far as I was concerned, she cursed that box. Cursed my life really. I knew she was going to really fuck me over someday."

"That fucking little bitch! Right? You wanted to kill her."

"I told you. She ran into those woods. I didn't touch her. Karen Sue Adams knows. She saw the whole thing."

"Really? How do you know?"

"A couple of weeks after Remy disappeared, I got a call from Karen Sue. I was in Boston, at med school."

"What did she want?"

"She asked did I know Remy had been reported missing by her father. She said she followed me and Remy that night. She was parked in the trees watching. She saw Remy run out of the house into the woods, me chasing her."

"With the knife, right?"

"I told her I didn't do anything to Remy."

"She said, 'But who's going to believe you?'"

"She was trying to blackmail you?"

"Maybe she was just offering me some friendly advice. What do you think?"

"I'm not the guy who was chasing a woman into the woods with a knife in his hand."

"I asked her if she could use a new client."

"She asked you for money?"

"No. I offered to put her on retainer to watch out for my best interests."

"What did she say?"

"It was up to me."

"So you've kept her on retainer for all these years?"

"Yes."

"She gets $10,000 a year. For what?"

"My peace of mind."

"Aren't you the lucky guy?"

No answer.

"Doc?"

"Yeah?"

"You know the Princess was pregnant? You knock her up?"

• • • • •

"So … maybe you're having second thoughts now, Counselor … about ever telling us the knife-chasing story?"

"What?"

"Didn't you know we would challenge Alpin with it and eventually the heat would come back at you?"

Adams' lower lip curls. Like maybe she's angry, ripped at herself, or a little panicked. Ripped at herself for not fully thinking things through before she blurted out her story about witnessing the knife-chasing scene. Maybe pissed about something even more mercurial that she has put at risk.

"You think your little financial arrangement with Alpin, the way the doc paints it, might look like obstruction of justice and conspiracy to a jury?" Colón sits on the edge of the park bench, eyebrows raised, watching the sun set over the Providence skyline. Mosquitoes buzzing around their ears now. "Want to square things before it all gets away from us and onto the DA's desk?"

The attorney runs her hands down her hips as if her thighs have suddenly started sweating and her skirt's too tight. "Spence Alpin's right, ok ...? As I told you before. I saw him chase her across the lawn. She threw a book at him. Zinged him in the face, knocked him off his stride. She ran into the woods. He tried to follow her, but she must have hidden from him."

"How do you know this? You didn't tell us about this hiding part before? Are you sure?" Johnny Match has his face right up in hers.

Adams squirms. "I'm sure."

"How do we know he didn't kill her in the woods? Or did the two of you do her?"

"I saw her later."

Colón puckers her lips, makes a low whistle. At last.

Slowly, she's making some headway with this chick. Making headway against a whole collection of suspects and material witnesses who persist in never telling the whole truth about anything, who keep trying to pass off the blame and save face. Her partner Lou Votolatto on the CPAC detail told her there would be cases like this. Cases when every day would be like you were a freaking dentist trying to pull the truth from some asshole's head as if it was an impacted tooth. It could drive you crazy, make you want to kill. Especially when the clock's counting down on the moment when your case and just about everything else in your life is going to blow itself all to hell.

"You want to tell us where you last saw Remy La Moreaux?"

"I think I need to talk to my attorney."

"Hija de puta."

48

THE NIGHT'S DARK, foggy when he finishes his fourth rum and coke at Captain Kidd's in Woods Hole and heads off-Cape for Weld Square.

He's drunk now, listening to an ancient Hall & Oats tape in the truck, trying to keep his ride between the white lines, swerving slightly down the interstate to the rhythm of "Man Eater." He has turned his phone off. Colón hates drunks, and he knows he cannot talk straight if she calls. Besides, he does not want to deal with her now. It has been a long time since he has gotten trashed like this. But now that he has started, he knows he has to see it through to the bitter end. Hook would say he's hell-bent, on a tear. A mission to see if he can do this thing one more time.

He strikes a bonanza in the second bar he hits, a block off Acushnet Avenue. It's a dark, narrow place calling itself a hotel, saloon, and restaurant. But the rooms upstairs are just flop pads for the regulars. Rummies, junkies. Rental cribs for the hookers and their Johns. The bar's crowded with good-time girls. Some Portuguese, some Latinas,

many the sexy, chocolate-skinned Cape Verdeans. It's a warm June
night. The costumes *du jour* are tank tops and short-shorts. Tiny gold
and green lights wink from around the edge of the long, tall mirror
behind the bar. Two old ladies serving drinks. One white. One black.

The men tonight are mostly working class in jeans and T-shirts.
All ages. Fishermen ashore between trips, lumpers from the docks, a
few young pimps with their dark hair jelled. A couple of guys selling
X, crank … junk. Some of the men play eight-ball at a table in the
back, cards at one of the tables. A lot of guys standing at the bar, sipping beer or shots, chatting up the whores.

The constant ring of their cell phones disturb the night, jarring
the melodies seeping from the juke box. Eighties love songs. A girl
gets a call and it's gotta-go-dolls. She disappears out the door for a
date. Every once in a while a couple disappears upstairs. Luther Van-
dross crooning "Here and Now." Corby blinks, staring down his own
face in the mirror behind the bar.

This is what he used to come to see. The shame, the wanderlust, the
fuck-all, cock-eyed grin of Richard Allen Church that he imagined staring back at him from the mirror. His father. The man who chucked his
marine insurance business and left his family in Wild Harbor for this.
The booze, the women, the sea. *Well watch me now, Dad. You bastard!*

• • • • •

Her name's Anjie, the one he picks. The one he buys a watered-down
Cosmo.

"What's the problem, blue eyes." She sits next to him at the bar.
Cape Verdean, barely the legal drinking age. Slender. Long, black hair
like Colón's. Gold lamé halter top offering breasts like peaches. Legs
long as swamp willows. Flip flops kicking him in the shin ever so
slightly.

"What makes you think I have a problem?"

Her eyes deep, black. Bottomless. "You don't come in here unless you got something you are trying to forget … something you lost … or something you just wish you had. Which is it?"

He looks up at the mirror, sees his father watching him. Then he pictures the Princess in here. Her red hair on fire in the twinkling lights. Her white, white skin a beacon among all of these dark women. *What a hell hole. A cage full of predators. And victims.* Remy. His dad. The rich guys from the multi-million-dollar homes of Padanaram, Mattapoisett, Slocums Harbor, further out on the Cape. The men who are slumming. The man in the mirror. The common denominator—death and destruction.

"Come on, cutie. What brings you out tonight?"

He rubs his lips with his hand, scratches the back of his neck. A monkey. "I don't know. You tell me."

She gives a big grin, teeth straight and white and perfectly formed. "Me. You came here looking for me! You want a date? You want to come back to my place for awhile? Smoke a little weed?"

• • • • •

Church can smell the sweet, resinous scent of pot even before he ties his skiff off the transom of the big, white sailing yacht and climbs aboard. Even in the darkness of Guana Cay the varnish glistens, the brass sparkles. This boat cost some serious scratch, he thinks. These folks have the big bucks. Music drifts from inside the boat. Piano chords. Bruce Hornsby singing about going down the road. About the ages-old trade of love for money. About hookers and whore mongers.

Then he's crossing the deck, looking in on the main saloon through the aft companionway. And he sees her. Red hair sizzling. Buck naked. Facing him. Eyes closed. Straddling the dude's lap. Shouting ride 'em cowboy.

Her hips posting on his loins. Him grinning like a fool, bawling at his drunken wife. "Take the fucking pictures, Bitsy you whore!" The Polaroid flashes. Lightning strike after strike.

Between clicks the Princess opens her eyes, sees him standing up here on deck. Stares at him like he's the angel of vengeance or a character who has walked off the screen of a very different movie. A witness.

• • • • •

"Hey, blue eyes. Let's go?" Anjie has his hand.

He looks around at the bar. It seems changed. The lights brighter or something. His own face, his father's face, stares back at him from the mirror behind the bar. Pale. Blotchy. Trying to say something, warn him maybe.

"You coming?"

His vision still locks on the man in the mirror. The mariner, the runner, the whore monger, the amazing invisible dad. But he sees something else too. The guilt. The shame. The broken pieces of a family. And the urge to be something more than a ghost in someone's life.

"Hey, love, let's ..."

"I wish ..." The words come into his mouth from someplace across time, space.

Suddenly he thinks he knows the only way to cast off years of anger. At the world. At his father. "I wish ... I'm ..."

"What?"

"I'm soooooooooo sorry ..."

She looks at him. Dumfounded. "Why?"

"I've got to tell Yemanjá!"

"What the hell are you talking about?"

He wants to say he was in the wrong place at the wrong time. But what he says is, "I saw something ... I saw *Sinbad*."

49

"I GOT A TIP, CHIEF." Colón stands before her boss's desk, trying to look humble. "I'm going to need your help on this."

Chi Chi Bugatti leans back in his chair and rubs his belly with both hands, seems to enjoy the way the starch in his uniform has been holding its press for the past seven hours on the job today.

"We're running out of time, Colón. This better be good. I put my ass on the line with the DA to get you those warrants. You get enough leverage to bring in the doctor, Alpin? I'm liking him for the Princess murder. In fact, I think I'm liking him for the serial jobs. Whore mongering little prick. Cocky piece of Ivy League trash, isn't he?"

She nods. *Like ok, yeah, but* "Johnny and I don't think he did it."

"Excuse me. First you write off the drug dealer as a suspect based on the testimony of the local liars club. Then you excuse Church and his buddy the boat builder. Forget about Karen Sue Adams, says Johnny Match, she doesn't do boats, couldn't have disposed of the body. So that leaves us with Alpin. He had motive, opportunity and means."

"Yeah, but consider this, Chief. He more-or-less admits to chasing her with a carving knife. You got a weapon like that and an itch to kill, why not cut her throat and be done with it? Why the hell would you try to strangle her? Hit her with something upside the head. And what about those ancient handcuffs. That ring we found in her belly?"

Bugatti, rolls his eyes. "Listen, *guapa*, let the DA and the jury work that out. Alpin's our most viable suspect. We are only a couple of days away from political meltdown … and unemployment. I'm telling you. The media has been calling me all day for comments. Your friend the celebrity attorney is shouting police harassment again. As soon as tomorrow's papers come out we're going to have the DA and the governor on the line screaming bloody murder."

"That bitch! We have a warrant. We got probable cause. She's dirty as hell, Chief, and she's still holding back. This harassment drill of hers is a smoke screen."

"Welcome to the big leagues. You want to bring her in on accessory to murder?"

She sees how it will go. *Claro*. She and Johnny have her cold on conspiracy and obstruction. Everything on tape. But the accessory charge is flimsy, circumstantial.

"She's a junkyard dog," says the chief. "And she's connected at the highest levels. She'll find a way to beat the charges. Bring a bonfire down on us."

Colón takes a deep breath. "I think she's protecting someone. Let me work this from another angle. Corby Church gave me something pretty interesting this morning."

"Oh, Christ! That name has been a thorn in my ass all day. The selectman have decided he's a liability. They are firing him as we speak."

She looks stunned.

"You can't save him ... I already tried. It's *adios* time. What did he give you?"

"There was a sex party one night in the Bahamas."

"When you were there?"

"No. Winter of '87-'88. When the Princess and her boys were doing the drug deal."

"Yeah?"

"Well, turns out they met up with another boat from Buzzards Bay down there and had a little *fiesta*."

"What boat?"

"Called the *Sinbad*. From Slocums Harbor."

"So ..."

"So the boat's still around. The owners are still around."

"Who?"

"You're not going to believe this ..."

An impatient look riddles the chief's face.

"Mr. and Mrs. Henry James Cabot IV."

"Hank?"

"And Betty Lou. Bitsy, I believe they call her."

Bugatti's dark cheeks are starting to turn pink. "Forget it, Colón. I've known Hank Cabot for thirty years. Jesus Christ. He's a select-man. Head of the archeological society. He's squeaky clean."

"I don't think so. Corby Church said he saw Cabot's wife, in the buff, shooting Polaroids of her husband having sex with our victim on board the *Sinbad*."

The chief's face is the color of red clay. "What the hell does that have to do with our murder? You really think I'd let you go to the Cabots asking them about what they did behind closed doors on a va-cation like twenty-two years ago. You must be fucking daft!"

"There's more."

"What?"

She says Cabot had a thing for Remy. It was clear to Church in the Bahamas. She played Cabot for favors for a couple of weeks, until his wife put a stop to it and made the *cabrón* sail over the horizon. The next summer when everybody was back north on Buzzards Bay, Hanky Boy started sniffing around again. Church thinks Remy was doing him.

"And I think he gave her money to buy blow. That bartender Chelsea, Corby—even Paolo Costa—say she acted like she had a sugar daddy."

Bugatti has his fat, ruddy-brown cheeks in his hands. "You think he knocked her up and killed her to keep her quiet?"

"It's possible. We should talk to the wife. I think the Princess could have gone to Cabot's house after she left Alpin the night she vanished. Johnny and I have been nosing around all day. We've heard some rumors. Cabot chases women. Always has. Bitsy drinks herself into oblivion, probably to cope. Maybe she's so pissed off and hurt she's ready to talk."

A grunt. "You're wasting your time, and mine. Yes, Bitsy Cabot has a problem with booze, but she's been in AA for years."

"So you know what I'm telling you is true. Slocums Harbor's model citizens have skeletons in the closet?"

"Goddamit! Let it go, Detective. Everybody has skeletons in the closet. What the hell do you call all that voodoo shit your crazy grandmother is into? Skeletons in the closet don't make people into murderers."

She says that Johnny Match called her fifteen minutes ago. That's why she came to see the chief. Match used to date a data analyst from the Cabots' bank. The analyst did him a favor, looked into their records. It turns out that every year for the last five, the Cabot household has been writing checks to Adams' law firm. Twenty thousand dollars every February First.

"Fuck!"

She hears a new note in his voice. It isn't attitude or defensiveness. It sounds like sorrow. A wound. "What's the matter, Chief?"

No answer.

"Chief?"

"I've been a fool?"

She can't believe what she's hearing. She's afraid to speak.

"Hank came in here right after we found the body. 'Bring me up-to-date, Chi Chi,' he said. 'The selectmen want to stay on top of every development. It's got the town in the spotlight. We're a quiet place. An historic little seaport. An oasis from big city problems. We're not used to this kind of attention. Folks don't like it. We have to make sure this case gets solved with as little hullabaloo as possible.' That's what he said. The son of a bitch. I briefed him. Every day I've been briefing him. I've been such a *pendejo*."

"I don't understand."

"He's the snitch. Deep throat. All those leaks to the press. He's playing his own game here. Bet on it. Creating smoke screens, as you say. Just like that arrogant, little rich-bitch lawyer. They've been using us. They don't give a shit about what happens to us. We're not like them. We're not rich. We're not white. We're disposable."

"And Remy La Moreaux?"

"She was a toy."

"Like all the others."

"What?"

"All those dead women left along the highways."

Bugatti pops up out of his chair, a wave of energy rushing through him. "Let's take these bastards down, Detective. *Vamos.*"

"*Sí, claro … hombre.*"

"We can start with Bitsy. She's a tough old girl. But she might talk." He straps on his holster and gun, turns for the door. "You and Johnny Mack meet me at St. Billy's church in Wareham. Side door. Seven o'clock sharp."

"What's there?"

"Bitsy Cabot."

"I don't understand."

"Seven o'clock. That's when AA lets out."

"Really?"

"I've been there every Friday for twenty-seven years, four months, nineteen days. I was a drunk, Colón. I almost killed somebody."

She feels her guts twisting. *Him on her. A* caballo. *Burning her. Until she is clawing at his back. Screaming in her head. You dirty, drunken bastard.* Borracho carbon …

"Colón. Seven o'clock sharp, got that?"

She blinks, coming out of her memory. Looks at her watch. It's almost four in the afternoon. "Right, Chief. Seven o'clock."

But first she has a bucket of stuff to do. She needs to make a phone call to an insurance company about the ring discovered in Remy's belly and run down some other stuff online about Bitsy Cabot's genealogy. Then she has to talk to the saints again.

50

A JUNE AFTERNOON, a northeast storm howling outside. And Abuela's shrine room reeks with the sweet scent of blood.

Thank the saints, it's strangely cool weather, or the whole apartment would smell like death. Ricky would throw a fit if he came home from his music enrichment camp and smelled this. Even Abuela understands, grudgingly. "He's an American boy," she has said. "People here think *Santería* is devil worship. He will grow up, godless, like a shadow."

"I hate this part."

"*Dejalo, nena*. Nobody ever said serving the *orishas* would be easy. Just hold the body. Hold it while I catch the blood." The two women kneel on the floor as Abuela cuts off the chicken's head with one swing of a meat cleaver.

Colón can feel the hot body of the chicken struggling in her hands. Even without its head, it wants to escape. It takes her tight grip, one hand on the legs and the other on the body, to keep the bird from breaking free as its neck squirts rich, red life into Abuela's clay bowl. The blood is the base for sacred paste.

The old lady has the sleeves of her white robe pulled up to her elbows to avoid the splattering blood. But it gets on her anyway, even flecks the white turban on her head.

"*Ibarakoo molumba Elegguá* ..." Abuela invokes the god of the crossroads.

From his place on the floor behind the door, Ellegguá scowls with his eyes of cowrie shells, a black, clay head on his plastic tray. The three horns sticking out of the head, sharp as blades this afternoon.

"Ooooooooooh!" The grandmother's free hand rises to cover her eyes.

"What?" The chicken's body is pumping its legs and wings. With a strength Colón can't believe.

"*El Nene* is very *duro* today. Very angry with you. The dead have followed you here. They are a torment to him. Their voices."

Do you want me, mi amor? Me quieres? Venga, pendejo. *Do you want to feast on me?*

"What do I do? *Por favor.*"

"You must make peace with the dead, *nena.*"

"How? Another chicken? Does he want another chicken?"

Suddenly the body in her hands breaks free, tumbles across the floor, rights itself and starts running around the room, flapping its wings colliding with the tureens, shrines of the *orishas*, splattering blood. Headless.

Abuela lunges from her knees, makes a dive, catching the chicken by one wing. "Run. *Fuera*, Daughter of Changó."

"Where?"

"Shake off the dead."

"How?"

The old lady lies on her side atop the sacred straw mat. The chicken's dancing in her hand. Its head in the clay bowl of blood, eyes blinking, the beak opening and closing greedily as if means to swallow its own life.

"I don't know. But do something fast."

• • • • •

He's in the wheelhouse of the *Brutus* when she throws herself into his arms. She feels like something tiny and broken to him, her sobs tearing holes in the air.

"What's the matter?"

A long, wailing sob. "I'm evil."

He takes a deep breath, exhales, lets her body mold to his. Holds her this way until her convulsing burns itself out.

"I thought if … I could find the killer … I could make everything right. But … but now the saints, the dead …" Her voice chokes on the words.

He wants to sooth her, says the only words that come into his head. "It's not your fault."

"Fuck you." She roars, pushing him away. Her eyes black lasers. This is not the same person who was crumbling in his arms a few seconds ago.

"Hey …?"

"Fuck you, *cabrón.*"

"What …?"

She wheels back with her right arm, spins. Nails him with her fist in the soft spot between the heel of his jaw and his ear.

Something cracks in the middle of his head. His vision blurs, his knees start to buckle. He reels back, tries to keep his footing as she stalks him, her arms flailing blades.

"Come on." Her fists are up, challenging. "Hit me *cabrón.*"

He doesn't understand. Is she asking for a beating?

"Hit me. *Venga, pendejo* ... Or I'll kill you, kill you tonight, you dirty, drunken bastard." Sobs. *"Borracho."*

The words sound strange. Not her own, like she's reciting from a script.

Her eyes are big as half-dollars. Her voice thunders curses in Spanish as she attacks.

But he sidesteps her, tackles her around the waist as she charges. They both go down on the floor. Her screaming as he wraps her in a bear hug from behind. "STOP."

She tries to elbow him in the groin. But he holds her too tightly. She just keeps ramming him in the hips.

"WHAT'S WRONG WITH YOU?"

She's sobbing again.

"Talk to me, Yemanjá."

"I saw him." Her voice is different again, almost a child's. Full of fear. "I saw him. I saw Papi from the doorway to my room ... from the shadows. The sun was setting over the little *isla* outside. The fishing boats on their moorings. The room on fire with light. He came home from the *taberna*. Drunk. *Borracho. Mi papi.* My dad!"

He holds her as tightly as he can. When he is with her, it seems he's always doing this. But he does not know what else to do. He feels that if he lets her go, he will lose her forever. Already she's in another place, another time. Seeing ghosts.

"I heard my *mami* say, 'Do you want me, *mi amor? Me quieres?* Do you want to feast on me? Eat my flesh?' And him on her. My *mami.* A *caballo.* Burning her. Searing her with his slick, brown body. His tongue in her mouth. His *bicho* inside her. Until she's clawing at his back. Screaming. '*Venga, pendejo.* Fuck me 'til I die. I'll kill you, kill you tonight, you dirty, drunken bastard.'

"Then his hands are on her throat. Eyes closed. Fingers tightening. As she goes down to her death. Gasping. Down to her death with my *papi*. I saw her die in his arms. His beautiful, strong, brown, drunken arms. Why did you kill her, Papi? Why did you tell me Mami died in her sleep?

"And why did I keep your secret? Even later. After you put the gun to your head. After you killed yourself. Killed me. Left me. A child with a broken soul on the beach. A burden for Abuela. Another ghost to wander in her house of saints. You bastard. *Cabrón*! Why?"

"Because of love," he says. "Because your *papi* loved you ... And I love you." These are not his words. At least not from his conscious mind. But they come out of his mouth. The way the voices of the long dead—Sinatra, Holiday, Marley—come out of the radio. The way they live again in redemption songs. Freedom songs.

She has begun to settle against his chest.

"I'm going to let you go now," he says, relaxing his grip. "I love you. Your mother loves you, too."

He does not know why he says this last part. But from the tenor of her sigh, he knows something like a current running through her has turned. At least for a while.

51

CHI CHI BUGATTI and Bitsy Cabot emerge together from the small door on the shady side of St. Billy's by the parking lot. He looks odd. Sheepish, eyes on the ground. A bit pale. Dusky.

As if he has lost the anger and indignation he had shown his detective back at the station. As if this Cabot lady has drugged him with the secret aura that the rich and the white excrete to make the rest of the world tremble with uneasiness.

"He's losing his *cojones*," she says to Johnny Match. "Come on, he's going to cave in and warn her about us, give her time to arm herself against our questions." She jumps out of the Honda parked at the curb, races up the walk, Johnny Match at her heels.

"Chief …"

He jumps, looks at her and her partner as if they are aliens. "Not now, Colón. I can handle this."

"Handle what?" Bitsy Cabot's face is one big question. "Handle what, Chi Chi? Who are these people?" The question on her face already beginning to dissolve into a sneer. Her back straightening until she looks imperial. A sixty-three-year-old society matron. Tall, slender. Very Vogue in her gold Christian Dior pants suit. Size four.

A large sapphire pendant on her permanently suntanned chest. Diamonds sparking from her ears, highlighting the perfect streaks of blond and silver in her bobbed hair. Her face must have been that of a world-class beauty once … with those high cheeks. A Lauren Becall. But now she's gaunt. The lips thin, too thickly glossed. The eyeliner just a touch over-done, but still not enough to distract you from the red veins around those gray eyes. Calling cards of way too much champagne and expensive coñac.

She extends her hand. "I'm Detective Colón, Mrs. Cabot. This is my partner Officer Machico."

Bitsy Cabot looks at the extended hand. Its dark skin possibly something she would only touch with a glove on. The long, bright red nails. "Excuse me?" Then to Bugatti: "They work for you?"

He's flustered, starting to blush, glares at the officers. "I said I've got this covered, Detective. We've just had a misunderstanding, Bitsy."

She feels the pounding of her heart crushing her eardrums. "No we haven't, Chief. You told us to meet you here. We need to ask you some important questions, Mrs. Cabot."

"I'll see you tomorrow in the office, Detective." Bugatti giving her the evil eye. Like get lost, *chica*.

Bitsy Cabot takes a step back from the three cops. "What kind of questions? What kind of questions give you the right to stalk me when I am here and—?"

"Questions about the murder of Remy La Moreaux."

The other attendees of the AA meeting sense the tension, flee to their cars. Some already probably thinking about stopping at a bar on the way home … just to wash away the stress, the stench of cops and suspect head-to-head on the sidewalk at St. Billy's.

"Who? What …? Chi Chi, make this rude, young thing go away. How dare you, you—"

"Cut the crap, Mrs. Cabot. You knew your husband was screwing Remy La Moreaux. You knew all that summer of 1988. And the night she came to your house on Labor Day weekend. It made you so angry."

"You're crazy. She's talking crazy. Chi Chi!"

The chief closes his eyes, maybe praying this nightmare will end. That the saints will vaporize Colón before Bitsy Cabot pulls out her cell phone, calls her husband and a legion of lawyers. Johnny Match plows the sweat from his scalp with his fingers, maybe thinking his partner has really screwed the pooch this time, not a single fact to back up her accusations. She's just winging it.

"No I'm not crazy, Mrs. Cabot. It made you furious, didn't it? I understand fury." There's a note of confession in Colón's voice, and maybe a sense of new self-awareness. As if she's finally starting to come to terms with her own demons. "That cheap slut was blackmailing your husband, wasn't she? Because of the sex … and something else. What else?"

Cabot stares at her with frozen eyes.

"I know what it's like to have a cheating man. The shame just eats you up. You'll do anything to stop it. And you want to kill her, *could* kill her if you ever have the chance. Could kill him and yourself too. Am I right?"

Cabot's shoulders slump.

"The bastard invades your sleep, stinking of whiskey and the scent of cheap perfume, lipstick, sex. You don't know what time it is. Don't want to know. The middle of the night. His hot hand plunging between your legs. And that bitch still right there on your property. You can smell her. Know he's going back to her after fucking you."

"No!" She's biting her lower lip, eyes darting around looking for some place to run, to hide.

The detective can't stop herself, her old anger's rising again. She's picturing the deed. Murder. Wanting to kill Jorge. Kill her *papi*. Kill the whores. Kill and be killed.

"Yes, Mrs. Cabot. Yes! You hate them. Those filthy fucks. And you want to get even. So when he leaves you again, you follow him. Follow him to his love nest. Stand at the door. In the dark. And you see them. Shadows pawing each other. The rage, the betrayal like stones against your teeth. You swing at him with something. Maybe a bottle. But you miss. Hit her. You think she's dead. He does too, your husband the *cabrón*, the goat. That's how it was, right? An accident? Just a terrible accident."

"Leave me alone!" Cabot's in tears, still backing away from the cops, trying to retreat inside St. Billy's.

"Who had the idea of putting her in the shackles and burying the body out on Bird Island? Your sorry-ass whore monger of a husband? Because he thought that if anybody ever found her bones out there, bound in those antique shackles, they would think she was the Moore lady in the old stories? That's what happened to Remy La Moreaux. We've got the picture, don't we?"

"No." A spark flashes in Cabot's eyes. Maybe a recognition. As if she has just seen through the detective's bluff.

"It was the perfect crime ... Except that you didn't realize that Remy La Moreaux was a klepto. She was like one of those birds. A raven. She loved bright, shiny things. She bought them. She stole them. And sometimes she ate them. She had a ring in her belly when we found her. Did you know that? A gold antique costume ring inscribed to 'KGF.' I've done my homework. Johnny has done his homework. We've talked to your insurance company. We've checked out your genealogy. You submitted an insurance claim in December 1989 for a gold antique costume ring from the French West Indies, engraved with the letters 'KGF.' Wasn't your great-grandmother from the French West Indies? Wasn't her name Katrina Garland Fitzgerald?"

Cabot, back against the side door to St. Billy's, raises her fists alongside her face and shrieks. "No. No. I didn't kill that slut ... But I wish I had. She was there. I knew it. I could smell her on him. And smell the stench of her cheap perfume and sex in the boathouse. She was there at least once every week that summer. His whore right there under my nose when they thought I was asleep. Taking Hank away from me. Taking him into that awful world."

"What world?"

A look of panic, pale and trembling, streaks across Cabot's face. Vanishes.

"What world?"

"The two of them without shame."

The detective sees the goat mounting the ewe, hears the static building in her own head. She has missed something here. Some inference. Maybe not just to sex. But she has lost her train of thought. *Damn*! She has to ask another question, take a different tack. "What about the ring?"

"I had taken it off to go sailing that Saturday, ladies' races in our little Herreshoffs. The ring wouldn't fit inside my sailing gloves. So I left it on the wet bar in the boathouse. The next day, Sunday I guess, I went to look for it, but it was gone. That slut was gone. So were a set of very valuable eighteenth century shackles from my collection of early-American nautical antiques. That's what I know. Now leave me alone!"

There is something *fingido*, bogus, in this story. The *cabrón*, Hank Cabot, still unaccounted for. And the remark about the "awful world"? She wants to press harder. She wants this pathetic woman to give up her husband for the crime. The killer. She thinks of the Princess and all of those violets, the roses, those poor young women, so long ago. Cut down. She wants to drive a stake through his black heart.

But she can feel something rising deep out of Bitsy Cabot, a strength that has been growing with the spark in her eyes. A woman's urge to protect the family. Protect the home. Keep it all intact, no matter what. No matter what a cheating *cabrón* you have for a mate. No matter what private shame she must live with. Her *mami* all over again. Herself. Bitsy Cabot. Victims of the same impulse. A bloody wall against reason. A silence broken only by sobs in the night.

"How do I know you're telling me the truth?"

Cabot's shoulders are rising a little out of their slump, her chest filling. Contempt … maybe even triumph … in those gray eyes.

"You can ask that divorce lawyer Karen Sue Adams. The one that's always on TV. She saw that red-haired tramp leave our house that night. Very much alive. I looked out the window. Saw a little red sports car parked just up the street. Like someone had been following that wench. And when the slut sneaked out into the streetlights and headed away up Water Street, I saw a young woman following her. On foot."

"Really? Did you know it was Adams?"

"Well … no. Not then. Only later."

"What do you mean?"

"I met her at the Whaling Museum in New Bedford, at a benefit. I thought she was flirting with Hank. But he told me she wasn't flirting. She was squeezing him for money. Threatening to go public with information about his thing with that bitch, about what she saw."

Bugatti suddenly raises an eyebrow. Shoots a look at his detective. Like heads up, *nena*.

"I don't get it. Why would your husband pay her off if you have nothing to hide?" Johnny Match has found his voice.

Cabot glares. "We can't afford the kind of scandal that would come from being connected to that tramp. Imagine being dragged into that awful world of hers. We have a certain status in the community. Henry, a selectman for all these years. Me in all of the clubs. Our friends would desert us, and then where would we be? Slocums Harbor is a small town. You make waves here, you have to move away. You'll see. Your days are numbered. I mean all of you."

52

"YOU'RE UNDER ARREST for conspiracy, obstruction, extortion and—"

"Please, Detective Colón. This is getting tiresome. How many ways do I have to sue you and expose your bullying and incompetence to make you go away?"

It's ten o'clock on Saturday morning. Karen Sue Adams is still in her rosy silk bathrobe as she stands at the door of her condo facing Goat Island in Newport.

"And the murder of Remy La Moreaux," says Johnny Match. A uniformed officer from Newport PD locks a plastic handcuff over the attorney's wrist.

"What?" Her face is puffy from sleep, circles under her eyes from last night's party with her congressman. She stares at the detectives and the local cop who's here to cover the jurisdictional bases. This is Rhode Island, after all. Not Massachusetts. "Are you insane?"

"We have our own sources in the press, you know. And unless you want to be front-page news in the Sunday papers, I suggest you invite us in to hear your side of the story right now."

Colón says that Adams might start by telling how her red MGB came to be parked outside the Cabot estate on Harbor Lane in Slocums Harbor at three in the morning on the day when Remy La Moreaux disappeared.

"Excuse me?"

"We had a rather enlightening conversation with Mrs. Henry James Cabot IV last night."

Adams' eyes turn stony. She nods for the three officers to enter. "Do we really need the cuffs?" she asks in a low, ragged voice.

• • • • •

"I was heading back to my parents' place in Pocasset when I saw her pop out of the bushes along Fox Road and head down Beach Street."

"La Moreaux?"

"Yes."

"You mean you didn't follow her from the Alpin place?"

"No. I already told you I had lost sight of her and Spence Alpin when they went into the woods. I was just going home. I felt like shit."

The three officers are sitting on a couch in the living room scrutinizing Adams as she sits in a plush, purple, wingback chair. Eyes on her hands clasped in her lap. The cuffs gone. At her back, sailing yachts glide back and forth across the harbor that lies beyond the sliding glass door leading to the second-floor deck.

"Was Alpin still following her?"

"I didn't see him."

"So you started to follow her again."

"Yes."

"Why? You wanted to kill her?"

"No! I don't know. I can't imagine how I would do such a thing.

It was like after everything I had seen that night, I was entranced. Curious. I even felt a little sorry for her. Especially after I had seen Spence Alpin trying to work her over. I wasn't exactly sober. It was almost as if I was watching a movie, you know?"

"No. Why don't you tell me? A movie?" Colón waves a hand in front of her face as if to shoo off a fly. "Never mind. Just tell me. You were in a car? Did she see you?"

"No. I don't think so. I turned my lights off, hung back on Cove Road until she was well down the hill on Beach Lane. Just a shadow."

"Then what?"

"I saw her head over to Harbor Lane. She was walking pretty fast. You know, power walking. Striding out. On a mission."

"You were where? Still in your car?"

"Yes. Maybe a half block behind her."

"Where did she go?"

"You already know. She went down the driveway of an estate. Into what looked like a boathouse."

"The Cabots' place."

"Yes, I guess. I didn't know the Cabots."

"Back then."

"Right."

"But you didn't leave?"

"No. I told you. I was fascinated. This girl. The mystery. So I parked down the street. Watched. Had a couple of sips of some peppermint schnapps I kept in the car. After a while a light came on in the boathouse at the estate. Only for a minute or two. Then it went out."

"Where were you now?"

"I got out of my car and jumped the stone wall onto the estate grounds. Just a little wall."

"What time was this?"

"I don't know. Definitely after three."

"What did you expect to do?"

"I don't know. She had become larger than life to me. In just one night I had watched this little tramp doing her thing with my fiancé, flirting and fighting with Spence Alpin. Now break into the Cabots' boathouse. It was like I wanted to know how low she would go. I wanted to throw all her trash in Corby's face to see if he was involved."

"What do you mean, her trash? You mean with Alpin and the Cabots? You suspected drugs or something?"

"I didn't want him to ever even talk to her again."

"You like to hold people's secrets against them, don't you?" She really wants to take a bite out of this woman. A big bloody chunk of flesh.

"What?"

"Forget it," says Johnny Match. "Just tell us what you saw next."

"I didn't see anything for a long time. Maybe a half hour or more. I just leaned against a big tree and watched the stars, the moon reflecting on the water out in the harbor."

"Why didn't you leave?"

"She came out of the boathouse."

"Alone?"

"There was a man, too. I could hear him whispering. I couldn't see him. He was telling her he could get her money. Told her to go up the street to the yacht club and wait."

"Did she?"

"I followed her on foot. It was hard because there were streetlights. She kept turning around and looking back, like she was suspicious someone was behind her. I had to stay in the shadows of the hedges and bushes that line the street."

"But you saw her at the yacht club?"

"She was sitting on the dock, sandals off, swishing her toes through the water in long arcs. Almost like she was dancing. Singing to herself. I thought she was nervous, trying to keep herself company."

"Really? You know the song she was singing?"

"Everybody does. 'No Woman No Cry.' Her head was back, tilted up at the stars. She seemed lost to the world until he broke the spell."

"Who?"

"A man. He surprised her. She literally jumped to her feet when she saw him."

"The same man from the boathouse? Did you recognize him?"

"I don't know. It was pretty dark."

"But it was Cabot?"

"I can't say for sure."

The detective growls a bit under her breath. "Where was this man when you saw him?"

"In a little rowboat. Very pretty. You could see the wood in the moonlight. Like it was all varnished. He came rowing out of the shadows from somewhere down the shore."

"From the direction of the Cabots' house?"

"I guess. Maybe. I never heard him coming. Not a sound. And it was a late-summer night. Crickets going wild with their chirps."

"Then what?"

"He said something and she got in the back of the rowboat. Sat."

"What did he say?"

"I couldn't tell. I was watching from the porch of the main clubhouse. It's pretty far from the dock."

"Why don't I believe you?" Agitation in the detective's voice.

Adams shrugs. Like so what?

Match tries to get things back on track. "What did they do next?"

"He turned the boat and started rowing out into the harbor."

"Which way?"

"I don't know. I'm not that good with directions."

The detective, who has been writing on a legal pad, throws down her pen. It rebounds off the green carpet, smacks the leg of a coffee table. "Think. Dammit."

"You don't have to swear. I'm doing the best I can. This was twenty-some years ago, ok?"

"No! *Puta!* You want to go to jail? You want your face all over the papers? Keep it up, Counselor. I've had enough of your half-truths, your creating suspicion around somebody new every time we talk. You think I don't know what you're up to? Sending us out on fools' errands to interview this person and that person. You think I don't know you're trying to run out the clock on my game so you can walk?"

Adams grits her teeth, glares at this Latina bitch hustling her.

"How many other people are you extorting, Ms. Adams? Besides Spencer Alpin and the Cabots? How many will step forward after we break the stories of your little shake-down racket in the papers? This has to be a million-dollar condo. And I bet it's paid for. Where did you get all that money? I don't think that even divorce and personal injury law pays so well."

"Piss off!"

"What?" The detective is on her feet.

"You heard me."

Colón turns to Johnny Match and the Newport cop. "I'm going to beat the ever-living shit out of this *jeba!*"

Adams jumps up, a glass orb—a paper weight from the coffee table—in her hand. A missile ready to launch.

Johnny Match throws himself between the two women. He straight-arms Adams so hard where her neck meets her chest she

crumbles back into her chair with a grunt. Then he spins on his partner who looks like she might be going for her gun. "Everybody just
sit the hell down!"

The two women look at him, eyes wide.

"Don't speak unless you want to see me go bat shit on the two of
you. Right here. Right now we get to the bottom of this nightmare.
I'm fucking sick of your cat fights and everything else." The veins on
his neck are red and throbbing. "One last time, Counselor. Was the
man in the boat Hank Cabot?"

Adams inhales, hand at her throat, still trying to catch her breath.
Finally nods yes.

"Where did he take La Moreaux in the rowboat? Pull any
punches and you are going to jail in cuffs. Am I clear?" He looks at
the officer in blue for confirmation.

She hesitates. Her voice little more than a whisper when she
speaks. "They headed straight out into the harbor."

"We can't hear you. What? Where?"

"They went straight out into the harbor to a big white sailboat."

"You know the boat?"

She coughs, almost chokes on the name. "The *Sinbad*."

"How do you know that was the name?"

"I heard him say it. When he surprised her at the dock, he said,
'The money's on the *Sinbad*.'"

"Why didn't you just tell us that in the first place? Like weeks
ago? Counselor?"

She looks at Colón then back at Johnny Match and the local cop.
Her blue eyes cold as a snake's. "Think about it! Do you have any
idea what kind of mess you're stirring up?"

"Are we talking about eleven dead girls and narcotics trafficking?"

Remy's voice is rising in her head.

• • • • •

"What about the money?" Remy nuzzles his neck.

"You're not trying to blackmail me, are you?"

"I'm pregnant."

"Nonsense."

"I want to keep the baby."

He groans. "I had a vasectomy ten years ago. I'm not anybody's daddy."

She feels foiled. Desperate. Sits up on the couch. "You made me a promise. Are you changing your mind? It's now or never. You've got to get me out of here. The cops have been all over me for the last week. They know about me. Maybe us."

"You think?"

She sighs. She's got him back on the hook again, throws her arms around him. "It's just a matter of time 'til they bust me. Or both of us. What are you going to do if the police come rolling up to your place asking why a known drug addict from Weld Square has been spending the night here once a week since the Fourth of July? What if the police start asking me about your sideshow in Nu Bej? About what you keep hidden in the bowels of the Sinbad?"

"Ok." He pauses, like he sees how things stand. "Don't worry. Go down to the dinghy dock at the yacht club and wait for me. It will take me an hour or so to get some things together, to get the money. I thought we had another month or two. But ... but what the hell. Time to cut our losses, right?"

"Exactly."

53

"YOU THINK she could have been a runner for some drug dealer?" Johnny Match takes a sip of his coffee. Scowls, perhaps wishing it were a Sam Adams.

His eyes flick back and forth between Corby Church and his partner as they sit at the counter of the Fish Monger Café in Woods Hole. Their sandwich plates empty, the Saturday lunch crowd all but gone.

She leans back on the barstool, crosses her arms under her breasts. "You think Hank Cabot was, or is, into the drug scene?"

Corby Church stares at the glass of ice water in his hand. Says nothing. Just tries to think. Tries to walk back twenty-two years in his mind.

"Did he set up something with Paolo Costa when you all were down there together in '88, Corby?"

He puts his napkin on his plate with the crusty remains of a sandwich. "I kind of doubt it. At least the Costa-connection part."

RANDALL PEFFER

"But they were both into Remy."

"Or … she was into both of them. Like what do those guys have in common, coming from different sides of the tracks? Just her. You think a business partnership could last very long? Guys like that from separate worlds, someone like Remy in between them, stirring things up?"

"Maybe that's why she got killed," says Colón.

"You ever see anything down there in the Bahamas, Corby?" Match is stroking the dark whiskers on his cleft chin. "Any connection between the two guys? Or any sign that Cabot was down there doing his own drug deal? It was the '80s. Before the mob and the cartels really cornered the market. Plenty of freelancers in the narco trade, back then, right? Maybe Cabot was one of them. Still is."

"You think he needs money … with a blue blood name like Cabot? The way I hear it, he's a fifth-generation trust-fund baby, and so is his wife. Like he's got controlling interest in a top yacht-building yard in Rhode Island, a toxic waste disposal company, and a fleet of off-shore lobster boats. Why would he need to get messed up in drug trafficking? Not his kind of people, too much risk, too much danger, unsavory characters. You know?"

She feels something nagging at her. Shadows. Dreams. "Unless he was desperate for money. And had a connection. Somebody who knew the territory. Could introduce him around … and do the dirty work."

"Remy?"

"Why not? It's pretty clear that she lived the last months of her life, at least partially, on the *entrañas* of Weld Square."

"The what?"

"Entrails."

He shakes his head. "I think you're stretching. Slocums Harbor's a small town. You hear things about people. The only thing I've ever heard about Hank Cabot is that he chases women. And that's what I saw in the Bahamas. Him drooling over the Princess. Nothing about drugs. I swear. But plenty of booze, no question."

"So you think Cabot and his wife were just on a sailing vacation down there in the islands? Rum in the sun? Occasional sport fucking? Swinging? No hidden agenda?" Johnny Match has a squint-eyed look, as if trying to see through thick fog.

"People do it all the time. At least the boating part. Hundreds, maybe thousands a year."

She frowns.

He wants to help. "Why don't you just arrest him?"

"No solid motive," says Johnny Match.

"What about a lover's quarrel?"

"We've got no direct evidence. The ring and the shackles belonged to his wife. All we have is your ex's testimony about seeing her go off with him in a rowboat to the *Sinbad*. That makes him a suspect. It doesn't convince the court to issue us a warrant. We need something more." Her voice sounds flat, far away.

"Is there anything I can do?" He means it. Knows now that there will be no peace, no future, for him and Colón until the killer is brought to justice.

"Think about the last time you saw the Princess, maybe she said something you have forgotten to tell us."

She was a wreck ...

· · · · ·

Remy stumbles up the gangway to the tug, shouting his name. Meets him on the deck, throwing herself into his arms. "Help me. Please?"

He holds her, stares out at Quissett Harbor. "I don't know. This is a bad time, Remy. I'm getting married ..."

It is like she does not hear him. She pulls her head back from his chest, takes his face in her hands, searches his eyes. Starts kissing him all over his face. His cheeks, his chin, his nose, his lips. "I need to tell you ..."

Then she slides back into his arms. Collapses.

He catches her. One arm beneath her knees, one behind her back as she falls. Red hair sweeping almost to the ground.

Her eyes are closed, tears sliding down the sides of her cheeks. "Remember that night on the beach in the Bahamas?"

His throat goes dry.

"I'm five months pregnant."

He cannot say anything. What's there to say? She's beyond wasted. On the jagged edge. Dreaming maybe. Jonesing as the blow wears off and all the booze starts her into a tailspin. Hardly a responsible mother ... but maybe she aims to change her game. He can't tell. Not now. She has just put an icicle through the center of his heart. He cannot be the father of her child. But Jesus. The timing's right. Five months ago. April. A walk along the empty beach in the starshine. The sarong off her hips, trailing from her free hand. Indigo swells rolling in white plumes over the outer reef. A promontory of high, blue rocks. A grotto under the crags. A place to get out of the wind. A place to lie down.

The only noise the sowing of the warm breeze in the trees. Her legs locking around his hips, welding herself to him as she tears at the back of his neck, drawing his lips to hers. Paolo shouting out her name, cursing her, coming closer down the beach. "Don't stop! Jesus god almighty, not now. Not now." And then her calling him that strange name. Jared! His mind, his body, crashing, a flaming meteor.

Christ.

He feels dazed as he slides her into the passenger seat. Straps the seat-belt across her lap. She's nearly passed out.

In his mind he hears his father calling him ten times the dumb fuck, the little shit-ass.

"We could go back to Guana Cay. I could run a little beach bar, raise the baby." Her voice a murmur. "You could take the tug, set up an island freight business. I know where I can get us money. And not just my stash from Spence and Paolo. A lot of money. I got a connection. Good as gold. Old money gold. Hanky's gold. The snowman's gold."

54

"SHE CALLED HIM THE SNOWMAN?"

He nods. It's Monday, almost noon. The detectives eye Church over the wooden skeleton for a new day sailer in the lofting shed at the boatyard. He's covered in wood shavings, a chisel in his hand; he's been fitting frames since sunrise. He called her, asked them to come. He has remembered these things from the last night he saw the Princess.

"She actually mentioned his name?" Colón's voice has a wild note in it. She smells the rank scent of rodents on the run.

"Yes."

"Anything else?"

He swallows hard. "No. Not really."

She looks at him, knows he's lying to her yet again. But she sees the pain in his eyes and decides not to push her luck. Figures she doesn't want to know what's tearing at his heart right now. Doesn't even want to guess. She will not force him to share it with her partner. Something terrible. Something personal. After she closes the case ... then there will be time. There has to be time.

"What do you think, Johnny?"

"You ever hear of O'Keefe & Sons, Corby?"

"The sail makers? In Scotland or something. Yeah, Why?"

"I can't tell you yet. Sorry."

She gives her partner a sharp look, is not following him. She knows that he has been phone freaking again … and surfing the web for the last thirty-six hours. Sometimes the guy's such a nerd. Just a mystery. "What's this all about?"

"Grommets. I found the source of the grommets from the grave."

She still doesn't get it.

"Sail bags have grommets on them. For the draw string, right, Corby?"

He nods.

"You think you could fit someone in a sail bag for a fifty-foot boat?"

She sees the body curled into a ball, fetal position. The head bent forward. Chin on chest and twisted to the side. Mouth gaping open. Red hair winding its way down and around the neck. The eyes like green holes.

The inside of her cheeks feel like someone has scorched them with a blow torch.

• • • • •

Her tongue's swollen, raw, caught in the sticky after-taste of his dark rum. She tries to open her eyes, and maybe she does. Still, everything is ink black. She tries to raise her right hand to her face to feel if her eyes are open. But her hand can only move an inch or two before something seizes it by the wrist and holds it still. It's the same for the left hand.

She wiggles her fingers, tries to wrench her hands free of whatever it is that's holding them. They feel cloth, maybe her clothes, maybe not, all around them. Like large gloves. No, more like a sheet. Her fingers tear, stretch until they feel something live and hard and frantic. Contact. Her right hand clasps her left.

Even working together, pulling toward her face with all her might, they are stuck. Her fingernails scrape against her ankles, her shins. Something is binding her hands to her lower legs or her feet.

She tries to roll her shoulders, arch her back to shake them loose. But nothing moves more than a few inches. She feels caught in a net. The right side of her body stiff and damp. Suddenly she knows that she's lying on her side, something hard beneath her. It's the cabin sole of the Sinbad. *She's still on Hanky's boat. Her knees pulled up tight against her face. Just like the baby growing in her belly. She can hardly breathe like this, and she wonders if it's the same for her child. Will it suffocate if she cannot break free?*

55

"I WANT TO TALK to that *hijo de puta*, Hank Cabot." Her words are more a threat than a declaration.

Chi Chi Bugatti shakes his head. "After the way you came on to his wife last Friday night, you don't have a prayer. He's circled the wagons. Called me less than an hour ago. Mentioned a conference with his lawyers three times."

Damn. She was hoping this would be the moment when the chief explains why he chickened out after the AA meeting and didn't back her up, why he just sort of buckled in the face of Bitsy Cabot's money and priviledge. But forget about a confession. His shame around being a mouse in the face of the Cabots' power is too deep to face. And, right now, the man's on a freaking tear.

"I'm not talking Karen Sue Adams, Detective. I mean some big hitters from Boston. Including the former attorney general—of the United States, not Massachusetts. He says his lawyers want to avoid legal action. But that pretty much depends on whether I have fired you or not."

"Well, have you?" Her black eyes stare at the chief. The air-conditioner rumbles, but the atmosphere in the tiny office feels hot and fetid, like *la Isla* … during an August heat wave.

"Yeah," he says. "You want to give me your badge and gun?"

Something squeezes her heart. She thought she was ready for this. How many times has she dreamed of this moment? Dreamed of telling this fat, little *pendejo* to take his Keystone Cops and shove them? But now …

"Detective?"

"Just give me one more chance. Just 'til tomorrow, Chief. 'Til Tuesday. I'm so close I …"

He holds out his hand, wants her gun. "You're off the job, Colón."

She feels the sweat starting to run down her back, soaking her bra and the white summer blouse beneath the shoulder holster. "Don't let him walk, Chief. You know it's Cabot. He's the one who killed the Princess. And maybe all of the others girls."

"Come on, Colón, hand it over, will ya, so that …?"

"You've seen the evidence. And Adams' testimony," she says.

Evidence such as the grommets from canvas bags for sails like the ones Cabot bought in 1985. And the financials that she ran down last night. Cabot's fiberglass boat-building company was going down the tubes in 1988 … until it mysteriously came up with ten million to retool in 1989. Just after he bought the offshore lobster fleet. Coincidence? Does anyone think those lobster boats are just catching seafood? Or might foreign freighters coming into Boston and Providence be dropping little cocaine surprises out there on the fishing grounds for the lobster boys to find and bring home? For Hank Cabot to distribute and sell to the locals in Weld Square and other places?

The toxic waste company's probably a front to launder drug profits and maybe a place to hide the product.

Bugatti rises out of his swivel chair and faces her, his hands and fingers feeling the air in front of him as if he's preparing to tear back an invisible curtain.

She tries to step back.

But she's not fast enough. Suddenly he reaches out toward her left breast.

"*Coño!*"

He snags the Glock from her shoulder holster.

"Exactly ... Now get out of here and let me do this my way! Send in your pal Johnny. That boy and I have things to do."

56

"WHAT I DON'T UNDERSTAND is how he got her to the island. Or why he ever took her there." Colón climbs up the ladder to the deck of an old, wooden schooner in a boat shed.

Corby Church is sawing something by hand in the cockpit.

He puts down his tool. "I'm sorry you lost your job, Yemanjá. I really am. It sucks ... But maybe you have to let it go. That's what I'm doing, letting it go. Messing around with boats."

She scrambles onto the dusty deck and into the cockpit of the schooner. At first he thinks she wants a hug. He wants to give her a hug. But he can see the taut chords in her neck, knows she's all business right now.

"Listen. There's a killer loose. Maybe a serial killer. We can't know until we have time to see if Hank Cabot's DNA show's up on any of the evidence collected from Remy and those other dead girls. I can't just walk away from this case with what I know. *No puedo*. It's still my case."

He rubs sawdust from his eyes, looks at her. *Like what now?*

"I need some of your insight. I need to know about how boat

guys operate. He whacked her on the *Sinbad*. With some kind of heavy metal object. A boat tool or something. I know it." She has a faraway look in her eyes, picturing a dream or memory. "That's where he got the sail bag. On the boat. He hit her then he cuffed her in those old manacles and put her in a bag."

"How do you know?"

She can't really say she has been listening to the dead. It would sound too crazy.

"He took the manacles from home. They were antiques. But the boat was a better place to kill than the house. He had more control over the environment, and there was no place for the victim to run. But ... if he had her body in a bag on the boat, why wouldn't he just weight it down with something and sink it somewhere no one would ever find it? Why take her to the island at all? Why risk discovery?"

"I don't know. What's it matter? You just have to prove that he killed her."

"When you don't have eyewitnesses, nailing down the how and why is everything. If you can't do that, any jury, maybe even the DA, will let him walk."

"Oh."

"Right: oh! Look ... You're my boat guy. Come on. Think. Why the island?"

He shrugs. "Maybe he already had a plan. Cabot's the kind of guy who probably always has a plan. And a back-up plan. He's a sailor. Sailors are planners. They always have to be thinking ahead, preparing for the contingencies of wind and weather and unfamiliar landfalls and fog and ... Sort of like playing chess. You see what I mean? Sailors plan for safety. For escape. For survival."

"And attack."

"Some people say that boat racing is like war."

"And these sailors … they like to rely on plans, on strategies, that have worked before?"

"It is a big temptation. Trust me. Most mariners are conservative. We stick with the tried and the true. The familiar."

She's sitting on the bench seat in the cockpit of the schooner, arms out behind her bracing herself as she leans back, facing the roof of the boat shed, eyes closed.

"*Papi Elleguá,* help me now. *Ibarakou mollumba Elleguá ibaco* …" Her voice trails off.

"What?"

"I'm having a bad feeling. Let me think."

"Sorry."

"You said sailors stick with the familiar."

"Yeah. You're out at sea, a storm comes up. There is a strong impulse to run for home, even if it's not the best move. There's this persistent belief that local knowledge can save you."

"So if a boat guy, for some reason sails to some particular island, say Bird Island, all the time … or uses the exit ramps to Reed Road off I-195 on a daily basis. He has what you call local knowledge. The place makes him feel safe. These places are his *querencias.*"

"What?"

"His territories."

"Yeah I guess so. What's this have to do with Reed Road?"

"Three bodies of women killed during the summer of 1988 were found around the exit ramps at Reed Road. It was the killer's *querencia.*"

"Cabot's?"

"I don't know. Maybe. Maybe he has business over that way. Maybe his toxic waste company or something. I don't know." She catches herself, feels her old anger and dread resurfacing. Tries to refocus. "Let's not get ahead of ourselves. One case at a time. We need justice and closure for Remy. First things first … Bird Island. I thought you were the only person who goes out there on a regular basis."

"Usually, yeah."

"Cabot ever go out to the island before this spring? That time I went along?"

"A few times I know of. It was when we were getting ready to re-light the lighthouse. The archeology society was a big supporter. They helped us raise funds."

"That was in 1997. And Hank Cabot was the president of the town's archeological society?"

"Yeah."

"He show any special interest in Bird Island?"

"You could say that. He helped us put together a pamphlet on is-land history and legends."

She remembers back in April, Cabot and Corby's competing sto-ries about the disappearance of the first lighthouse keeper's wife. "The mysterious Mrs. Moore."

"Yeah. Vanished into thin air."

"She thought it was the end of the world. That island. A hostile place."

"You've been there. What do you think?"

She closes her eyes, pictures a skull wreathed in muddy, red hair. Attacking birds. The mornful cry of gulls. The smell of decay. "So why was Cabot so interested in the place?"

"I actually asked him that once. On one of our boat rides out to the island."

"Well?"

"He said he had been on the race committee for the yacht club for years. A lot of the sailboat races start and end near the island. So he had to spend hours out there in the committee boat at anchor, killing time. Sometimes the island just captured his imagination, he said. You know, the Mrs. Moore story."

"He had a lot of time to study the island then."

"I guess."

"Time to get local knowledge?"

"Yeah."

"Time to conceive a plan to dispose of a body and make it look like an historic grave?"

"If that's what was on his mind."

"Could he have taken the *Sinbad* out there the night Remy disappeared?"

"It wouldn't have been easy. There's only one place to anchor and it can be sketchy, a bunch of underwater boulders that can snag a big sailboat. But, sure, a good mariner, if he had local knowledge, he could do it. Still, someone might see him in a boat like the *Sinbad*. That would kind of defeat the purpose if he was trying to get rid of a body."

"How would *you* get a body out there undercover?"

"Take it in a dinghy from the main harbor. It's less than a three-mile trip."

"Row? We heard he picked her up at the yacht club in a row boat?"

"It would take a long time. I would take an inflatable."

"What?"

"A rubber boat with an outboard engine."

"He has one of those?'

"He did in 1988 in the Bahamas. A big, orange Zodiac."

Colón jumps to her feet. Nearly hits her head on one of the rafters in the boat shed.

"What's the matter?"

"He's probably out on Bird Island right now. With the chief and Johnny."

She says that Match told her that they were going. It's this crazy
plan of the chief's to back Cabot into a corner at the scene of the
crime and make him confess. Really amateur and kind of Hollywood.
Bugatti wants to look like a star, some kind of Dirty Harry. Setting
Cabot up and catching him in a flurry of drama. But what if Cabot
knows it?

"How could he not guess? What if he's going along with the chief
and Johnny Match because he has already thought about this possibility, already has a Plan B for escape?"

Church opens his mouth to answer—but she can't stop spewing
out her thoughts. "We've got to get out there!"

57

"WHAT THE HELL'S GOING ON?" Hank Cabot looks around the musty cave that's the ground floor of the stone lighthouse. The building is empty except for a roll of wire fence and some signs on posts saying KEEP OUT. "You said we came here to look at a strong box your detectives found on the island. I don't see any strong box."

"We need to talk, Hank." The chief pushes his sunglasses up on the top of his head, has a solemn look on his face.

Johnny Match pulls the iron door closed. Puts his back to the exit and crosses his arms. Nobody's leaving. The room's dark except for a thin shaft of light filtering down from somewhere higher up in the tower.

"Are you trying to intimidate me, Chi Chi?" Cabot has not moved. He's still standing in the center of the small circular room.

"Take a seat, Hank. Like I said, I just want to have a little chat." He nods to the granite steps that circle the interior and spiral up to the light, thirty feet overhead. The steps are the only place to sit.

Cabot prefers to stand. "You sure put us all to a lot of trouble. We could have done this back in town. You didn't have to lie to me about finding a strong box or bring me out here just to get me to talk."

"Yes I did. I want you to see something. And I want you to see it here." He opens the briefcase he has been carrying and pulls out an eight-by-ten-inch manila envelope. "I've been talking to Bitsy."

"Haven't we already had this conversation? Didn't I tell you that if you, or anyone who works for you, bother my wife, you better find a new place to live?"

"She called me last night while you were at your race committee get-together at the yacht club."

"What? You must be dreaming."

"She said she really felt like drinking. Was already a half a bottle into the cooking sherry. Asked me to go with her to a meeting."

"Oh, Jesus. Not again!"

"Yes, again. But give her credit. She called me for help."

"Wasn't that sweet."

"I tanked her up on coffee and took her to a meeting in Marston Mills."

"Ok, Chi Chi. I owe you one, alright? I'm sorry my wife can be such a miserable pain in the ass. But surely you didn't bring me out here to tell me you had to drag that lush out of a bottle again."

"She gave me these. She said that she stole them from you years ago. She said she has been keeping them as insurance."

"Insurance against what?"

"She said you'd understand." He hands the envelope to Cabot who finally sits down on the dusty steps, shakes the manila packet.

A handful of cracked and discolored Polaroid pictures fall out.

"That woman's crazy."

"You better have a look." The chief sits down on the steps too.

Cabot pulls on his reading glasses. Stares at the first snapshot. Sees Remy. Red hair on fire. Buck naked. Her back to the camera. But her head turned so you can see her face. Mouth open, as if she's shouting. Her hips posting on his loins. Him grinning to beat the band.

"Well?"

He throws the pictures on the floor. His face pale as the stone walls of the lighthouse. "What do you want me to say?"

"You had an affair with Remy La Moreaux ... And you killed her."

"I don't think so."

"Then what happened that night she came to your house on Labor Day weekend at three AM? You took her out to your sailboat, the *Sinbad*. Karen Sue Adams will testify to it."

"She doesn't know squat. She's been pinching me for years about this. I should never have given her anything. She has no idea what was going on ... Ok, so I took a few tumbles with Remy. From what I hear, a lot of guys did. That's not against the law."

"Remy La Moreaux was a drug connection for you that summer wasn't she, Mr. Cabot?" Johnny Match has taken a couple of steps away from the door into the center of the room.

"Nonsense."

"She was your link to the pushers and users in Weld Square. To the distributors on the Cape, too. She took the product to them, brought the money back, right? You paid her in free blow."

"You're dreaming."

"Corporal Machico here has been doing a little investigation into your offshore lobster company."

"So?"

"So I see your business is kind of a co-op of independent fishermen. You don't really own the boats. You buy the catch and market the lobsters."

"Right. What's wrong with that?"

"What's wrong is that there's a big turn-over in the boats that fish with you. Like most guys don't stay with you longer than a year. It must be tough not being able to count on a stable fleet. How come there's no loyalty?"

Cabot grunts. "Fishermen. Independent sons of bitches."

"I don't think that's why they leave," says Johnny Match.

"What are you saying?"

The chief stands up. "He's saying that the lobstermen quit because you're not legit."

"What?"

"Because you asked them to bring home more than lobsters. Nice, tightly-packed, little plastic barrels of cocaine paste. They don't like being your drug mules."

Cabot gets to his feet, dusting off the seat of his shorts, eyes wide, nostrils flaring. He's moving toward the door. "I'm out of here. Take me back ashore, Chi Chi. Don't let this half-assed detective brainwash you. Do you know how close you are to losing your job? And your pension?"

Johnny Match steps back, guarding the exit again. "You think Detective Colón and I haven't been talking to your ex-lobstermen?"

"They don't have anything to say."

"That's what you think. You'd be surprised what people say when you show them a badge and offer them immunity."

"Take me home, Chi Chi. If you want any future at all."

The chief's shoulders slouch, his barrel chest starting to collapse into itself. His mouth gulping for air ...

Suddenly, his body jolts as if some remarkable change of polarity has occurred in his soul. Some deep rage has begun to fume, and he's shouting into Cabot's face. "Don't fuck with me you arrogant piece

of shit! Don't ever try to fuck with me again! I swear to you by all your hoity toity, blue blood ancestors, you're not leaving this place until you tell us how that poor girl—"

The first shot rips right through the chief's left wrist. Continues through his neck. He's not dead when he hits the floor. But he is too far gone to even hear the pop of Cabot's Walther as it blows the right eyeball out of Johnny Match's head.

58

THE DOOR TO THE LIGHTHOUSE is open when they get there, someone moaning from inside.

"Oh, Jesus, help me."

Colón pictures Johnny, and something claws at her guts. She forgets everything she ever learned in basic training at the state police academy, forgets the son of a bitch is still on the island. She runs into the tower, a pistol in her hand. Her personal .32 H&R magnum revolver that she's been carrying since turning in the Glock. In her state of mind, the gun's merely something for her fingers to hold onto to feel real.

Church is right behind her. On a mission, too. He has her back. Hook's Remington pump gun is in his hands as he follows her into the darkened chamber at the bottom of the tower.

"Drop your gun." A voice in the dark, to her right. Near. "Put your hands over your head … and back against the wall."

She squints, her eyes not adjusted to the lack of light. Smells mold, *guano*, something sweet. Her left foot slips in it. A pool of blood. The shadows are beginning to resolve into shapes. She sees Johnny Match's body face down in the middle of the room. The chief curled into the fetal position, hugging his throat, a bloody, blue windbreaker pulled up over his face. Moaning.

Colón's lost in the moaning when Cabot grabs her from behind, choking her with his left arm. His right hand holding his pistol to her head. Her gun drops on the floor at her feet.

"Don't do what he says, Corby." Her throat burns.

• • • • •

Cabot shoves Church forward. "Ok. Now up the stairs. Slowly. You first, Corby. Keep your hands on your head."

He does not know what else to do, cannot think. So he starts, hoping the climb up the stairs will buy him some time to get his brain working again. Collect his courage.

The gunman keeps pushing his hostages until they reach the top of the stairs. "Stop. Keep your hands over your heads. Face the bay! Face the sun!"

They are in the light gallery atop the tower. The space no longer filled with an antique Fresnel lens the size of an oven, or lit by an oil lamp. There is just a bank of storage batteries and a small electric light fixed on a metal pedestal in the center of the floor.

The wind's up now with its usual afternoon fury, whistling. Whirring over and around about a hundred panes of glass that make this turret. There's a narrow iron catwalk around the outside. Beyond that, the waves roiling up Buzzards Bay … steep chains of combers under fuming white, crashing on the southwest shore of the island. They tear at the remains of the stone seawall.

"Open the door, Corby." Cabot nods at the metal frame, filled with panes of glass, the gate to this bird cage, leading out onto the catwalk.

"You mean to the outside?" A stupid question. He's stalling for time, trying to come up with a plan.

"Do it!" Cabot still has her in a strangle hold, gun to her head.

"What are you going to …?" Her voice echoes in the tower for a second, then carries away in the sighing of the wind outside.

"Open the goddamn door."

Against the silver cresting of the waves out on the bay, the blinding flash of the sun on a sea of jagged glass, Church pictures it. Pushed and falling from this tower. Spinning, tumbling through the air. And Colón right behind him. Her hair a comet's tail. The ground rising up. Green, muddy.

"Now, man! Or I'm going to blow her brains all over this lighthouse."

"It's not too late. You don't have to do this." His words sound pathetic.

"What the hell do you know about anything?" The man suddenly eases his choke hold on Colón, steps away from her. His gun now turning toward this lighthouse keeper, the tugboat dweller.

He reaches out, grabs the iron latch. Twists.

The wind slams the door wide open to the bay. The gallery is filling with a blizzard of twigs, feathers from bird nests out on the catwalk.

This is his chance. Church strikes.

A wicked chop with both arms, his hands fused together as if in prayer or handcuffs. They hammer the gunman's wrist. The pistol sails out the open door.

Cabot watches the gun. A silhouette against the sky. Then just a speck. Falling. He turns to the detective, his gray eyes locking with hers. His lips curling. Almost a smile, but not a smile. The look of someone deep in a memory or a vision … Amused, maybe. Or lost.

"She set me up. That's what you bitches do isn't it …?" His voice is raw, bitter as he glares at Colón. "Well fuck you all."

And just like that, with the bitter smile still on his lips, he jumps.

• • • • •

Colón sees the leap, feels the flight. It's like Remy's flight.

Better, for a while, than having wings. That's how Remy feels after the first wet, cold clods of earth crash down on her. After she raises her manacled hands to shelter her head. After she pulls into a tight ball. A baby protecting her baby. And the dreaming starts. The skating.

This skating with her Jared of the night. Jared of the fog. Jared of sad-eyed vulnerability, Jared full of grace. Jared who never kisses her anymore. Jared who feels her pain. Who brings her pleasure. Even as he is about to leave her. Jared who kisses boys.

He breaks the rhythm. Pulls his face away from her cheek, looks around. "I'm going to miss this."

"Don't … Please!"

She tries to inhale as deeply as she can to gather her strength, hold onto this moment. The air bright, ice smoke in her chest.

Then comes the keening of her heart. Almost a command to find her will, focus. To pry herself loose. She must stretch and give herself up to the arms of this man, must leave the earth below. One last time.

She pictures it, pictures herself, as she strains to break free of the ice, lift in his arms. Her partner. Her one and only. His smooth pink face, the strong hands on her waist. Her blue, chiffon skater's dress flashing as the spotlight finds her rising. Finds them flying together in the dark over the ice.

Red curls lifting in the air as they speed toward center ice, the music filling in from a dozen speakers. Bob Marley's "No Woman No Cry." She can hear the crowd cheering in the arena, over the sound system. Knows that this is the long live version. And that she has nearly an eternity to soar in his arms ...

Before he leaves her for the boys he loves. Leaves her feeling her broken wings. Picturing her rummy father. Picturing Chelsea. And many, many men. Forever.

Epilogue

"WHAT DO YOU THINK he meant by that remark, Mrs. Cabot? 'She set me up'?"

Colon's on the prowl again. At Bitsy Cabot's harbor-front estate. The detective has her old job back, but she's not loving it. Yes, the remaining two Slocums Harbor selectmen have told her and the media how proud they are of her. But now the selectmen are leaning on her. Like wrap up the case, please. Slocums Harbor has seen enough of tragedy. Let the chief mend in peace from his nearly mortal wound. Johnny Match is three weeks dead, buried with military and police honors. Machico's killer Hank Cabot is dead, too, after his leap from the lighthouse. Was his jump an escape attempt gone wrong … or an act of self-destruction? No one knows. But the fall killed him.

So … put it behind you, Detective. This little seaside town needs to return to its peaceful ways again, say the Slocums Harbor selectmen. The drama's over. Don't go digging into connections to the serial killings. Don't start looking for links between Hank Cabot and the disappearance of Remy's cold case file at the New Bedford Police

Department. Don't look for evidence linking Cabot's drug business and those eleven dead addicts, those poor women. Let the dead rest in peace.

Colón's not buying that, really not liking the politics of small-town police work. She's not ready to walk away from this case yet. Too many loose ends. She has to see where they intersect. That's what Johnny Match would have done, what he would have wanted her to do. She thinks about her dead partner. He was so conscientious, with such a strong sense of right and wrong. For two months he shared the load of this terrible case with her. He was her friend.

So get on it, jeba, she tells herself. *To hell with the selectmen.*

"What do you think, Mrs. Cabot?"

The heiress in the turquoise bathing suit, tortoiseshell shades, stretches her shoulders. Does not respond to the question. Her body's still trim, muscles toned from daily visits to the gym. But her skin's a farm of sun freckles. Her face a net of broken blood vessels, of drink. She adjusts her position in the chaise, an old lioness at leisure, warming her bones in the sun.

The southwest breeze blows off the bay and harbor, across the lawn of the Cabot compound. Gusts ripple the water on the swimming pool, carrying away most of the heat on this July day.

"Help me out, here. Who do you think he was talking about when he said that—'She set me up'?"

The widow inhales slowly, raises her head a little to look at the speaker. Flashes a smile, her thin, glossed lips pressed tightly together. "I can only guess,Detective. But I'd say he was talking about that little slut. The one he killed. But maybe he was talking about Karen Sue Adams, the blackmailer. Or maybe one of those other poor women from New Bedford who died that terrible summer. But what does it matter? Hank has already paid for his sins."

"I think he was talking about you."

"Don't be ridiculous."

"We found strands of another woman's hair among the remains of Remy La Moreaux. It matches hair that Chi Coco Bugatti got off your coat one night at an AA meeting." She has been waiting to say this since the news of the hair match came back from the lab earlier this morning.

Cabot drops her head back down on her pillow, looks away. Then reaches down to the pool deck for a tall, green, plastic glass. Takes a long sip if its golden liquid, what they call a Yellowbird in the Caribbean. Orange juice, Galeano, lots of rum.

"That whore was diddling my husband in my daybed in the boat-house. Of course she would have my hair on her. I took a nap in that bed almost every afternoon. My hair's always shedding. You can ask our plumber. It's a curse to the drain in my shower. Now … why don't you go away and leave me alone. Be glad that you got your killer."

"We have a tape, Mrs. Cabot. Chi Chi Bugatti was wired with a tape recorder."

"What are you talking about?"

"The day of the shooting out on Bird Island. The day your husband died. The day he killed my partner. The chief had a tape recorder running. The whole time. Would you like to hear it?"

"Why are you doing this to me? You think a wife wants to hear a live recording of her husband's death? Maybe women where you come from enjoy that sort of thing, but, trust me, the idea of you even asking me to listen is appalling."

"*Cayate su boca y escuchame, bruja!*"

"What?"

"Just listen."

The tape player clicks on.

"You're not leaving this place until you tell us how that poor girl —"

The sound of gun shots. Moans. Fumbling around. The sound of Hank Cabot swearing to himself.

"Christ, Jesus Christ. Shit."

Then Chi Chi Bugatti's voice again:

"Why? Oh, god … why?"

"You dumb son of a bitch, you should have kept your nose out of this. Now look what you've made me do."

"Help me, I'm dying." Choking, coughing. "I can't breath. My neck. You shot me in the fucking neck. *Madre mia*!"

The sound of clothes rustling. "Here. Put your head on this. My windbreaker. Close your eyes. I'm going to get you some help."

"Don't go. I don't want to die alone."

"I didn't mean for any of this to happen. Things just got out of control. That sweet wreck of a girl. I had the money for her. For us. Lots of money. I was ready to run off with her that night. Just cut loose. Head for the Bahamas. That's what she wanted. I didn't care. I was ready. To hell with Slocums Harbor, you know? Do you have any idea how insane life with Bitsy can be?"

A pause. The screech of terns. The chief choking. Finally his voice. "She killed La Moreaux?"

Another pause. The sounds of wind humming around the tower. More choking. Deeper, almost as if the sounds are coming from underwater.

"Somehow she got out to the *Sinbad* before we did. Took her kayak from the dock at the house while I was rowing to the yacht club to pick up Remy. But she set her kayak adrift before we got to the sailboat. We didn't know she was there. Oh Christ, it was awful! One second I was hugging Remy right there in the starshine in the middle of the main saloon. The next thing I know Bitsy jumps out of the fo'castle, raps her on the side of the head with a bilge pump handle, starts choking her with her own hair. Jesus. Even before she hit the floor."

"You made him bury her, didn't you, Mrs. Cabot ...? You told him to use the handcuffs. Your shackles. They were an afterthought, weren't they? You knew about his fetish for the island and the vanished Mrs. Moore. You played right into that. You wanted this all to look like his work, like he planned it all. If anyone ever found her, you wanted the evidence to point to that cheating son of a bitch, not you. And maybe you even knew that she was still alive."

"You think any court will ever believe that, Detective? The words of a killer, the desperate fabrications of a guilty man?"

"A judge in district court has already issued a warrant."

The older lady, who has had her back to Colón this entire time, turns, sits up in her chaise, pulls off her sunglasses and glares back. "That tramp deserved what she got. Just like you. Just like all of the sluts who should suffocate in their own stench ... You stray mutts ...! Strays who don't know where—"

"Where we belong? Is that what you were going to say, Mrs. Cabot? You mean with our legs spread and your husband fucking us like a split mango? Killing us with his lust. That's where we belong?"

"Bitch!" Cabot plunges her hand into the straw beach bag beside the chair. Feeling for something, maybe a weapon. "I ought to do you like I did that—"

"Drop it, Mrs. Cabot. Take your hand out of that bag. Slowly." Colón has her Glock out, pointed.

There's a rustle in the bushes behind her. "I've got your back, Yemanjá." Corby Church's voice. He has Hook Henry's pump gun again.

"Where did you come from?" She's as surprised as Bitsy Cabot to see this man in a sawdust-sprinkled T-shirt and shorts, straight from the boat shop.

He nods over his shoulder to the screen of *arbor vitae* shielding the pool from the driveway. "I was worried about you."

Cabot sees his cockeyed grin, the look of a man on a mission … and proud of it. "I think he likes you, Detective. What do you think of that?"

Colón senses a sudden loss of pressure right behind her eyes.

The heiress still has an amused look on her face. "You're just like Hank. You always were, Corby. A sucker for thrift-shop pussy. You had it bad for that Cocaine Sally in the Bahamas didn't you?"

The detective feels an almost irresistible urge to pull the trigger. Just let a few rounds go to get everyone's attention. *Coño carajo.*

"She talked about Corby, you know, Detective? Right at the end. I heard her."

"What?"

"Yes, that red-haired wench. Hank had her in a sail bag. He thought she was dead. He was dragging her up the beach on Bird Island. From the Zodiac. And suddenly she made a noise. Began to mumble. Your boyfriend's name."

"You're lying!" She feels sweat pouring from behind her ears. Hears the cry of a baby. Remy's child. Her child, too. Ricky. Across time. Across space.

"Am I, Corby? Do you think I'm just saying this to piss your sweetie off? You want to shoot me now? One of you want to pump one into me?" She's daring someone to shoot. Either the Lancelot or the Latina. *Like goddamn shoot. Shoot and wreck the whole case. Right here, right now.*

"Go ahead and shoot." Cabot's reaching for her bag again.

"No." Colón surges forward. Two steps in quick succession.

A hard, sweeping kick from her right leg knocks the beach bag out of Cabot's grasp. It arcs a few feet through the air, hits the concrete pool deck. Tumbles, scattering its contents. The cigarettes, the pint of rum, the make-up, the compact, the cell phone, the pistol.

"Don't move an inch, Mrs. Cabot! Or your head is next. You're under arrest."

The heiress is sitting up in her chaise, bent over at the waist, squeezing her left wrist with her right hand. "I think you broke my arm."

"My heart bleeds for you!" Colón wheels toward Church. Gives him a look like *watch this bitch*. "I need some space."

She marches away, across the lawn toward the water. Just stares out at the harbor. Out at the sailboats slipping off to sea. They heel over under the press of hot wind. Beating past Bird Island toward open water beyond.

Her eyes flash with the fire of a memory. Her lips quiver as she passes her Glock back and forth between her hands.

She sees that Bitsy Cabot is not the only wounded person here. All three of them are broken in one way or another. And, right now, it will take a total sea change to set things right.

• • • • •

She watches the sailboats, sees their foaming trails leading from Slocums Harbor out to who-knows-where. The stiff southwest breeze brushes her cheeks. Her eyes close. And she sees Remy.

Dancing with a dark figure. A beach in the moonlight. Off in the distance, from a beach bar, from Nipper's, come the strains of a love song. Marley asking to turn the lights down low ...

The dancers multiply in her mind. Females. First Remy. Then herself. Then the faces of eleven women from New Bedford rising out of the purple dark. One by one. Fallen flowers. The ones Bitsy Cabot

probably did not kill. But someone did. She's not ruling out Hank
Cabot … with that fierce hatred of women she heard in his voice just
before the end. With his whoring and his drug business.

And now the music is changing. Whitney Houston. "Saving All
My Love For You" is soaring through the night, the day, her head.
Like too much Stoli.

*Strong hands, restless hands sliding behind her neck. Gliding over
her shoulders. Lips kissing away the tears. The softest skin, the wettest
skin.*

Something's rupturing in her head, the roots of her hair explod-
ing in sharp little snaps.

She gasps for breath … Knows.

Johnny Match does not rest in peace. Her heart trembles for him.
For the innocence of her son Ricky. For the Princess. For the skater's
lost lover Jared. For Remy's dead baby. And for the others. For all the
sisters. The mothers.

The case is not closed. The *orishas* are declaring it. With voices
shrill and full of longing. Swelling in her with anger. Her mother's.
Her own. Her lovers'. The violets. The roses. The dead.

A long road of cold cases lies ahead. If the selectmen will not
abide her pursuing the murders of all those lost girls, then to hell with
them. Maybe she will have earned enough cred by bringing the
Cabots to account that her old partner Lou Votolatto and the Cape
CPAC unit will take her back. Maybe they will forgive her for certain
indiscretions. The ones she will never talk about, not even to the
saints. The ones last October when she was out of her mind with a
fatal attraction to poor, broken Michael Decastro.

She slides her left hand into her jacket pocket, fingers the golden
ring that she ought to have returned to Bitsy Cabot. The antique wedding band. The ring found with Remy's bones. The one that red-

haired siren swallowed so long ago on a dark night in her lover's nest on the edge of Slocums Harbor. Surely, swallowing that ring had something to do with control, with taking back the power. From Hank Cabot and Bitsy Cabot ... and all their money and privilege. From the Man.

Now she takes it, almost a wafer in her fingers. Raises it to her lips. Slips it in her mouth.

Corby Church has reached her side.

"Yemanjá, are you ok?"

She nods. Swallows. The ring's a frozen sliver going down. A piece of Slocums Harbor treasure that the selectmen owe her.

"Yemanjá?"

She tries to inhale as deeply as she can to gather *fuerza* and *color*. Heat. The ring is ice beneath her breasts.

For just a second she pictures the dancers on the night beach again. Feels Church's strong hands on her waist. Trade winds beginning to catch in her hair. Warming her chest at last. Smelling of coconut. The music reggae, or salsa. From a band she has never heard before. *Sí coño.* She's going to quit this freaking job. Stop whoring for the Man. Today. Get away from Slocums Harbor. And run from the dead for a while, too. Sometimes she thinks they want too much from her, that they won't let her be until they get every last bit of her stuffed in a sail bag, buried on an island. She needs to call time out and rest ... gather her strength before she faces any of those cold cases that lie ahead. Strength for the nights when she hears the lost girls and the saints whispering again. Strength to skate again.

"Give me your hand, Corby," she says to him. "Want to go back to Guana Cay?"

RANDALL PEFFER is an instructor at Phillips Academy in Andover, Massachusetts. He is the author of the Cape Islands Mystery Series, including *Killling Neptune's Daughter, Provincetown Follies/Bangkok Blues, Old School Bones,* and *Bangkok Dragons/Cape Cod Tears.* He is also the author of *Southern Seahawk.* His nonfiction books include *Logs of the Dead Pirate Society* and *Watermen.*